SUSPICION

Leigh Russell

Also by Leigh Russell

The Adulterer's Wife

Praise For Leigh Russell

The author had me hooked and intrigued very early on . Her style of writing is excellent. The story is very well put together with the characters and scenes flowing well. I'll definitely be reading other novels by her. **Donna Wilbor – Amazon Reviewer**

Unable to put the book down. Fast-paced gripping storyline. I have always enjoyed any books I have read by Leigh Russell. **Jenny Wren – Amazon Reviewer**

The Adulterers Wife is a nice departure for Leigh Russell but she done so without losing that magic touch her fans have come to expect from her previous books. A well written, fast paced and engaging psychological thriller **Joanne Roberston – Goodreads Reviewer**

For a first stab at psychological thriller, Leigh has done a damn good job, all that is left for Leigh to do is to go onwards and upwards, I'm sure her next psychological thriller will be bigger and better than the first. **Diane Hogg – Goodreads Reviewer**

Chapter 1

The girl greeted us in a low voice, her English as flawless as her complexion.

'Thank you, Mizuki, we're pleased to meet you too,' Nick replied, 'and we're very happy to be here.'

That was certainly true, as we had travelled a long way. Now that we had arrived, it seemed appropriate for my husband talk for both of us.

The Japanese girl was captivating, with alluring almond-shaped eyes in a pale oval face. Seemingly oblivious of my admiring gaze, she smiled politely at me and bowed. 'Good afternoon, Mrs Kelly, and welcome to Tokyo. I hope you had a good journey. I myself studied at boarding school in England. It was similar to your own, and I was very happy there.'

My husband beamed. He had recently been appointed headmaster of a public school in the Home Counties, and we had come to Japan to promote our establishment to parents of prospective students.

'We mustn't get carried away by the fees we can attract from wealthy Japanese families,' Nick had explained to me before our trip. 'We're only interested in recruiting the most academically able pupils. It's potential we're looking for, potential.' He was not telling me anything new, but I listened in silence, understanding that he was not speaking for my benefit. 'We can't take on too many pupils from overseas, but some of these kids are extremely clever, and they have an impressive work ethic.'

'Unlike the home-grown variety,' I murmured.

Nick grunted. 'Not necessarily. But that's not the point. We want to be able to select the best students from as wide a pool as possible.'

With boarding dwindling in popularity among English families, Nick's predecessor had set about forging links with recruitment agencies in overseas territories. The purpose of our present trip was to strengthen our connection with the agency based in Tokyo and encourage them to continue recommending our school. If the numbers of families seeking to send their children to study in England was growing, so too was the competition from other public schools. So while I was excited about going to Japan, Nick remained focused on our objective.

'This is business, not pleasure,' he had insisted before we arrived in Tokyo.

I repeated his words in my head while Mizuki led us to our hotel room. As graceful in motion as she was exquisite at rest, she glided along the corridor in front of us. A European girl with her delicate figure might have looked unhealthy, but Mizuki's tiny waist and narrow hips somehow gave an impression of femininity.

'This is where you will be staying,' our guide said, before she slipped away.

'I can't believe we're actually in Japan,' I said when Nick and I were finally alone, and he smiled at my enthusiasm.

Staring around the luxuriously appointed room, I felt my spirits soar. The decor was very simple, with drapes and bed linen matching the ivory-coloured walls. The absence of any clutter gave a sense of space and freedom, as though I was floating in the sky. Nick went over to the window to look out. I joined him and we stood, side by side, gazing out at the lights of Tokyo. He put his arm around my shoulders and pulled me close.

'Yes,' he said, 'we're in Japan.'

That night I barely slept, excited by the strangeness of it all and slightly befuddled by jet lag. Taking everything in his stride, Nick snored softly all night long, a faint smile on his lips. The following morning he worked through breakfast in our room, responding to urgent emails and preparing for the day ahead.

It was very early when Mizuki arrived to accompany us to several well-known sites of Tokyo. In the colourful bustle of the Fish Market, our guide vanished from view only to reappear in front of us moments later, her movements unhurried and her smile enigmatic, as though she had never lost sight of us. After the commotion of the Fish Market, we visited intricate and spectacular temples, and beautiful manicured gardens where peace seemed to float above us like an invisible dome. Nick and I sat on a bench and he took my hand as though we were alone, yet all the time Mizuki hovered nearby, watching over us.

Meanwhile, we gazed around at the beautiful gardens, and at one another, as though we were on a second honeymoon. In a way more surprising than the spectacular tourist sites were some of the everyday sights. In contrast to humdrum grey manhole covers serving obscure functions in England, the manhole covers in Tokyo were works of art. More than merely colourful and decorative, they showed recognisable images such as a fireman with a hose, making them practical as well as beautiful. I was aware of the Japanese reputation for cleanliness, but the toilets in Tokyo took hygiene to a whole new level.

Wherever we went, Mizuki escorted us, charming and unruffled, allowing us to enjoy the tour without having to work out where we were going. After a magical weekend of sightseeing, we arrived at the purpose of our visit and met the manager of the UK branch of the Sekai Educational Agency. The director, Mr Tanaka, was a dapper Japanese man who spoke very little while Nick and his contact, Suzuki, discussed various proposals.

With her rapid speech and lively gesticulation, Suzuki seemed very excitable beside the other members of the Japanese team we had encountered: Mizuki with her serene grace, and Mr Tanaka, silent and smiling. The director and I sat quietly as Nick and Suzuki discussed requirements, laid out expectations, and negotiated terms, while Mizuki waited patiently to serve tea.

Seated beside Nick on the plane home, I listened to him chatting cheerfully about our visit. It felt as though we had been away for months, although the whole trip had lasted little more than a week. As far as Nick was concerned, it had been a resounding success.

'At any rate, we're likely to attract a few very strong candidates as a direct result of our visit. Tanaka was definitely impressed,' he said. 'I'm confident the governors will agree it was worthwhile.'

Nodding my agreement, I smiled. Nick tended to be confident about everything, but his positive attitude had not done us any harm.

'It was certainly very different there,' I replied. 'It makes you realise what a culture shock it must be for pupils arriving from overseas. Perhaps we should introduce some kind of buddy system to help them settle in.'

'That's definitely something we ought to look into. Someone friendly who speaks the same language can make a huge difference. Perhaps that's something we can discuss with our Japanese agent over here. And we should ask her to write to Mr Tanaka and tell him our door is always open to any of his employees who visit the UK.'

'You can leave it to me to draft an email, if you like.'

Nick smiled. He was an attractive man, with penetrating blue eyes that seemed to hold a hint of mischief even when he was looking serious. Sometimes I felt a flutter of desire just looking at his lean body, his biceps straining the fabric of his shirt sleeves. Now that he was a headmaster, he had acquired the added allure of power and I returned his smile, thinking how lucky we were to have found each other.

Chapter 2

I watched Rosie as she glanced around Nick's study, taking in the high bookshelves and imposing leather-topped desk. Her eyes lingered on a vase of tall lilies, waxlike against the high window, before looking past them to admire the view.

'You know, I've driven past here so many times, but I never stopped to find out what's hidden away behind those high walls,' she said. 'You'd think a journalist would be more curious.'

'I hope you like what you've seen so far.'

She nodded. 'I can't believe I never so much as poked my head through the gates before. It's magnificent.'

She was right; the grounds of the school had been designed to impress. My husband's windows looked out across a cricket pitch where we could see boys practising against a backdrop of rhododendrons and overhanging lilacs. It was not yet June but summer had come early and, in the halcyon May sunshine, the scene was an Arcadian idyll of innocence and tranquillity.

'It's quintessentially English,' she added, gazing through the window.

'We like to think so,' I replied. 'Certainly we try to send our boys out into the world armed with a clear sense of right and wrong.'

The words I had heard so often in my husband's speeches sounded pompous on my lips. As I hesitated, wondering whether to continue, the sound of cheering reached us faintly from the cricket pitch.

'Someone's out,' Rosie said.

'You're familiar with the rules of the game?'

She smiled at my raised eyebrows. 'I know someone who's a keen amateur.'

I turned to glance through the window at the boys on the far pitch. Doubtless grass stained and grubby, from this distance their whites appeared immaculate. Even the disused cricket pavilion looked picturesque in the glow of the afternoon sunlight.

Rosie's voice recalled me from my musings. 'You've talked a lot about the benefits of life in a public school.' Suddenly brisk, she brushed her long dark fringe out of her eyes and fixed me with a penetrating stare. 'You've told me how pleased you are with the house that comes with the job, the overseas travel to market the school, and the gardens here which I can see are truly spectacular. Now,' she leaned forward, an encouraging smile softening her narrow features, 'what can you tell me about the disadvantages? You must be planning to make some changes.'

Thrown off my script by the unexpected direction the interview was taking, I shook my head.

'Don't tell me there aren't even a few little niggles.'

She must have known I would be too well prepared to speak freely to a journalist.

'Really, there aren't any downsides. My husband has an important and demanding job as headmaster, and I'm happy to support him. Naturally he's planning some changes, but I'm sure he talked about them when you interviewed him.'

'What kind of changes are we talking about?'

'He intends to modernise the facilities here.'

'Yes, but I'm not asking you about the buildings, or about your husband's plans. I want to know about *you*, Louise Kelly, the woman behind the public image. You gave up your own job as an IT teacher when your husband was appointed headmaster of Edleybury, didn't you? How did you feel about your career being sidelined?'

Actually, it had been a welcome respite to take a break and devote myself to my new role. Apart from my duties as the headmaster's wife, and the demands of settling into a new area, finding the shops, and overseeing the running of our home, there were people to charm, as Nick put it. In reality, he was the charmer, not me, with his glib tongue and ready wit, inherited no doubt from an Irish grandfather. By contrast, I was introverted, although teaching had helped to bring me out of my shell. You cannot survive long in a classroom without opening your mouth. If it had not been for Nick's plans, teaching would probably not have been my chosen job, but we had agreed that my experience of the profession would help to further his career, and that decision had paid off.

'It's true. I've taken a break from teaching because my duties as the headmaster's wife are keeping me busy,' I replied. 'I may go back once we're settled, but for the moment we're focusing our energies on establishing ourselves. We haven't even completed our first year, and so far we've spent most of our time here on the school site. Over the summer, we plan to explore the area.'

'You're not from Hertfordshire are you?'

'No. But we really like what we've seen of it so far,' I said politely.

'You certainly seem to enjoy being married to the head of such a busy and flourishing school.'

I smiled my appreciation, relieved that she appeared to have dropped her slightly intrusive line of questioning, and hoping she would use those words to describe Edleybury in her article in the Hertfordshire Style magazine.

'Was it a difficult adjustment from being a class teacher? Do you miss the contact with pupils?'

'You know, I wouldn't put it like that, because I do see a lot of the boys and girls here.'

I trotted out my prepared response, and she smiled and nodded and checked her recording device. Easing into our new roles had been relatively straightforward, I said, thanks to the wonderful support we had received, and continued to receive, from the rest of the staff. We were particularly grateful, I said, to the deputy head, David Lancaster, and to my husband's secretary, Sue, both of whom had exceeded their duties by assisting and advising me as well as Nick.

'Helping you is really the same as helping Nick,' Sue had insisted when I attempted to thank her for spending time with me. 'It's all part of my job. I'm more than happy to do whatever I can to make the transition a smooth one.' She smiled kindly at me. 'We're all in this together.' It was the kind of comment Nick would have made.

Sue was the person who explained to me how the school had been run before our arrival, and how much, or how little, the previous headmaster's wife had involved herself in the daily affairs.

I repeated to Rosie what I had already told Sue, that I wanted to be as active as possible in supporting my husband.

'I get that,' Rosie replied with another smile. 'I'd be the same if I were in your position. And with your own career taking a back seat, how are you keeping yourself occupied? Perhaps hoping to start a family?'

Suppressing my indignation at the personal nature of her question, I continued our exchange of professional smiles. The years I had spent teaching had trained me to keep my feelings under control, at least outwardly. A successful teacher would make an effective poker player, or a spy. As the wife of a headmaster, it was more important than ever before to present an appropriate façade to the world. Besides, Rosie was there to interview me about being married to a head teacher. My private life was no concern of hers. Holding back from telling her exactly what she could do with her impertinent questions, I gave a measured response. Nick and I had to present ourselves to the world as a dignified and sympathetic couple, perfectly suited to leading and moulding young minds.

What I refrained from telling Rosie was that I would have liked a family, but Nick had always been interested in his career to the exclusion of all else. I didn't really mind. It wasn't as though we were delaying the decision to have a child for nothing. On the contrary, Nick's ambition had served us so well that, at the age of thirty-eight, he had gained the coveted post of Head of Edleybury. And we still had time. I was only thirty-six. For years we had schemed and worked towards him gaining a headship. Now that our hard work had finally paid off, it was hard to see how anyone could cope with bringing up children while married to the head of a thriving boarding school. The previous summer we had travelled to Japan where well-off families were increasingly looking to send their children to boarding school in England, and Nick was planning a future trip to China. Our lives were full enough without any more responsibilities.

I met Rosie's gaze with an equable smile. 'Nick and I have over eight hundred pupils in our care. I think you'll agree that's enough children for anyone! Nick is dedicated to his work.'

'Not to you?'

Her quick response made me wonder whether my words had betrayed an underlying wistfulness, but I kept my voice steady.

'We're a partnership. I admire what Nick does, and am happy to support him in his work.' That was an understatement.

Chapter 3

'Okay, that'll do.' Switching off her dictaphone, Rosie leaned back and her polished smile broadened into a grin. 'I think I've got everything I need. You've been a brick. Thanks so much. A photographer will be along tomorrow to take a few pictures of you and your husband together, perhaps outside on the lawn if it's not raining, and then we'll need a headshot of your husband and a picture of him at his desk. I'll come along as well, to make sure we get everything we need, so I'll see you in the morning.' Rising, she straightened her back, her close-fitting navy trousers emphasising her slim hips. 'It's not good to sit still for too long. I hope you didn't find my questions impertinent. I was just looking for a human touch, you know.'

'I hope you weren't disappointed with my answers,' I responded stiffly.

'Not at all. I'm sure readers will find your comments very engaging.'

Apart from a couple of slightly awkward moments, my first serious interview as a head's wife had gone smoothly. In fact, I had quite enjoyed talking to Rosie. It wasn't often that people were interested in me.

Leaving the building, I passed David, the deputy head, in the courtyard.

'How did your interview go today?' he asked.

'Fine. We talked about Nick, and his dedication to the school.'

David nodded. 'That's good. But I'm sure she was interested in you as well. The woman's angle and all that.'

'We touched on my role as Nick's wife. She said she was looking for a human touch.'

'A human touch,' he repeated, with a benevolent smile. 'I'm sure you were charming.'

Despite his faintly patronising way of speaking, David was a kind man. With a large square head and broad shoulders, he resembled a human teddy bear but, although he was not tall, he had an imposing presence that could be intimidating. In his forties and single, he had spent his life in the company of boys. It was no doubt a consequence of his blinkered experience that he addressed adults as though they were children, but he was that rare paradigm among teachers, a successful disciplinarian, both feared and adored by pupils. He had been at Edleybury for almost his entire career and his devotion to the school was obvious.

Nick had expressed his admiration for the deputy head to me on more than one occasion.

'It's one thing telling me, but have you told David? I'm sure he'd like to know how much you value his input.'

'Oh, I think he knows,' Nick had replied vaguely. 'And I'll certainly pay tribute to his contribution in my end-of-year speech. Everyone knows what an important role he plays in maintaining discipline without which we're nowhere. It would be Lord of the Flies in our quaint bubble in rural Hertfordshire.' He chuckled. 'That sad little character in Year Nine, you know the one I mean, Bertrand who's always running to the medical centre in tears, he'd be the first to be torn limb from limb. I know David's stamping down on the lads who have been giving him such a hard time, but some kids are just natural victims.'

'That's a bit harsh.'

'I wouldn't say it to anyone but you, but we all know it's true. The lads do bully him, but there are always two sides to every story.'

'Sometimes more than two,' I muttered, more to myself than to Nick.

'If only David didn't have such fixed ideas,' Nick added thoughtfully.

'Is that a problem?'

'Not for me,' Nick replied with a smile. 'I'm the headmaster so he'll back my plans, whether he agrees with them or not. His trouble is that he's been here too long, and he's set in his ways. But he'll come round.'

That evening Nick came home late, flung himself into an armchair in the living room, and loosened his tie. 'So, there's a photographer from the Hertfordshire Style coming tomorrow morning, and then we're done. I must say, David did us a favour.'

'How so?'

'It was David who arranged the interview. He knew the journalist from somewhere, I forget where, and he suggested she contact us.'

Although Nick didn't comment any further, I knew he was pleased to be featured in the annual educational supplement of the glossy county magazine. While I was content to hover in the background, Nick was always courting publicity for himself and the school. I sometimes wondered whether it was his sense of responsibility to the school, or his ego, that made him so hungry for attention. But knowing how hard he had fought to get this job, I understood his drive to succeed. In a competitive market place, even an established school relied heavily on marketing.

The following day was sunny again. I chose my outfit for the photographs carefully: a knee length summer dress, smart yet casual, and kitten heels. Rosie was waiting for me in the school reception area with the photographer, and together the three of us went to Nick's office.

While the photographer was busy with Nick, Rosie asked me quietly if she could have a word with me. Assuming there was a question she had forgotten to ask during our interview the previous day, I led her into the outer office where she closed the door.

'There's something I need to tell you,' she said, addressing me in a low hurried tone, and standing with her back to the door.

She looked agitated. Her eyes flicked around the room and she licked her lips nervously.

Waiting for her explanation, I began to share her unease, but I maintained the dignity appropriate at all times to the wife of a headmaster of a public school. 'Please, take a seat.'

She stepped forward and sat down with a jolt, twisting her fingers in her lap, and avoiding my eye.

'What was it you wanted to ask me?' I prompted her at last, glancing at my watch.

Rosie shook her head and sighed. 'This is so difficult. It's not a question actually. But there's something I need to tell you. That is, I feel I ought to share it because it's not fair for you, of all people, to be kept in the dark.'

'I'm listening.'

She glanced around. 'We won't be disturbed in here, will we?'

I shook my head, wondering what could possibly prompt such caution. She seemed very different to the confident journalist who had interviewed me the previous day as, clearing her throat, she uttered the most shocking words I had ever heard.

Chapter 4

'What do you mean?' Rising to my feet, I glanced at the door to make sure no one could overhear this gossip. 'That's impossible. I've never heard anything so outrageous. You couldn't be more wrong.'

'I'm not wrong,' she replied simply.

As though confronting an insolent pupil, I sat down and forced myself to remain calm, my voice level, my hands folded neatly in my lap. 'No, that's nonsense. My husband's not like that. I would have known if there was anything going on.'

Rosie shook her head. Looking askance at me through her long fringe, she repeated her accusation, adding, 'A wife is often the last person to know when her husband's seeing someone else.'

Even acknowledging the truth of her last remark, I was adamant that she must be mistaken.

'I'm sorry to be the one to have to tell you,' she said quietly. 'To be honest, I assumed you already knew, or at least had a pretty good idea. Surely you must have suspected something?'

Swallowing my anger, I dismissed the idea with a wave of my hand, as though swatting away an annoying fly. Apart from the fact that I trusted Nick when he told me he loved me, he couldn't possibly have time to be carrying on with another woman. An ambitious man, he thought of nothing but his career. Rosie's defamation of my husband's character was a deliberate attempt to undermine his position. All the same, I had to prevent her from mentioning it to anyone else. Gossip spread rapidly in a closed community like Edleybury.

'Where is this alleged affair supposed to be taking place?' I asked with a deliberate sneer in my voice.

Admittedly Nick and I weren't together every minute of the day, but the school was close knit. Like us, many of the teachers lived on site, in the boarding houses with the pupils, or in designated staff accommodation, a row of houses forming an imitation street in the grounds. There were bound to be rumours flying around if there was any hint of a scandal, especially one involving the headmaster.

'And what makes you think he's having an affair?' I demanded, my voice rising as I struggled to control my irritation.

'I saw something.'

'Oh, you saw something. So tell me, because I'm really curious, how would you have stumbled on this when no one else knows about it?' I stood up, finally losing my temper, but still keeping my voice low. 'How dare you come here and make these ridiculous allegations to me, of all people. Did you really believe I was going to take your derisory slander seriously?'

'I'm telling you because you have a right to know. You don't have to believe me, but I'm an investigative journalist. It's my job to discover the truth.'

Fabricating a scandal in order to make her name as a newshound was contemptible. Even if it was immediately discredited, an accusation like that could ruin my husband's reputation. For a moment, I was too furious to speak.

'You're interviewing head teachers and their spouses for a feature in a magazine,' I pointed out coldly, when I had regained my composure sufficiently to respond. 'That's hardly investigative journalism.'

'You don't have to believe a word I say, but I felt I ought to let you know.'

She explained that during the course of his interview with her, Nick had been called out of the room.

'I was left on my own in his office, sitting beside his desk.' She hesitated. 'The top drawer was open and I noticed a handwritten note. It caught my eye because ... because it was written on pink paper.'

Although I knew she was making it up as she went along, I had to admit she was convincing. Listening, I wondered if she believed her own lies.

'So I took a screenshot of it on my phone.'

'You had no right to do that! Delete the photo at once. How dare you go snooping–'

'Here you are,' she said, holding out her phone. 'Take a look for yourself.'

Against my better judgement, I glanced at the screen. The image appeared to show a rather passionate love note.

'But it's not addressed to anyone.'

As relief swept through me, I realised that her allegation had actually disturbed me quite considerably, in spite of my protestations to the contrary. I had noticed the way female members of staff clustered around Nick, hanging on his words and giggling at his jokes. He dismissed my concerns with a laugh, assuring me that the young teachers were currying favour in the hopes of gaining promotion or glowing references, and their attentions meant nothing to him. If anything, he said, he found them irksome. But having witnessed how he enjoyed their banter, I was uneasy. Anyone could be susceptible when tempted. Far better to avoid temptation than gamble with what fragile happiness we had.

Knowing my own suspicions were foolish and unfounded, I dismissed Rosie's allegation with a careless shrug. 'It could have been meant for anyone. There's nothing to suggest it has anything to do with Nick.'

'It was in his drawer. Why would I make up something like this?' She held out her phone again. 'Here, take another look.'

Shaking my head, I turned away from her. 'I'm not in the slightest bit interested in your malicious scandalmongering. It's time to rejoin my husband.'

The photographer had completed the shoot, and Nick chatted easily with the journalists, heedless of my silence. Watching him shake hands with Rosie, I kept quiet as he smiled at her and thanked her for her time, unaware that she had tried to stitch him up for the sake of a story.

'I'll email you,' Rosie muttered to me as she was leaving.

Giving her a frosty smile, I said nothing.

Although I did my best to put Rosie's accusation out of my mind, it rankled. It was difficult to stick to my decision to ignore what I had seen, and that night I barely slept. Every time I closed my eyes, I saw the note, neatly written on pink paper. There was no way that message could be misinterpreted, but it might have been intended for anyone. There was no reason to suppose it had anything to do with Nick, just because it had been seen in his desk. There was only a very slim chance that Rosie had drawn the correct conclusion. On the other hand, if she *was* right perhaps everyone at Edleybury knew that my husband was having an affair – everyone but me that is. As Rosie had pointed out, a wife is often the last person to know when her husband is seeing someone else.

The following afternoon I had arranged to play tennis with one of the PE teachers at the end of the school day. It was lovely weather for a game, bright but not too warm, with a gentle breeze sending clouds scudding across the sky to offer us some shelter from the sun which would otherwise have beaten down on us remorselessly. The conditions were perfect, yet I did not play well. Rosie's words kept running through my head: 'I'm sorry to be the one to have to tell you, but your husband's having an affair.'

'You're a bit off your game today,' my tennis partner, Angela, called out.

'Sorry.'

Not wanting to spoil the game for her, I focused on the ball. It wouldn't be much fun for my opponent if I failed to return a single serve, but it was an effort to pull myself back into the game, and I was relieved when it unexpectedly began to rain and we scurried off the court, passing a cluster of Japanese sixth formers hurrying towards one of the boarding houses.

'We ought to do more to encourage them to integrate,' Angela muttered as the boys went by, chattering in their native language.

Although my partner was older than me, she was a skilled tennis player, and moved effortlessly around the court. I had never been particularly good at sports, unlike my sister who had captained the girls' football team at school and had played in the netball team. It could easily have been embarrassing to be so outclassed on the tennis court, but Angela was generous enough to say she enjoyed playing with me, and she had the knack of putting me at my ease. In short, she was an excellent coach, feeding me simple shots and shouting encouragement rather than trying to win, although we both knew she could beat me without breaking into a sweat if she chose.

More interesting to me was the fact that, living on site, she was abreast of all the current gossip and often filled me in on what was being said about other members of staff. We had a good giggle over most of it.

'What's the latest on the Edleybury grapevine?' I asked her.

'Not a lot.'

A housemaster's wife was said to be having affair with a member of the PE department.

'But they're both married and they both live on site,' I protested.

'Of course there's not a word of truth in it, but I had you going for a minute there, didn't I.' She laughed. 'You'd be surprised at the stories the pupils make up.'

'I have worked in a school before. In my last place I was supposed to be a rampant lesbian, even though I'm happily married.'

'Oh yes, they'll have some story about you circulating by now. Last I heard, I'm supposed to be shagging David, along with most of the female staff, including Dot from the kitchen.' She laughed again. 'Teenage boys don't seem to be able to get their heads around the fact that a man can be happily single, and that it's actually possible for adults to be both healthy and celibate. I am, for one. I suppose I'd rather be with someone, as long as it was the right person, but I'm perfectly content to live alone. That's teenage boys for you. They have to pair us off together and have us shagging like rabbits. They just assume everyone is obsessed with sex.'

'Has David always been single?'

She nodded. 'There was supposed to be some girlfriend working in France, but I think he invented her for his application.'

'Application?'

'Yes, you know he applied for the headship when William retired?'

'Surely David knows they don't appoint internal candidates to headships.'

She shrugged. 'I guess he just thought he'd throw his hat into the ring, because you never know, do you?' She grinned. 'He dragged some woman into school and made out she was his girlfriend, but they didn't seem like a couple. When he brought her to the staff dining room and put his arm round her, they both looked pretty uncomfortable.' Angela chuckled at the memory. 'He made out they were planning to get married, but once he knew he hadn't got the job we never heard a word about her again. Apparently, they had conveniently 'split up', once he no longer needed to parade her around as his pretend fiancée. Sad and pathetic really.'

I thought about David, an old-fashioned schoolmaster perfectly suited to his current post, a vital disciplinarian in a school, but hardly a romantic figure.

'So what's the gossip about Nick?' I asked.

Angela shook her head. 'None as yet, but I've no doubt there will be. Just give it time.'

We laughed. Watching her closely, I believed she was telling the truth, but that didn't mean there was no hidden scandal about to break.

'And what about you?' I asked.

'What about me?'

'Is there anyone?'

She pulled a face. 'There was, but not anymore.'

'Oh, I'm sorry.'

'No, it's okay, we've been divorced forever. It was never really going anywhere. It was a mistake. Stupid, but there it is. I was happier on the day the divorce came through than I was on our wedding day.'

'Life can be a bitch,' I said, as though I had gone through a similar break up.

Actually, my own experience had been very different. Nick had proposed to me, in a manner of speaking, at the end of our first term at university. I was eighteen. To begin with I had been overawed by his attention. Everyone said he would go far, and the general faith in his abilities was borne out by his rapid progress from first year student representative to president of the students' union, while still managing to do well in his studies, eventually graduating with a first class Honours degree in History.

Attractive, intelligent and personable, as the son of a surgeon and a solicitor he had been raised by high-achieving parents who had managed to inculcate in him and his equally successful brother an unshakable self-confidence. We had waited for several years, but I had always known we would end up together. Only I was no longer sure that Nick was as committed to our relationship as I was. Doing my best to dismiss the idea that he could have the energy to chase another woman, I tried to forget about Rosie's allegation.

When Nick came home that evening, he was preoccupied with his work, talking at length about problem pupils, and troublesome parents who worried him more. I listened patiently to his complaints, pleased to provide him with a listening ear so he could vent his frustrations in confidence. On the pretext of not wanting to bother him, I shied away from challenging him about the note in his desk, refusing to acknowledge I was afraid of starting that conversation for fear of what it might reveal.

About a week passed before Rosie contacted me again.

'Can I see you?'

Immediately regretting having answered her call, I told her that I was extremely busy, which was true.

'I have the proof you asked for.'

'Proof?' I repeated, affecting not to know what she was talking about. 'Proof of what?'

'I thought you might want to see it.'

'Stop calling me.'

'I'm just telling you the truth. I don't think husbands who cheat should be allowed to get away with it.'

'Did your husband cheat on you?' I asked, noticing the bitterness in her voice.

'This isn't about me. I can go away and leave you alone, if you don't want to listen, but surely it's better to know the truth. Maybe you don't care if he's seeing someone else. This might not be the first time, for all I know, and if you're okay with it, that's up to you. I'm just telling you the truth, because you have a right to be aware of what's going on. Don't you want to be sure, one way or the other? I know I couldn't live with that sort of uncertainty.'

On the point of telling her to get lost, I hesitated. If the conversation ended right there, I would never find out what she had been going to say, and suspicion would eat away at me. It might be better to hear what she had to tell me, and put an end to her malicious gossip. So far, her "proof" had amounted to no more than a love letter that looked as though it had been written by a teenage girl to one of our sixth form boys. If that was all Rosie had to show me, her accusation would be quickly scotched, and I was keen to put an end to her lies. Even without any basis in fact, rumours could take hold.

Telling myself I was doing this to protect my husband's reputation, I agreed to see her. Keen that no one else should chance to overhear our conversation, I invited her to come to the house when Nick would be out attending a meeting with his departmental heads. Hanging up, I had an uneasy feeling that it was a mistake to see her again, but there was nothing else I could do. I had to know the truth.

Chapter 5

That night I slept badly, increasingly apprehensive about my meeting with Rosie and regretting the arrangement to see her again. It was too late to cancel her visit and besides, I *was* curious to hear what she had to say. The night passed slowly, but at last morning dawned on another beautiful sunny day. After watching Nick stride off to school, I tried to distract myself while I waited for Rosie, but my thoughts kept returning to her accusation. If it were true that my husband was having an affair, he might actually be seeing his mistress at that very moment. Horrible imaginings flashed through my mind until I was almost tempted to race over to his office to check that he was seated at his desk, focused on his computer screen or talking on the phone.

Admittedly, Nick was kept busy running the school – interviewing parents, writing reports, and discussing budgets for future projects – but at any particular time I had no idea what he was doing, and there were numerous places around the site where two people could slip away to spend an hour together unseen. The wording of the pink note Rosie had shown me on her phone seemed indelibly stamped on my brain: "Can't wait to be alone with you, my love, and feel you inside me again." The more I ran over the message in my mind, the less it sounded like something written by a teenage girl who would be more likely to use language like "make out" or "cock".

By the time Rosie arrived, I was tense with worry that she wasn't going to turn up and, what was even worse, fear about what she would tell me if she did. The bell rang promptly at ten o'clock, as we had arranged, and we sat down on a sofa in the living room. Without offering her anything to drink, I asked her what she wanted.

This time Rosie had brought a series of images. With a feeling that she was leading me to the edge of a precipice, I looked at the phone she had placed on the table in front of me. The screen showed my husband with his arm around his personal assistant, Sue. Rosie reached out and scrolled onto the next photo, which showed them kissing.

Shocked, I looked back at the first image to check the couple really were Nick and Sue, then went forward to the second one. This was no friendly peck on the cheek. The third image was even more compromising. With a low cry, I pushed the phone away from me and stared out through the window, trying to blot the image from my mind.

For an instant the room seemed to go black, but the upholstered seat of the sofa was pressing against my back, and Rosie's sphinx-like eyes were fixed on me, dark and inscrutable.

Recovered from my initial shock, I could only assume that the photographs were fake and said so. There was no reason to trust Rosie. For all I knew, she had a personal grudge against Nick. She could have been the mother of a child who had been expelled from the school, or bullied, like Bertrand in Year Nine. On the point of asking her if she had a son, I held back, because that information could be found in the school records. What I needed to discover was whether Rosie herself had any history with my husband, and that could only be learned from her.

Hard as it was to believe a complete stranger would have taken the trouble to mock up images of my husband having sex with his secretary, the only other possible reason for the photos was that he was actually having an affair. He wouldn't be the first man to have been seduced by someone he worked with so closely, and Sue was attractive. Whatever the truth, every explanation was disturbing.

Switching off the phone, Rosie slipped it back in her bag. 'You can have copies of the photos if you like. I can easily print them off for you.'

'Why would I want to look at them again?' I watched her closely. 'So let's have it. Where did you get hold of them?'

She nodded as though she had been expecting the question. 'As you know, I'm an investigative reporter. After coming across the note in your husband's desk, I decided to follow him around for a few days and see what I could find out. I'm so sorry, but this is where it led me.' She tapped her bag where she had put her phone. 'I'm a reporter,' she repeated. 'I have a nose for stories.'

'Stories?' I repeated scornfully.

This was my life she was dismissing as a "story". I could imagine the headlines. *Headmaster of public school caught with his pants down.* It was the kind of careless falsehood that destroys lives. On the other hand, if Rosie's allegation turned out to be true, then perhaps Nick *should* be exposed for the adulterer he was, hardly the kind of man to be head of a prestigious school.

While deriding her scandalous allegation as slander, I was also weighing up the implications should the accusation prove to be true. If Rosie published her photos, my whole way of life would be threatened: the money, the house, the travel, the pension for our old age. Everything would be snatched away from us. Whatever happened, this allegation must never become public. To protect my marriage and my status, I had to ensure Rosie never published her story or showed the photos of my husband to anyone else.

'What are you after?' I asked. 'Are you intending to blackmail us? Because you won't get away with it.'

She gaped at me in genuine surprise. 'Do you think I want to be paid to keep quiet about this? Listen, Louise, we're not discussing whether to expose a crime, are we? I mean, it's not as if your husband's been interfering with little boys. A man takes a mistress. It's hardly big news.' She shook her head. 'I don't think it would even make the front page of the local paper. The photos aren't exactly titillating, are they? Two adults shagging between the sheets.'

I shuddered. This was my husband she was talking about, the man I loved more than anyone or anything else in the world.

'What are you doing here then? What do you want?'

'It's like I told you, I think you have the right to know what's going on. This is about you, Louise. It's your life. If you want to sweep this under the carpet, that's up to you. For all I know, you've been in this position before and have made a deliberate choice to turn a blind eye to your husband's goings on. You wouldn't be the first woman to put up with a partner playing away from home. You can forget about it, if you like. I'm not planning to tell anyone. As far as I'm concerned, this is a private matter between you and your husband. It's really not that interesting to anyone else.'

We both knew that wasn't exactly true. The police might not attach any importance to my husband's affair, but the school governors would react very decisively to the discovery that the head of Edleybury was an adulterer.

'I'll let myself out, shall I?' she said, standing up.

I had no intention of offering her tea. 'I'll see you to the door,' I replied stiffly, and heard myself thanking her politely as she left.

I was still undecided what to do when Nick came home.

'How was your day?' I enquired.

As usual, he reeled off a series of meetings and incidents.

'So what have you been up to?' he asked, when he had finished.

'Nothing out of the ordinary,' I lied, as though hearing he was unfaithful was an everyday occurrence. 'I played tennis with Angela and then sent out a batch of emails about a gathering I'm arranging with the parents association. Did you eat at school or shall I make you something?'

'I ate earlier.' He peered at me. 'Are you all right?'

'Sure. I'm just a bit tired. Were you pleased with the way the interview went the other day?' I asked, unable to restrain myself from touching on the subject.

'You mean the interview we did for the magazine?'

I nodded.

'It should be fine. Why?'

'No reason. Just that the feature is due to come out soon.' I hesitated, doing my best to sound casual. 'Had you met her before?'

'Who?'

'The reporter. The one who interviewed us.'

'Do you mean before she came here to do the interview?'

'Yes.'

'No, not that I recall. Why? Should I have known her from somewhere?'

'You tell me.'

'I just said, I don't ever remember seeing her before we did the interview. Why do you ask?'

'No reason. Only she seemed to know you.'

He nodded, without showing much interest. 'That's just her patter, isn't it. It's not so very different to my giving parents the impression I know who they are, and know all about their precious sons. I'm an experienced liar too.' He laughed. 'A professional liar. It's what I'm paid to do.'

'So you've never met her before?'

'No. Why, should I have done?' He was frowning, mildly irritated. 'What's this about?'

I shook my head. 'Oh, nothing. Just that she seemed to know you, that's all.'

'Of course, she would have read up about me before coming here,' he replied, with unconscious arrogance.

He sounded so indifferent, it was hard to believe he had met Rosie before, let alone had any kind of relationship with her. I wondered whether some other experience could have prompted her to want to wreck our marriage. Nick and I had been together since we met in our first year at university. It was inconceivable he could have a jealous ex-girlfriend. The most likely explanation was that Rosie was an aggrieved mother who blamed us for her child's academic failure.

I spent the following day tracking down the names of every pupil Nick and I had ever taught, without once coming across a mother called Rosie White. I even looked up the records of Bertrand in Year Nine, in case he had any relations called White. Realising this accusation against my husband was taking up far too much of my time, I resolved to put the whole thing out of my mind, once and for all, simply refusing to entertain the idea that he was unfaithful. He told me he had never met Rosie White before, and there was no reason to doubt his sincerity.

Only now it was Nick's words that kept repeating in my head: 'I'm a professional liar.' After an admission like that, how could I trust anything he said?

Chapter 6

However hard I tried to forget about it, Rosie's accusation blistered at the back of my mind. No matter how many times I told myself Sue couldn't possibly be Nick's mistress, my dreams were plagued with images of them together. When I finally determined to approach him about it, I floundered. To be fair, the opportunity to broach the subject rarely presented itself. When he wasn't busy, he was preoccupied. In the end I resolved to stop giving any credence to what was no more than idle tittle-tattle passed onto me by a stranger. If Nick and Sue were having sex they could hardly have kept it hidden from the whole school. Someone would have noticed or heard something, and rumours would have been rife. Yet no one had intimated by so much as a glance, a lowered voice or a raised eyebrow, that there was something going on of which I should – or shouldn't – be aware.

The truth was, I didn't have enough to occupy my mind and, as a consequence, my thoughts were meandering off in all sorts of foolish directions. Realising I needed something else to focus on, I went to ask the person who was best placed to advise me. Sue had been recruited by the previous headmaster and had been in her post as his secretary for just over seven years when Nick had inherited her with the job. Keeping her on as a useful source of information about the school system, he was soon telling me that she was a valuable asset to him in his new role.

'No point in reinventing the wheel,' he told me cheerily. It was one of his favourite sayings.

For my part, I had been pleased that Sue was there, making Nick's life easier. She was thirty-five and single. Attractive, blonde, trim and pretty, it had never occurred to me to view her as a possible rival for my husband's affection until Rosie had planted the thought in my mind, but it seemed perfectly reasonable to suppose there might be a mutual attraction. They certainly had ample opportunity for intimacy, meeting as they did before the school day began.

Since January, Nick had taken to going to his office as early as half past six to confer with her, before going to breakfast in the main dining room where he often ate, as he thought it was good to show himself around the school as much as possible. While I had previously agreed with his decision, I began to speculate about what he and Sue got up to while the rest of the school was still asleep. Banishing such uncomfortable thoughts from my mind, I entered her office, which was adjacent to Nick's.

'Nick's interviewing prospective parents,' she told me, assuming I was there to see my husband. 'He should be done in about half an hour. That's if they don't overrun.'

'Actually, it wasn't Nick I wanted to see. I came to speak to you.'

Sue smiled, without any appearance of surprise. People were always popping into her office with queries, and she made it her business to know and welcome everyone. She was the perfect head's secretary, skilled at protecting him from unwanted visitors without causing offence. She was so charming, it seemed incredible that I had never before questioned whether she might have cast her spell over my husband.

'So, how's everything going with you?' she asked me, appearing genuinely interested.

'I'm hoping you can give me some pointers on what to do. With the Gala Dinner and Ball coming up at the end of term, it feels as though I ought to be doing more than I am. To be honest, I'm kicking my heels and it doesn't seem right. I mean, now we're settled in the house and everything, I sometimes feel a bit like a spare part. You're always so frantically busy, I really want to help as much as possible.'

'I hope I don't give the impression that I'm frantic,' she replied, with her disarming smile. 'If I were you, I'd enjoy it if you have a little breathing space. You'll be busy enough when the new year starts, I'm sure.'

Registering how perfectly white her teeth were, I wondered whether she kept herself looking so spruce for a particular man in her life: my husband. With her quick smile and soft voice, she was an easy person to like, and clearly dedicated to her job, but I wondered whether her commitment was actually to the school, or to its head. Up until then Sue and I had developed a good working relationship. To be fair, I got on well with all of my new colleagues, which I hoped wasn't solely on account of my position as the headmaster's wife. I had always been too quiet and retiring to be particularly popular, but people generally seemed to like me well enough.

'What about the arrangements for the end of term?' I tried again. 'There must be something I can do to help.'

'It's all under control. At least, that's what I tell myself.' She gave a little laugh.

'That's good to hear.'

What I would really have liked was her honest advice about what to wear for the Gala Dinner and Ball which was, by all accounts, a glamorous occasion, the most talked-about event in the school year. It was daunting, yet thrilling, to think that everyone would be looking at me, as the new headmaster's wife. I might be attractive, but I needed to look like more than a trophy wife. I wanted to make Nick proud of me and, as his consort, to be the envy of every other woman in the room. It was vain of me, I know, but we had worked hard to achieve our status in life, and deserved to enjoy our success. Given her position as Nick's secretary, Sue seemed an appropriate person to consult, yet I held back, conscious that she might actually be more to him than that. Before the silence threatened to become awkward, Sue spoke to keep the conversation flowing. In some ways she would have made a far better headmaster's wife than me.

'I think we're nearly ready,' she said. 'Which means I haven't packed yet. But Nick's well prepared, of course. He's checked his notes and they seem to be okay, which is a relief.' She smiled and nodded agreeably at me.

'Yes, he can be a bit of a stickler,' I agreed, wondering what she was talking about and reluctant to betray my perplexity.

'Anyway, I'm sure he'll be brilliant,' she added. 'He always is. But you should know. You usually go with him to these conferences, don't you? Of course, it's going to be different this time, with him being a headmaster.'

She referred to Nick with a touch of what sounded like proprietorial pride, which made me uneasy. I realised she was referring to the coming weekend, when Nick would be going to a headmaster's conference, giving his first speech as a member of that august group. He had been a deputy head for four years but was young to be appointed as a headmaster and was nervous about giving his first speech to his more-experienced peers. It had been a mutual decision for me to stay at home and, as Nick put it, "hold the fort".

'I want you to call me every evening,' he had said. 'Even if there's nothing to report, I want to know that everything's all right here.'

Sue had mentioned her own packing, so I assumed she was going away for the weekend as well. It made sense for her to take the opportunity to have a couple of days off while Nick was out of school. Her absence would leave me without her back up if anything should go wrong, but that wasn't really a problem. The deputy head would be around, and he was a capable man, and besides, Nick was only on the other end of a phone.

'So where are you off to?' I asked breezily.

Her ready smile wavered, and I sensed it was her turn to be baffled. With a horrible jolt, I listened to her chatter on, confirming my sudden suspicion. I did my best not to look startled when the penny finally dropped.

'Didn't Nick tell you I was going with him to Derby?'

'Oh yes, of course,' I replied, speaking too loudly, and laughing to hide my consternation at the bombshell she had just dropped.

I left the room before she could see that I was upset. Nick had told me all about the weekend conference in Derby, but he had never mentioned he was taking Sue with him. That was a clear indication that he wanted to spend time alone with her, without my knowledge. I resolved to tackle him about it, head on, that evening.

'You're off to Derby this weekend, aren't you?' I asked him, in as casual a tone as I could muster.

He grunted.

'Why don't I come with you?' I went on brightly.

I had thought better of confronting him directly about Sue, choosing instead to approach the issue in a more roundabout way. There was still a slim chance I had misunderstood the situation, but Nick's frown fed my growing agitation.

'I thought we agreed that you would stay here to be my eyes and ears while I'm away.'

'If we did, I don't remember.'

'You said it was one thing coming with me to Japan, but Derby was just too far to travel.' He chuckled.

Recollecting saying that the last time he had gone to London, I gave a noncommittal nod.

'I can't say I blame you,' he went on. 'Derby wouldn't be my first choice of places to visit. I mean, the school itself is beautiful, but it's stuck right outside the town, miles away from anywhere, and there'll be nothing for you to do there. You'd be bored silly. No, I don't blame you for not wanting to come.'

'I just thought it might be nice to spend the weekend with you.'

'It wouldn't be nice,' he replied impatiently. 'You know I'll be tied up all day in meetings, and at dinner in the evenings.'

'So you're going on your own?'

His eyes glittered as though he realised I was trying to catch him out, and was calculating his next move.

'Sue's coming with me. She's been on a training course about data security so she's the obvious person to attend a conference like this. In fact, I'll be largely redundant as I won't understand most of what they're talking about. It's all very technical, to do with General Data Protection Regulations and the internet, very boring stuff but essential. It's a legal requirement so we have to get it right. It's a nuisance and I wish we didn't have to waste time on it, but everyone's in the same boat and it's got to be done.'

He was trying too hard to justify his choice and I knew then that I had been stupid, shutting my eyes to what had been going on under my nose. In themselves, his words could have been perfectly innocent but, under the circumstances, I was convinced he was lying about his reason for wanting Sue to accompany him to Derby. My attempt to dismiss any thoughts of Nick and Sue together vanished in that moment.

'I hope it won't be too dull for you,' I said.

I have no idea how I kept my composure, while inwardly seething with rage and disappointment.

'I expect I'll manage.'

'I'm sure you will,' I muttered sourly as I stalked out of the room.

Glancing over my shoulder, I saw Nick sit down at his desk and switch on his laptop. I hovered in the doorway for a second, but he didn't look up.

Maybe I overreacted. After all, a lot of husbands cheat, leaving their wives with two choices: end the marriage or tolerate the infidelity. But perhaps the only reason most women don't plan a revenge like mine is that they lack the skill to carry it out.

Chapter 7

One of my roles in my previous school had been keeping track of pupils who went on the internet during lessons to visit social media sites, view inappropriate images, and communicate with their friends. Once in a while, a capable pupil would set up a fake account in order to visit unauthorised sites, or bully other pupils online. Trained in IT, I knew how to work my way around the system. In fact, before meeting Nick, I had considered pursuing a career in cyber security. The idea of becoming a government spook, tracking terrorist activity on the internet, had appealed to me. It might have been an easier life than struggling to control classes of rowdy teenagers. Now I decided to put my knowledge to use once again, but this time I was going to exploit my expertise in secret.

The closed-access Edleybury site was relatively easy to negotiate, compared to an open public system. Having cracked the main passwords, my next task was to create a fake ID that couldn't be traced back to any particular user. It took a while to set up, working around hoops that couldn't be jumped through, but however circuitous a route I took, there was always a risk the IT technicians would be able to track me down. Eventually, after a series of adjustments, I was able to log onto the school intranet from my own laptop independently of the system, but there remained a risk that the source of my trespass could be traced. For what I had planned, I needed to become an anonymous intruder in the school intranet, leaving no trail, so that no one would even know I was there. Working like an invisible virus inside the system, it had taken me nearly an hour to get past the first security hurdle. It was crucial to the success of my plans that I moved around without alerting the IT support technicians to my presence.

If I could have been left alone in the IT office for just a few hours it would have been possible to set up my fake identity in such a way as to avoid detection, but I couldn't risk anyone noticing me. Then it struck me that Nick would be away in Derby for two nights. This could be my chance to enter the IT office without anyone knowing, because staff only worked there during the school day. Very rarely were the technicians required to carry out maintenance at night; most of the routine servicing took place in the holidays.

Nick and Sue left for Derby on Thursday afternoon. Having waved my husband off, I went indoors and set my alarm for one thirty in the morning. It was an unnecessary precaution, as I didn't fall asleep that night. Dressed in dark jeans and a black shirt, with a navy scarf covering my fair hair, I left the house at two o'clock and headed towards the main school compound. It was warm during the day but, after the sun set, the temperature dropped significantly. It may have been the slight chill in the air that made me shiver as I hurried across the moonlit grass.

My heart pounded as I stole between trees that bordered the path between our house and the main school site. Although I had done nothing wrong, and even my planned transgression wasn't exactly illegal, I felt like a criminal. Had I been challenged, I would have said that I was taking a walk, unable to sleep while Nick was away. It would sound perfectly plausible. There was no call for me to feel frightened.

A few light clouds scudded slowly across a startlingly bright moon. I crept on, moving stealthily even though there was no one there to witness my silent progress towards the school. Suddenly a bird screeched. It must have been an owl that made the harsh cry, sounding like a terrified woman. I started and nearly let out a shriek of my own. Trembling, I stood perfectly still for a moment, struggling to recover my self-control. There was no reason why the headmaster's wife shouldn't take an innocent walk around the grounds at night, I told myself fiercely. And so far, I had done nothing else.

The clouds drifted across the moon as I reached the main school building, allowing me to walk towards the IT block in almost complete darkness, until my movement set off the security lights. Cursing my oversight, I pressed myself against a wall of bricks still warm after the heat of the day. There was no response to the lights coming on. If the security guard who occasionally patrolled the site had noticed, he would probably have assumed a cat, or perhaps a fox, was responsible. Fortunately for me, he spent most of his time indoors, relying on the alarm system to alert him to any intruders. All the same, I stayed close to the wall and tried to stay out of sight in case anyone happened to look out.

Reaching the main block without hindrance, I made my way around the side of the building to the computer suite. Fumbling in the darkness, I pulled on rubber gloves and reached out to switch off the alarm. For a terrifying instant all was silent and I was afraid someone else was there, but then I heard the reassuring beep of the alarm as it was deactivated, signalling that the office was unoccupied. I hoped no one would decide to try their luck at burgling the computer building that night, while the alarm was turned off. It had been a target for attempted break-ins in the past. But even if it was discovered that the alarm was not on, no one could point a finger at me as the culprit. I had my story ready, in case of disturbance, but no one challenged me as I entered the IT office.

Safely inside, I worked fast, and before five o'clock was back home, trembling but safe. No one had spotted me resetting the alarm and stealing away across the grass, leaving an invisible trace of my unauthorised intrusion, a false identity embedded in the system. I called myself Avenger which was not merely appropriate, but was the kind of name a boy might choose. The pupils gave themselves many such nicknames, but mine was the only one not linked to a real account. If someone happened to come across Avenger roaming around in the system, they would hopefully assume my fake identity was one of the many names innocently dreamed up by pupils. It was concealed in an army of names like Darklord, Warrior and Champion, along with the less imaginative accounts listed under the users' real names: Partridge Jake, and Wolsey Daniel.

With everything in place, I waited until Nick was back from Derby before typing my first email, sending it to all the staff, both academic and ancillary. My initial sally was fairly tame; I just wanted to see what kind of reaction it would provoke: "Sue Ross is a dirty slut".

Even though I was fully committed to what I had written, my finger seemed to act independently of my will, hesitating to touch the "send" icon. Then, with one tiny tap, it was done. A burst of elation surged through me, like a mind-altering drug. I may have actually laughed out loud. The sense of liberation was almost overwhelming. And then, just as rapidly, my mood changed. Aghast at what I had done, I switched off my laptop and concealed it under a pile of underwear in a drawer in my bedroom, telling myself that was the end of it, I had sent my email, and had my fun. But by the time I left the bedroom, my nerves had calmed, and I knew that my hate campaign had only just begun.

They say a murderer always returns to the scene of the crime. I hadn't committed a crime, yet I felt compelled to see the effect my email had on Sue. With my laptop safely hidden, I walked to the main school compound to look for her, and found her seated at her desk. Even if I hadn't known already, I would have realised at once that something was amiss. Usually cheerful and lively, Sue was staring in dismay at her screen, her face pale.

'Are you all right?' I asked, stifling my glee.

She didn't respond.

'Are you all right?' I repeated, leaning forward over her desk and raising my voice slightly.

'What? Oh yes.' She sat up with a start, as though she had only just noticed me standing there. 'Yes, some stupid nonsense one of the pupils is getting up to. It's nothing.'

I pressed my lips together, forcing myself to act as though I knew nothing about the email.

'What sort of nonsense? Is something bothering you? Sue, is something wrong?'

She hesitated, then beckoned me to go round behind her desk to look at her screen.

'You're going to see it soon enough anyway,' she said. 'It's addressed to all staff. Everyone's going to know about it before long.'

'Oh my God,' I blurted out, feigning surprise at what I had seen. 'How stupid.'

'Isn't it just.'

'What evil little minds some of these kids have, spreading insults like that. I'm sure Nick will find out who's behind it.'

'I hope whoever's responsible for it is thrown out.'

She seemed far more upset than I would have expected if she were truly innocent. With any luck, she would think twice before messing around with my husband again.

'I'm sure whoever did it will be expelled,' I reassured her. 'This is completely out of order. I'll make sure Nick looks into it straight away and puts a stop to it. We can't have emails like that being sent round.'

Sue thanked me for my sympathy and I gave an appropriately gracious response before walking out of her office, trying not to smile, and hugging my secret to myself.

Chapter 8

Already I was thinking how that one short email could be the start of an extended campaign, and it was going to be brilliant. In addition to the challenge of going undetected, revenge, I discovered, was fun. Any fleeting sympathy I had felt for Sue was quickly dispelled in a tide of jealous rage. A woman who slept with my husband deserved to be punished and, with any luck, her discomfort would drive her to resign.

Thinking up other messages I could send, I made my way to the staff room, a small brick building situated between the library and the science block. Under no circumstances were pupils allowed to cross the threshold, and that in itself was sufficient reason for most of the staff to gather there at break times. Unless they were on duty, they would sit indoors, whatever the weather, drinking tepid coffee, and grumbling companionably about the pupils.

Perching on a lumpy upholstered bench reminded me of my own years in the classroom. In some ways I missed the banter with pupils, but by and large I considered myself well out of it. Every year there had always been at least one pupil who had bugged me. I might only see that particular boy or girl twice a week, in a class of thirty other pupils, but that one unwelcome presence could be enough to cast a blight over my whole week. Knowing that I would never again have to handle my worst-behaved pupils gave me a frisson of relief.

The Edleybury staff looked increasingly browbeaten as the term wore on, and already an air of gritty exhaustion hung around them. Their complaints sounded familiar: an uncontrollable boy in Year Nine, a gang of bullies flexing their muscles in Year Ten, a disaffected sixth former, an incompetent head of department. Then there were the clusters of keen teachers discussing arrangements for outings and trips, while others argued earnestly about government policies and incessant syllabus changes from examination boards, devised by people who had never set foot in a classroom. One cabal of grey-haired men dropped their voices at my approach, and I knew they must be criticising my husband. I didn't mind. It wasn't long since I had been in their shoes. Pleased to have escaped from the classroom myself, I pitied them all. Even the newly qualified ones, barely out of the sixth form, spoke more cautiously than they had done at the beginning of the year, when they had arrived glowing with naive enthusiasm.

Beneath a general air of camaraderie, rivalries and disagreements flourished. One of the points of contention was the installation of interactive whiteboards which enabled the use of online resources. The History Department was a case in point, with a clear split between a teacher close to retirement who insisted on encouraging the habit of studying from books, and his younger colleagues who taught using interactive lessons downloaded from the internet. This particular division of opinion provoked heated discussions in the staff room, in which David was the champion of traditional teaching.

As I crossed the room to find a seat, my attention was caught by one of the English department talking animatedly. 'They're sent here for an English education and what happens? They end up spending all their free time hanging around with other Japanese students talking in Japanese. And we're expected to get them up to speed with their language. They might as well stay at home and spend the money on one-to-one English tutoring there.'

One of his colleagues laughed. 'The fees here would buy a hell of a lot of private lessons!'

'But they don't only come here to learn English, it's also an opportunity to experience the culture,' another teacher pointed out.

'Culture? What culture?'

'We take them to London, and they learn English manners and customs just by being here.'

'The only thing they learn...'

The sound of the discussion faded, swallowed up in the general buzz of voices as I moved further away. I refrained from pausing to interrupt them to tell them that Nick had plans to increase the number of overseas students attending the school. There were other matters on which I was less reticent, and the responses I received were also irritatingly familiar. A recurrent topic of conversation was the quality of coffee available at break times: tasteless and often lukewarm.

'You ought to do something about the staff room tea trolley,' I told Nick that evening.

'The tea trolley? What's wrong with the tea trolley?'

'It's heavy, and someone has to wheel it all the way from the kitchen to the staff room every day.'

'That's their job.'

'I just think we could have a more efficient way of delivering coffee to the staff at break time. Why can't they have a proper coffee machine?'

He shook his head. 'A staff coffee machine is hardly top of my list of priorities. If that's the way it's always been done here, I see no reason to worry about it right now. There are more important changes I need to implement before I can turn my attention to that kind of trivia.'

I decided to mention it to David, but he gave me the same answer as Nick.

'That's what we do here.'

For a few days after my insulting email, the teachers talked about little else. I listened to as much of the gossip as I could, joining in but guarding against showing an undue interest in the topic. The consensus among the staff was that only a moronic pupil would have sent so puerile an email, and I concurred with the general censure of the adolescent author of the message. Anything that diverted attention away from the truth was fine by me.

'It's vile,' was the general view, summed up by one of the older teachers.

'Yes, to target an individual like that is nasty,' a member of his department agreed.

'It's bullying of the worst kind,' a younger colleague said.

'Cowardly,' another teacher added. 'Sending anonymous emails is the pathetic action of a coward.'

'And to target Sue, of all people,' the art teacher commented. 'She's the most inoffensive person imaginable.'

'It's irrelevant who the victim is,' someone else said. 'It's unacceptable whoever it's aimed at, and the head needs to do something about it.'

'But what can he do if we don't know who sent it?' David chimed in.

Just as the chatter was beginning to die down, a sixth former found out about the email and the word quickly spread. By the end of the day, even the least clued-up pupil had heard about it. That started the chatter all over again, only this time the staff were incensed that the information had been leaked to pupils. From the little I was able to gather, older members of staff blamed their younger colleagues for becoming overfamiliar with some of the sixth form.

'We're their teachers, not their mates,' the grey-haired head of science said to one of his cronies.

Everyone knew what he was talking about.

'Bunch of cantankerous curmudgeons,' a young history teacher muttered as she walked past.

It was an argument I had heard many times before, and I paid scant attention to it once I was satisfied that no one had come close to guessing the identity of the author of the email.

Nick was furious the pupils had found out. He talked about little else at home for a couple of days. Finally he issued a memo to the staff highlighting the need to behave professionally at all times, and to bear in mind that they were responsible for maintaining an appropriate relationship with the pupils in their care. After that, the fuss died down, and other issues took over, with a Year Eleven parents' evening looming.

All the time this had been going on I had been wildly excited, because I alone knew the truth. Even Nick hadn't unmasked me. At the same time, the fear of discovery was somehow thrilling. I had never before realised how similar terror was to exhilaration. I had to watch what I said, and continued to listen out for any hint of suspicion against me, but another week passed and nothing happened. Soon I began to miss the adrenaline rush of my secret attack, so I sent another message, reasoning that one more couldn't do any harm. The damage had already been done.

Nick stormed into the house that evening, red faced with anger.

'There's been another one.'

He glared at me so furiously, I was afraid he had discovered the truth.

'Another what?' I stammered, stalling for time as I tried to think. 'Come inside and take your jacket off. Cool down, and tell me what's happened.'

Ignoring my exhortations to remove his jacket and tie, he flung himself down on a chair and told me a second insulting email about Sue had gone around the school. 'This one calls her a whore!' he cried out, incandescent with rage. 'I'm going to find out who's behind it, and he – or she – is going to be expelled. No second chances. No wriggle room. I don't care who it is. That stupid child is going to be sent packing.'

'He's hardly stupid if he's managed to send an email to the whole staff without being caught,' I pointed out quietly, carefully sticking to the idea that the author of the email was a boy. 'Can't the IT technicians find out who it is? Surely they can trace all the passwords.'

'Yes, well, apparently they can't,' Nick replied crossly. 'Somehow the little bastard's managed to conceal his identity.' Nick looked at me, his eyes suddenly bright. 'You!'

I seemed to be drowning, gasping for air. 'What do you mean?'

Nick was too wound up in his own feelings to notice my agitation, but I vowed that if I managed to talk my way out of this, I would never send another clandestine email again. No amount of excitement was worth terror like this. My whole life was about to crash around me, and I could do nothing to stop the disaster. Worse, I had brought it on myself by my arrogant belief that I was too clever to be detected. Now that Nick knew, the repercussions would be catastrophic.

'You,' Nick repeated.

'Me?' I stammered. 'I don't... I never... '

'Yes, you could find out who did this,' Nick said. 'That's what you did in your last school, isn't it? When that sixth form boy sent round a pornographic image. You tracked him down, didn't you?'

'Yes, I managed to trace him. It wasn't that difficult because he had created a new identity using his own laptop. He was clumsy, very clumsy. So yes, of course I'll do what I can. You know that. Whatever I can do to help. You don't even need to ask. That is, you only had to ask.' Exuberant in my relief, I was talking too much. Adopting an earnest expression, I slowed down and took a deep breath. 'Obviously this has to be stopped and I'll do whatever I can to help. But if the culprit has been using the school system, I'll need access to the IT office,' I added thoughtfully.

'Of course, of course. You can have the run of the place at lunchtime. I'll have a word with Don.'

The next day, while the IT team were at lunch, I scheduled Avenger's next email to go out in the evening, while pupils would be enjoying free time before lights out, and I would be at home with my husband. I hesitated over the wording. Having used "slut" and "whore", I settled for calling her a "slag". It wasn't very imaginative, but it would hopefully be enough to put pressure on Sue to look for another job, while no hint of suspicion fell on me.

Chapter 9

As well as obtaining compromising photos of my husband and his secretary, Rosie had found a note which she claimed Sue had written to Nick. It was difficult to know whether to believe that since I had never seen a sample of Sue's handwriting, with communication at school being almost exclusively electronic. As long as he had no reason to suppose anyone suspected him of adultery, Nick might have felt no need to hide the note, so it was probably still in his drawer. If I could find that note and somehow have it forensically checked for fingerprints, it might be possible to establish whether or not Sue had been romantically involved with my husband, but I had no contacts in the police. Even so, I wanted to look at the note, in the probably vain hope that it might reveal something about the writer. Waiting until Nick was out having lunch with the senior management team, I slipped into the main administration block.

No one took any notice of me as I made my way along the corridor to Nick's office. Turning the key silently, I glanced around before slipping through the door and locking it behind me. Safely inside, I dashed over to the desk and pulled open the top drawer. Carefully emptying it, I put all the contents down on the top of the desk in the exact same order that I had removed them so they could be replaced without Nick noticing anyone had been rummaging around inside his desk. A pile of letters which I flicked through quickly, a handful of pens, loose paper clips, a six-inch ruler, a couple of propelling pencils, and other assorted small items of stationery were soon stacked neatly on the desk.

There was no sign of a love note anywhere, but I did find a pink envelope. It had Nick's initials on it and looked as though it was the same colour as the image I had seen on Rosie's phone. Sick with excitement at my trivial theft, I hid the envelope in my bag and carefully returned all the other items to the drawer. Then I left the office, anxious not to be seen. I could explain my presence quite easily by claiming to have been looking for my husband but if he learned about my trespass, and realised the envelope had vanished, he might suspect I had taken it.

Returning home, I went into the bedroom, wondering where to conceal the envelope while I thought about how to establish whether it had come from Sue. Having considered hiding it under the mattress, or in the bathroom cabinet, or in one of the drawers of my wardrobe, I decided finally that my jewellery case was the only place where no one else might possibly chance to look. Tipping a string of pearls and matching earrings onto the bed, along with a diamond pendant, and all of my less expensive necklaces and jewellery, I raised the velvet base of the box, slid the envelope underneath it out of sight, replaced the black velvet square, and put all my jewellery back in the box. As it turned out, I finished just in time, because shortly after I put my jewellery away I heard the front door slam.

I hurried downstairs to greet Nick in the hall and enquire how his latest meeting had gone.

'Same old, same old.' He smiled. 'It was a very pleasant lunch. Charlie did an excellent job – veal escalope, dauphinoise potatoes, asparagus – it was really very good. How was your morning?'

My preoccupation with searching Nick's desk, and settling on a hiding place for what I had found there, meant I hadn't eaten since breakfast. I mumbled vaguely about eggs, but it didn't matter what I said, because he wasn't listening.

'We talked mainly about staffing issues,' he continued with his own train of thought. 'Appointing a new head of maths in a year's time could be a problem because the department is so well established, and they're all a load of stick-in-the-muds, so it's going to be a tough call for a newcomer to lead them, but none of them wants to step up to the mark. I'm tempted to appoint a young woman. That would shake them up a bit.' Nick grinned. 'But we've got time. There's no immediate panic.'

He seemed so focused on school matters, it was almost impossible to believe he was having an affair. Yet I knew how easily lies slipped from his lips. Watching his well-loved face, I longed to forget all about Sue and the hideous photos and return to how we were before Rosie had aroused my suspicions. I wanted my life back. Meanwhile, the stolen envelope lay concealed beneath all the glittering jewellery Nick had given me. Had I been more courageous I might have confronted my husband then and there, or driven straight to Sue's house and asked her whether she had sent the love note. Instead, I asked Nick what he would like for dinner.

'I can make you something light later on,' I suggested, cursing myself for my cowardice.

I was relieved when he told me he had a meeting with the school bursar that afternoon, followed by dinner with the governors.

'I did tell you I was going out,' he said. 'This is where we get down to the nuts and bolts of discussions about the future of the school. The changes I'm proposing are going to mean a lot of work, but it will be worth it in the end. I'm planning to complete the foundations for the new building next summer, so we're going to need to reach a decision very soon.'

'It will be a culture change for some of the staff,' I said. 'Especially the older ones.'

'They're due to go out to pasture soon anyway, most of them. We can't be held back by a few old codgers.'

'Good luck with the meeting. I'm going shopping. Do you need anything?'

With the Gala Dinner approaching, we had no official engagements coming up at the weekend, because everyone was busy with preparations for the dinner and ball. Before I drove to the nearest shopping mall, I considered slipping back into Nick's office in his absence, to return the envelope to the desk drawer. There was a risk I would be spotted, but as long as the envelope was safely back in place, it hardly mattered if someone saw me entering my husband's office. There could be any number of innocent reasons why I might want to go in there.

The thought of the envelope hidden in my bedroom was making me jumpy. In any case, even if I managed to establish that Sue's fingerprints were on the envelope, that would prove only that she had handled it, as she did all Nick's post. There was no point in hanging onto it. I had been an idiot to take it in the first place. Once I reached my decision, I couldn't wait to get rid of it. I wasn't ready to confront Nick, nor was I going to speak to Sue about it.

Sitting on the bed, I saw that my hand was shaking as I held the wretched pink envelope. My first thought was to burn it. That way, even if Nick realised it had gone, he would never be able to trace the theft back to me. But if he knew it had been hidden at the back of his drawer before he had gone to lunch, and later discovered it was missing, he would have very few suspects because only I, the school caretaker, and Sue had keys to his office. And there was still an outside chance someone had seen me go to his office that morning. My only really safe option was to put the envelope back where I had found it.

Hurriedly making my way to the administration block, I entered Nick's office. This time I didn't care if I was seen. It was the work of a second to pull open the drawer and replace the envelope underneath a few other papers. With the drawer safely shut, anyone could find me in there and it wouldn't matter. Even so, I had an excuse ready, but no one challenged me, or even saw me as I left.

I could have confronted Nick about the love note, but had chosen not to. It was irrational, but returning the envelope seemed to have drawn a line under what had been going on. I just wanted to put some distance between myself and the scene of my recent misery. Relieved at my decision, and also slightly regretting my cowardice, I set off for the nearest shopping centre, a quarter of an hour's drive away. The school was set in acres of woods and farmland in a relatively isolated spot, making it difficult to go anywhere without a car. The location kept the pupils on site, except for a few sixth formers who had their own cars, but it also meant that security was an issue, and the computer labs had been broken into several times.

A weight seemed to lift from my shoulders as I left the school premises behind me. Driving through open fields, with the sun beating down, I felt a sense of freedom, and was convinced that my emails would succeed in deterring Sue from her pursuit of my husband. Certainly they would have made him think twice about continuing his adulterous relationship. If the school governors heard a whisper of a scandal involving him, he would lose his job. He might find another teaching post, but he would never gain another headship. However much he liked Sue, he had too much to lose by screwing around.

As I drove further away from the school, I endeavoured to find a way to forgive Nick, if not his mistress. With his appointment going to his head, he had lost sight of what mattered to him, but our marriage was strong enough to withstand that one brief aberration. Admittedly I had used devious means to achieve my purpose, but that didn't matter. I had been perfectly within my rights to do everything in my power to protect my marriage, and I had succeeded. The affair was over. From now on I was going to put it behind me and pretend it had never happened, and Nick would never know that I had found out, or what I had done to bring matters to a satisfactory conclusion. The only loser in all this would be Sue, who might end up out of a job if she didn't find another position soon. But that was her own fault for having messed around with my husband.

'Get your own husband,' I muttered to myself as I drove. 'Nick's mine.'

Chapter 10

At morning assembly, on the Monday after I had sent the third email, Nick addressed the whole school, insisting the vexatious emails stop at once. He promised to carry out an intensive investigation throughout the whole school, urging those responsible to come forward, and threatening to involve the police if the situation wasn't resolved by the end of the week.

'Bullying of any kind will not be tolerated here at Edleybury,' he declared, with a lot more rhetoric along the same lines, all designed to terrify the culprit into owning up. 'This abuse of a valued member of staff will not go unpunished.'

When he had finished his diatribe, David, the deputy head, took over, reinforcing the message. 'Rest assured we will track down whoever did this. If you come forward first and give yourself up, you will be suspended, but if you continue to skulk and hide, you will be expelled when we find you. And we will find you, and if appropriate we will report this matter to the police. We have IT experts searching the system right now, tracking you. Remember, there will be no second chance if you don't give yourself up. I expect to see whoever did this in my office immediately after assembly. I'll be waiting. However this ends, whether you choose to ruin your school career or salvage it, we will find you.'

Sitting at the side of the school hall with other staff, I had been observing the pupils' reaction to Nick's speech. Some of the younger boys looked anxious, but the majority of the pupils were sniggering. Clearly they were as entertained by the situation as I was. The main differences between us were that I knew the exhortations of the headmaster and his deputy would be fruitless, and I considered it politic to hide my amusement.

Some staff expressed the opinion that it would have been better if less attention had been paid to the emails, but Nick felt he had to do something. Accustomed to being in control, his fury at being unable to discover and discipline the miscreant was eating away at him. It gave me considerable satisfaction to witness his frustration. It served him right for cheating on me. Like his simpering mistress, he deserved to be thoroughly castigated for his adultery, but his punishment had to be meted out anonymously.

After assembly, I went along to Sue's office. Although I should have kept away from her, it was impossible to contain my curiosity.

'Just popping in to see how the arrangements for the end of year dinner are going,' I fibbed, 'and to ask what I can do to help.'

'What you can do?'

'Yes, what I can do to help out with the preparations. I know you've assured me everything's under control, but it's part of my remit to help with plans for the end of the year. You can't do everything yourself.'

Taking a seat with my back to the window, I gazed at her, noting how pale and tired she looked.

'Oh, seriously, everything's in hand, but it's very kind of you to offer,' she replied.

'You look worn out. I hope Nick's not making you work too hard? Seriously, Sue, he's a workaholic and that's his choice, to some extent, but it's up to you to make sure his expectations of you don't become unreasonable. You have to take care of yourself.' I approached her desk. 'Are you sure you're all right?'

For answer, she just shook her head mumbling inaudibly.

'Whatever's the matter?' I asked. 'What's happened? Sue, talk to me.'

Without warning, she burst into tears. Caught off guard, I felt a spasm of guilt in case my emails had really upset her. I used to tell my pupils to be careful what they said. 'You never know what other people are going through. A comment you find funny might be really hurtful to someone else, even if you think it's just a joke.' Now I had done exactly that, posting abusive messages without any consideration for Sue's feelings. Like a thoughtless teenager, I hadn't stopped to find out what else might be going on in her life.

'There's been another one,' she said.

I thought it best to pretend not to understand what she meant straight away. 'Another one? Another what?'

'You know, those emails about me. There's been another one.'

'Oh that.' I brushed it aside with a quick shake of my head. 'I really wouldn't take any notice of them. No one else does. It's just kids being stupid.'

'I know you're right, but you know how people think. There's no smoke without fire and all that. *You* don't think there's any truth in what they're saying, do you?'

I frowned. '*Is* there any truth to it?'

My question upset her all over again. Her eyes welled up and tears trickled down her pale cheeks. Somehow the anticipation of my revenge had been far more enjoyable than the reality.

'No, no, there isn't. Oh God, that's just what I mean. Even you suspect me of being–'

'Of course I don't,' I assured her, guilt momentarily dispelling my distrust. 'We had a similar episode in my last school. Seriously, Sue, no one took any notice. It was too stupid. Once the kids doing it realised their emails were being ignored, they got bored of it and stopped.'

'But they're not being ignored here, are they? Nick's told the school he's looking into it, and the police might be called in to investigate.' Her eyes filled with tears again and she flapped her hand, sniffing noisily. Having blown her nose, she added, 'I'm sorry, but your kindness just set me off.'

Seeing how distressed she was, I decided to change tack. Sending those emails had been a childish way to behave anyway and, although it had been gratifying to see both Nick and Sue disturbed by them, nothing had changed. In a way, I had scuppered myself. If I questioned Nick about having an affair, he might suspect I was responsible for sending those emails. I would have to keep silent for a while and then raise the subject with him indirectly, when an opportunity arose. Sooner or later I would have to learn the truth because this uncertainty was unbearable.

'Now that the head is taking it seriously,' I told Sue, 'and threatening to bring in the police, it's bound to stop. You'll see. Within a few days, everyone will have forgotten all about it.'

That evening Nick was at home. While we were having a drink before dinner, I couldn't resist broaching the subject in a roundabout way.

'You never told me about your weekend in Derby.'

He grunted. 'There wasn't much to say. It threatened to be dull as ditch water, and it was.'

'Did you miss me?'

He smiled. 'I was too busy to do anything but network and sleep,' he said. 'If there had been time to spend with you while I was there, I would have wanted you to come along. But no one else had their wives or partners with them.'

'It must have been helpful having Sue there,' I said, trying to sound casual.

He lowered his head to cough, and I suspected he was afraid his expression would give him away.

'I think it's those flowers,' he said.

'What?'

'Those flowers are making me cough. They have such a strong scent and I think it may be some sort of allergic reaction.' As though to underline his point, he coughed again.

'I'll get rid of them.'

'It's a pity because they are lovely, but...'

'Oh don't worry. They're past their best now anyway.'

He had succeeded in changing the subject, but I didn't intend to be put off that easily.

'So, you were telling me about Derby. How was it?'

'Just like I said, dull, although it was useful catching up with the other heads. I hadn't seen some of them since my appointment.'

He smiled. He might have been recalling the congratulations he had received from his peers, but the recollections making him smile could have been something very different.

'What are you thinking about?' was the closest I dared to go in challenging him about his weekend.

He shook his head. 'I was just thinking about the Gala Dinner and Ball at the end of term. Our first one. I can't believe it's nearly the end of our first year. What a year it's been!'

'A good year?'

'God yes! I mean, I knew it was going to be hard work, but I have to say I've loved every minute of it.'

'Even your dull weekend in Derby?' I asked as I picked up the heavy vase.

He laughed. 'Even my dull weekend in Derby.'

I turned away, imagining what was really going through his mind at that moment. But I couldn't harp on about Derby any longer without arousing his suspicion. As I took the flowers to the kitchen to throw them away, it struck me that the strongest scent came from a few lilies in the bunch. It was strange that the lilies in his office didn't affect him in the same way. While I was wrapping the flowers in a carrier bag, I heard Nick talking on the phone.

'I'm sorry,' he said. 'There's nothing else I can do.' He sounded stressed. 'This is just the way it's going to be from now on. I'm sorry, but things change, and that's all there is to it.'

The door to the living room closed, reducing his voice to a faint muffled drone, but what little I had been able to hear had given me hope. It sounded as though he might have been finishing his relationship with Sue. Despite everything he had made me suffer, I didn't want our marriage to end, and had already resigned myself to the fact that he had strayed. What I had to hang onto was that he had decided to bring his fling to an end, possibly spurred on by the emails suggesting that someone suspected what was going on. I would probably never get to the bottom of that, but the important thing was that the worry and strain of the situation were over. Nick was ending his affair and our marriage remained solid.

Chapter 11

While I was at the local village shop the following afternoon, my phone rang and I recognised Sue's extension. Normally I would have answered without a second thought, but the knowledge of the envelope stolen from Nick's desk made me jumpy, even though I was confident no one had seen me taking it or putting it back. Telling myself Sue couldn't possibly have discovered what I had done, I took the call.

'Hi Sue.' I forced myself to sound cheerful. 'How are you? Feeling any better?'

'Fine, I'm fine. Are you free this evening?'

Without knowing what she was going to suggest, that was a difficult question to answer. It was just as well she wasn't able to see the expression on my face.

'I think so,' I replied guardedly.

'Would you like to come round to my house?'

Having just told her I was free, it would be easy to go on to say that I needed to check my diary before committing myself, but there was no good reason to refuse. Besides, I was curious to know why she wanted to see me.

'Come for a bite of supper. About half past six? You know my address, don't you?'

Before I could reply she hung up, leaving me slightly surprised by the brevity of her call. Presumably she had to get back to work. I wondered whether it was wise to succumb to the temptation to see where she lived. The visit was bound to be awkward, but I wanted to know why she had asked to see me. With time to spare, I finished my shopping and then went home and put the kettle on.

Sitting over a mug of tea, I speculated about why my rival might want to see me at her house. If she wanted to discuss the plans for the end-of-term Gala Dinner and Ball, she would surely have done that at school. The most likely reason for her invitation was that she was simply being friendly, but the thought that she might want to talk about the emails made me shudder. I wracked my brains to think of any way she could have discovered what had happened, but I had left no telltale traces. Even if Sue had somehow cottoned onto the fact that I suspected her and Nick of having an affair, she would have no proof, and I had only to deny any accusations she might level at me.

With any luck, Sue would be upset by more than just a few emails, because I was fairly confident Nick had put an end to their affair. There was no way she would be able to talk about that situation openly with me, but she could talk about an unnamed man, or perhaps invent a name for her lover.

'The trouble is, he's married,' I imagined her telling me. 'His wife got at him and is forcing him to stop seeing me.'

It would be hard not to give away my feelings if she began talking along those lines.

'Does his wife know about you?' I might ask her.

And then I pictured her shaking her head, her blond hair fanning out around her face like a halo.

'No, I'm sure she doesn't know who I am, but I think she may have discovered he's having an affair.'

'What makes you say that?'

'Why else would he suddenly tell me he has to stop seeing me?'

'Perhaps he realised it was too great a risk.'

'A risk?'

'I mean, it would be a risk to carry on seeing you if he doesn't want his wife to find out.'

'But I think she knows.'

'Isn't that all the more reason why he would want to put a stop to it? Perhaps she threatened to expose him if he didn't, and then he'd lose his headship – that is, he might lose his job, whoever he is.'

I tried to imagine how the conversation would continue, but it might be something along those lines, and I would be walking on eggshells, making sure not to let on that I knew exactly who she was talking about. Although it seemed odd that she would want to talk about it with me, of all people, I supposed she might be hoping to pump me, in an attempt to find out whether I had discovered she had been having an affair with my husband. The more I thought about it, the more I realised it would be difficult not to reveal that I knew who she was talking about. But I was one step ahead of her, and would do everything possible to avoid the topic altogether.

As the time for our meeting approached, I drove to her house, feeling both agitated and curious. Sue lived in a nearby hamlet consisting of a few picturesque yellow-stone cottages, a pub that was popular with the staff at school, a small grocery store and a farm shop, all spread out beside a pond where white ducks paddled around, and an old and gnarled weeping willow tree drooped elegantly over the water. The streets were narrow and Sue's terraced cottage was perched half way up a hill which led away from the pond towards open fields.

Some unfathomable caution led me to park around the corner from her house and walk back down the hill. Carrying a bottle of wine, I went through the low wooden gate in her white picket fence, admiring the neatly kept front garden: a tiny lawn bordered with flowers. As I went up the path to the front door, I wondered how she managed to cut a patch of grass scarcely larger than most mowers. There was no answer when I rang the bell. Lifting the polished brass knocker, I rapped sharply on the door and was surprised to see it shift forwards. The door was not only unlocked, it had been left ajar. Puzzled, I pushed it open.

'Sue? Are you there?'

Obviously she was at home, or the door would have been locked. She must have left it open so I could let myself in. Even though I was there by invitation, it felt awkward entering the house without seeing anyone. The front door led directly into a square living room, comfortably furnished in an old-fashioned style, with embossed anaglypta wallpaper and armchairs upholstered in a flowery chintz material. There was no sign of Sue. I could imagine the rest of the house being equally orderly and, at the same time, fussy. A small white cat lying curled up in front of an ornate fireplace unfurled itself slowly and rose to its feet, glaring at me. It must have decided I posed no threat, and had brought no food, because it lay down on the hearth again and lazily closed its eyes.

'Sue?' I called out. 'It's me, Louise! I'm here!'

I closed the front door behind me and stepped into the middle of the room.

'Sue?'

Still there was no response. Even in such a small village, I couldn't imagine someone as organised as Sue would have gone out leaving the front door ajar. Wondering if she was waiting for me in the back garden, I crossed the room to an internal door which opened onto a long narrow kitchen with a breakfast bar that had space for one person to sit and eat. There was no sign of any food preparation, and the oven was switched off, which seemed strange, given that Sue had invited me over for supper. Possibly she had been intending that we should go out to eat. There was a pub within walking distance which might serve decent food. A small neat rear garden was visible through the window, but the back door was locked. This was becoming stranger by the minute.

I wondered whether I had the wrong day, but that didn't make sense because the front door had been left open, presumably for me. I called her again, but there was no response. I was beginning to grow uneasy. Leaving the bottle of wine on the breakfast bar, I went back into the living room and stood at the bottom of the stairs, calling out. 'Sue! It's Louise! I'm here! Sue!'

Still there was no answer. I had three choices: to sit down and wait for Sue to wake up or finish doing whatever was preventing her from hearing me shouting, abandon my visit altogether and go home, or look for her upstairs. The most likely explanation for her absence was that she had forgotten she had invited me over. But that didn't explain why her front door had been left open. If it hadn't been for that, I think I would have given up and gone home, taking my bottle of wine with me, but I was concerned that Sue might have fallen ill and be lying upstairs, unconscious. Far from feeling any goodwill towards her, I had every reason to wish her harm. So it was curiosity, rather than concern for her wellbeing, that led me to climb up the stairs in my rival's house.

Chapter 12

My feet made no sound on the thickly carpeted stairs. One tread creaked and I froze, listening, but there was no other sound. Feeling more than ever like an intruder, I called out loudly, but no one answered. It felt wrong to be going upstairs in her house without Sue knowing I was there. She could be asleep, and my unannounced appearance might shock her, even though my intentions were innocent and she had invited me to her house. Besides, it was possible that she was ill or had suffered some terrible accident. She might have slipped in the shower and hit her head, knocking herself out.

'Sue! Sue! Are you there? I'm coming upstairs. Sue!'

I continued up the stairs.

There were four doors leading off the landing. One on my left stood wide open. Inside was a bathroom with a sloping ceiling, neat and pretty enough, and spotless, but kitted out from a bygone era, with an avocado bath suite and white tiles dotted with yellow flowers. With its outmoded furnishings, the bathroom should have smelt of lavender and talcum powder instead of which there was a fresh tangy citrus scent. Gingerly I opened the second door to find a deep cupboard with a neat pile of pink and white towels.

The next door led to a small office with a pine desk and matching chair. A monitor, keyboard and lamp were neatly arranged on the desk, along with a stack of cardboard folders, an old-fashioned paper notebook and a painted ceramic pot of pens, and along one wall was a row of metal filing cabinets. Dark wooden beams across the ceiling looked as though they had been there for hundreds of years. Held back by embroidered sashes, pale curtains hung on either side of a lattice window, smaller than windows in modern houses. Approaching the desk, I saw that the notebook was in fact a black diary, with one week on display per page. Aware that Sue might come in at any moment, I glanced over my shoulder to check she wasn't watching before reaching for the book.

Several of the pages were blank. Others had cryptic notes about an unnamed man referred to only as "he" or "him", along with entries noting when she was due to see him and comments about gifts which "he" had given her. Some weeks there was no mention of "him" and once she had written that "he wants to stop". There was no explanation, but I assumed she meant he wanted to end the affair. I scanned through a whole month without finding anything to indicate who "he" was, but I could guess. Hearing a creaking noise, I hurriedly replaced the diary and moved away to continue my search for Sue.

The last door opened on a bedroom. Glancing inside, I barely noticed a flowery duvet cover and matching curtains, and hardly recognised my own shocked features glaring at me from the mirror above the dressing table on the wall opposite me. I have no idea how much time elapsed while I stood staring at the woman lying on a bed to my right. She was propped up against several pillows with her face turned towards the door, so that she appeared to be looking straight at me. Framed in blond hair, her face had a bluish tinge and she stared at me without blinking, her lips stretched in a horrible grimace. One glimpse of the distorted face was enough. I had found Sue.

For what felt like hours, I stood gazing at her in silence, my legs trembling. At last, I took a step towards her and called her name, in the desperate hope that she might still be alive. Not daring to touch her, I went no closer but stood, stupefied, calling her name. On the bedside table I saw a half empty bottle of whisky and a few white pills scattered beside a small bottle. A chair, upholstered in flowery fabric matching the duvet and curtains, lay on its side beside the bed. Without thinking, I reached out to set it upright then drew back in panic, aware that it would be wise to leave the house at once without touching anything else. Discovering the body of my husband's mistress was serious enough. If I was spotted at the scene of her death, and Nick and Sue's relationship subsequently came to light, my position could become extremely difficult.

No one but Rosie knew that I had learned about Nick's affair with Sue, but it took only one person to be indiscreet for a rumour to spread. I had to go and speak to Rosie at the first opportunity and persuade her not to tell anyone about our conversation. Or perhaps it might be better to say nothing and deny knowing anything about the affair, if Rosie went to the police or spoke to the papers. My urgent priority was to get away from Sue's house without being seen, and appear surprised and shocked when the news of her death reached us. If Nick learned where I had been on the afternoon of Sue's death, he might suspect I had discovered his infidelity and had gone there to kill her.

As I was running down the stairs, it struck me that when the police found Sue's body they were bound to come across her diary and discover she had a lover. Like me, they might wonder whether she was having an affair with her boss. They might even suspect he was responsible for killing her.

Feeling sick, I raced back up the stairs, grabbed the diary, shoved it in my bag, and dashed out of the house.

Once outside, I breathed a sigh of relief because there was no one in sight. Pulling up the hood of my jacket, I strode back up the hill to my car, crouched down behind the steering wheel, and drove away, restraining myself with difficulty from putting my foot down and exceeding the speed limit. The last thing I wanted was to be sighted anywhere near Sue's house, or caught on a security camera around there.

Driving away, I struggled to make sense of what had just happened. By the time I reached home, the front of my shirt was damp with my tears. Whatever she had done, however abominably she had behaved, Sue had not been a bad person. Her only transgression had been to fall in love with my husband. I, of all people, could hardly blame her for that, having succumbed to his charm and good looks myself.

Thanking my lucky stars that Nick was out for the evening, I had a shower. Locked in the bathroom, I studied the diary, page by page. According to the entries the affair had started after Christmas, four months into Nick's headship. I grew more convinced than ever that their affair had taken place in the mornings before the school day began. Hiding my distress was going to be difficult, but there was nothing to be gained by challenging Nick about his relationship with Sue. To do so would risk causing irreparable damage to our marriage, and there was no point now that she was dead.

I hid the diary at the back of a drawer, beneath my underwear, before making some supper, and forcing myself to eat. Whatever else happened, I had to keep a clear head and make sure no one had any reason to regard me as anything other than a dutiful wife to the headmaster. My husband, especially, must have no inkling that I had uncovered his secret.

If Nick had ended his affair with Sue as a result of my emails, as I had intended, she might have become depressed and committed suicide as a consequence of her disappointment. There was no way anyone could know that I had written those malicious emails, but Sue must have understood that Nick had chosen me over her. I had managed to work that much out, at least. I imagined her begging him to leave me, and his blunt refusal. Thinking about it, Nick never allowed anyone to deflect him from his purpose, an admirable determination that could also make him unsympathetic towards the needs of others.

If my emails had prompted him to end the affair, and she had killed herself as a result, then I would be indirectly responsible for her death. It was crazy that she had seen me as a rival for Nick's affections when he had only known her for a year, but it certainly seemed as though she had blamed me for the end of their affair.

The more I thought about it, the less I cared what had happened to her. She was a crazy predator, and a marriage wrecker, who had deserved to die in bitter despair after she had failed to steal my husband away from me. Not only that, but she had taken a particularly cruel revenge on me, making me feel responsible for her death when it had all been her own fault for seducing Nick in the first place. Perhaps she had intended to destroy me with guilt. I was stronger than she realised.

But every time I closed my eyes I saw her face, glaring and discoloured, until it was hard to convince myself that I was blameless. At the very least, I had tormented her during the last days of her life.

Chapter 13

It was hardly surprising that my sleep that night was disturbed by nightmares. After dozing restlessly for a couple of hours, I fell into a convoluted dream in which a scarecrow woman with a white face and stiff limbs stalked me around a school of interminable corridors. Her footsteps echoed behind me but every time I turned a corner, she hovered in front of me like a ghost. Although I dared not speak to her, I knew who she was. Once I saw Nick striding ahead of me, and called out to him to help me, but he vanished through one of the doors along the corridor and I couldn't find him although I searched in every room. I woke feeling drained, aware of my heart pounding. But at least I still had a beating heart.

My sister knew me better than anyone else. Although she was seven years older than me, we had been close when we were growing up, perhaps because we had lost our mother to cancer when we were only six and thirteen. It must have been hard for Jen, as a teenager, but I only ever remember my sister being strong and cheerful, a stabilising presence throughout my teens. She cared for me as a mother might have done, and the sister of my childhood memories was a comfortable plump figure, although she was tall and stringy as an adult. She assured me she had been a rebel, but her wild streak had passed me by, and I still regarded her as steady, someone to rely on in troubled times.

These days we didn't get to see one another as often as we would have liked. We both lived busy lives and had little time for social calls. Jen lived about thirty-five miles away and, with four children and a career as a part time GP, she was even busier than me, so we hadn't seen one another for six months, not since

Christmas. A week earlier she had called to say she was travelling to Northampton, leaving her children at home with their father.

'It's about time Tony did something around the house,' she had laughed down the phone. 'Not that he'll be much use. More likely the kids will be looking after him while he puts his feet up and complains about having too much to do.'

Jen had explained she was going to Northampton for a conference, and was keen to take advantage of the rare opportunity to stop off at Edleybury on the way, if I was free.

'It'll only be a flying visit,' she had said. 'Just for coffee. I have to be in Northampton for two.'

'You can stay for as long as you like. You know you're always welcome.'

'I wish I could stay longer, but you know how it is. Places to go, people to see, not enough hours in the day and all that jazz. But I couldn't travel north and not try to come and see you.'

When we had arranged Jen's visit I had been really excited about seeing her, but with all the drama taking place, I didn't feel like seeing anyone, least of all the one person who might see straight through my protestations that everything was fine.

My hopes of covering up my feelings evaporated as soon as she set eyes on me, and I knew straight away she was not fooled for a moment by my forced smile.

'Is everything all right?' she asked, pulling back from my embrace and screwing up her eyes to scrutinise my face. 'You look—' On the point of telling me I looked dreadful, she broke off. 'You look tired,' she concluded kindly. 'You look really tired. Have you been under the weather? You're not overdoing it, are you?'

'I'm fine, honestly I am. It's just nearly the end of term, you know, and the end of our first year here. It's been quite a – well, it's been a busy year.'

She gave me a guarded smile. 'It's more than that though, isn't it?'

I shook my head, not trusting myself to speak.

'Lou, what is it? Tell me what's wrong.'

I forced a laugh to conceal my distress. 'I'm fine, really.'

She stared at me for a moment. 'Okay,' she said at last. 'If you say so. But you will tell me if there's anything wrong, won't you.'

I nodded. 'Sure. You know I will. No secrets, eh? If there was anything seriously wrong, I promise you'd be the first to know.'

Seeing there was nothing to be learned by pressing me, she began to talk about her children, two of whom were at university while another was taking A Levels, and the youngest was doing his GCSEs. From what Jen told me, they seemed to be doing well, and she didn't appear worried about them.

'I've always told them, it's not about the performance on the day, it's about the preparation beforehand. And they've been hard at it for months. As long as they've done enough work, they'll sail through.'

I wished all the parents who sent their children to Edleybury shared Jen's philosophical attitude, but it was easy for her to be relaxed, with her bright and diligent children. Over coffee, she brought me up to date with news about her family, and her work, and a new kitchen she was having installed after a flood, before steering the conversation around to me again.

'I'm doing all the talking. Come on, what have you been up to?'

After learning my husband's been unfaithful, I sent insulting emails about his mistress to all the staff, and forced Nick to dump her unceremoniously, all of which drove her to commit suicide, I thought.

For a wild instant, I was tempted to tell Jen everything.

Instead I said, 'I've taken up tennis again. I play a regular weekly game with one of the PE teachers I'm friends with here, and it's taken a while to get to know the place, but recently we've all been preoccupied with getting ready for the end of year Gala Dinner and Ball, which is a massive deal here, the event of the year. You wouldn't believe the fuss that's made, or expense they go to. It's worse than planning a wedding. And then there are exam arrangements and parents' evenings, and Nick's having meetings with the governors and the bursar, and the marketing team, and goodness only knows who else besides, all working up to the end of the year. I've had to host an evening for the female staff – it's a bit sexist really, but they've always done it here, and the school is ruled by its traditions.'

'You could change the tradition,' she suggested drily.

I wasn't surprised. Jen had always been fiercely feminist. Although she was careful not to criticise my choices, it was clear to me that she had been bitterly disappointed at my ready acceptance of a role where my sole responsibility was to support my husband. Clearly it hadn't occurred to her that without my marriage I would still have been a class teacher answerable to my previous head of department, or some other petty egoist. At best I might have risen to become a head of department myself, struggling to impose my will on a few colleagues within the artificial bubble of another school. As things had turned out, I was in a privileged position, married to the headmaster of a prestigious public school, enjoying the status and the lifestyle that the role attracted.

'Nick's planning to make enough changes next year, without my adding to them,' I replied with a smile. 'The governors are a lot of old stick-in-the-muds and it's taken him a while to persuade them to agree to his vision for the future.'

'His vision?'

'Yes. Not many people know about this yet, apart from the governors and the senior management team, but he intends to make the school co-ed throughout, not just in the sixth form, and he's also planning to spread the responsibility around.'

'What do you mean, spread the responsibility around?'

'He's going to appoint a director of studies, so there'll effectively be two deputy heads instead of one. The director of studies will oversee academic affairs, and the existing deputy will be in charge of the pastoral side of things. Up until now, it's all been looked after by one deputy head, but Nick thinks, quite rightly, that it's too much for one person to do everything. A lot of schools have split the roles like that, and it seems to work.' On the spur of the moment, I added, 'I think he might want one of the deputies to be a woman.' That was a fib but I thought it would please Jen.

'Another break with tradition?'

'I should say so. Nick feels it's about time Edleybury moved into the twenty-first century.'

I paused, aware that I was parroting what Nick had said to me.

'So what will Nick do, if he isn't in charge of the academic and pastoral life of the pupils?'

'Oh, he'll still retain overall responsibility, of course, but these days the role of a head is more to do with marketing the school than with the day-to-day running of the place.'

'Does he mind?'

'The marketing? No, not at all. He enjoys it. And of course it involves a lot of travelling, for both of us.'

Hearing myself talk about Edleybury, my life sounded pretty dull. Introducing girls into a boys' school was hardly going to change the world, but Jen made a decent stab at looking interested.

'So they're keeping you busy,' she said, when I had finished my recitation. 'And you're still enjoying it here?'

I nodded.

'Louise, you would tell me if there was anything wrong, wouldn't you?'

'Of course,' I lied. 'I don't know why you keep going on about something being wrong. You know if there was anything, I'd tell you.'

Just then we heard the front door slam and Nick called out to us from the hall.

'Lou, I'm home. Is your sister still here?'

The opportunity to tell Jen about Sue had passed, and I was pleased I hadn't mentioned what had happened. The fewer people who knew about Nick's affair the better. But as we carried on chatting about our life at school, the corpse I had seen was never far from my thoughts, and I was grateful to Nick for keeping the conversation flowing. He didn't appear to notice anything unusual but Jen was observing me closely, and I could tell she was troubled.

For my part, I was partly preoccupied with wondering whether the body had been found yet.

'What's your conference about?' I asked, with a pretence at enthusiasm.

Jen told us, but I wasn't really listening to her answer. As a doctor she must have come across many dead bodies. I had just encountered my first. No one else knew about Sue's death or the horrific circumstances in which she had died, and I was entirely alone with my distress. I struggled to maintain a calm exterior until, at last, Jen had to leave. For the first time in my life I was pleased to see her go.

'Don't stay away so long in future,' Nick urged her as we stood on the doorstep watching her go. 'Louise loves seeing you.'

Chapter 14

Determined to get past my horror and spend a normal evening with my husband, as though nothing out of the ordinary had happened, I prepared a casserole and had just finished cooking it when he came into the kitchen, a look of horror on his face. A sick feeling hit me in my stomach as his words sank in. The body had been found. The words had been spoken aloud, and I was no longer alone with the terrible truth.

'Suicide?' I stammered. 'Sue's committed suicide?'

'Apparently so. It seems she took an overdose of sleeping pills washed down with half a bottle of whisky. A neighbour found her, because her front door was left open and they went in to check that everything was all right.'

'It sounds like she wanted to be found.'

Nick sighed. 'Perhaps.'

'In any case, they can't be sure she meant to kill herself, can they? She might not have taken too many pills intentionally.'

My interest in what had happened was a sham; I did not care whether the police thought Sue's death had been an accident or suicide. All that mattered was that they believed she had taken her own life, meaning my husband was in the clear, even if his affair came to light.

'She left a note of sorts,' he said, 'scribbled when she was clearly too drunk to write.'

'What did it say?'

'Just one word: sorry.'

'But suicide? How is that possible? Suicide?'

'Can you please stop repeating that,' he said, sinking onto a chair and reaching for the bottle.

Hoping I hadn't overdone my shocked reaction in my effort to conceal my relief, I sat down opposite him at the table.

'I spoke to her yesterday,' I said. 'She seemed all right,' I added uncertainly.

The lie slipped out, quite unintentionally, but there was no point in admitting how upset Sue had been about the emails. I didn't want to remember our last conversation, or her tears. Soon everyone would know that she had killed herself but I didn't want to think about her at all, because I knew it was my fault she was dead.

She must have been depressed when she had invited me to her house. Clearly she had been confused, not to say deranged, and I could only assume she had wanted to take some kind of revenge on me for Nick's refusal to leave me for her. But I had done nothing to initiate the situation, only reacting to her behaviour. If she hadn't chosen to have sex with my husband, none of this would have happened, so I felt justified in fighting off any feelings of guilt over her death. I was as much a victim of his deception as Sue. He had lied to me too. But I still had a chance to work out my problems with Nick and rebuild my shattered life. For Sue it was all over.

Given the circumstances, Nick's conduct was impressive. He gave dignified speeches to the whole school, and to the staff, expressing his sorrow and offering them comfort in theirs. Many of them had known Sue far longer than we had, and he paid respect to their feelings, as well as giving a fittingly glowing tribute to Sue's work. He also had the difficult task of writing a letter to her parents expressing his personal condolences. He discussed with me how to approach this, before consulting the senior staff about a suitable response from the school. Only I could have appreciated how hard Nick must have struggled to bear his grief in a manner appropriate to a boss who had lost his secretary, when their relationship had meant so much more to him than that. Like mine, his solemn demeanour hid a secret which he could never share.

Even at home, he expressed anger rather than grief.

'A suicide hardly fits with the image of a happy school community where everyone is cared for,' he fumed. 'How could this have happened without any warning? Did no one have the slightest inkling she was so unstable?'

'If anyone knew, surely it would have been you.'

He raised his eyebrows, looking straight at me, and I bottled it. 'What I mean is, you worked so closely with her. You saw her every day. Didn't you spot any signs?'

'What signs? What are you talking about? I'm not a mind reader.'

Just as well, I thought, but I kept that to myself.

'She was upset by those emails, but they were hardly something to be taken seriously...' He shook his head, baffled. 'She had no history of depression. I just don't understand how this could have happened.'

If I hadn't known how he had betrayed me, I might have felt sorry for him, a powerful confident man reduced to casting about helplessly, unable to make sense of the darkness that had unexpectedly descended on him.

'There must have been something else going on,' I said. 'Something we don't know about. Perhaps she was having an unhappy love affair.' I watched him closely as I spoke, but he didn't flinch. 'Did she have a boyfriend?'

He shrugged, as though that was unimportant. 'I don't know.'

'You worked with her for nearly a year and you don't know whether she was seeing anyone?'

'We didn't discuss personal matters. I was her boss, not her confidante.'

That was an outrageous remark from a man who had been so intimate with her.

'I wonder what will happen to her cat,' I said, changing the subject before my feelings became obvious.

'What cat?'

'She had a cat,' I said, thinking that either he was a better liar than I had given him credit for, or else he had never been to Sue's house. 'I wonder what will happen to it.'

'How do you know she had a cat?'

'She mentioned it.'

He shook his head. 'I dare say a neighbour will feed it. I think her cat is the least of our concerns.'

Nick and the senior management team agreed that Sue's death should be referred to as "a tragic accident". They felt there was no need to go into any more detail than that. Before any serious questions could be asked, the term would finish.

'By September, Sue will hopefully be buried and forgotten,' Nick told me.

I struggled to conceal my revulsion at his coldness but, on reflection, I supposed there was nothing else he could do, unless he broke down and openly confessed he had been having an affair with Sue. And, after all, there was no point in putting his career at risk for a woman who was dead. Even so, his words struck me as callous, and I wondered how he would react if I were to die. His ambition, and his determination to hold onto his position, seemed to have stamped out any vestige of humanity in him.

Chapter 15

It was hardly a surprise to learn that the Gala Dinner to celebrate the end of the school year was to go ahead as planned.

'No one wants to rock the boat,' Nick explained, with a composure I found hard to forgive.

The deputy head's secretary, Mandy, took over the running of the evening, and outwardly life continued as before, but without Sue. The nature of her job had meant she was in contact with everyone who worked at Edleybury and, as far as I could tell, she had been universally liked.

Angela and I discussed what had happened, and we agreed that Sue's popularity only made her suicide seem the more tragic. Among all the people she had communicated with on a daily basis, not one had offered her the support that might have saved her life. No one had known about the depression that was generally assumed to have led to her death.

The staff room was subdued and everyone walked around looking miserable. Sue's death had touched us all. Although we were not allowed to mention the word "suicide" in front of the pupils, it had been impossible to conceal the truth from her family, who were understandably distraught. Nick and I both dreaded having to meet them.

The next morning, on my way to Nick's office to meet Sue's family, I nipped into the ladies' toilet to prepare for this ordeal. Coming out of a cubicle, I yelped aloud in shock. Sue was standing in front of me, staring at her reflection in the mirror, tears trickling down her cheeks. For a few seconds I stood, paralysed with shock. The room spun around me and the neon lighting overhead quivered.

Catching sight of my shocked face behind her in the mirror, she turned, wiping her eyes.

'I'm sorry, I'm so sorry,' she said quickly. 'I didn't mean to startle you. I know I look like Sue. I'm her sister, Judy.'

She spoke in Sue's voice, but I saw that her hair was longer than Sue's had been, and she was plumper than her sister, and looked older.

'I'm– I'm Louise Kelly,' I replied, taking a deep breath and fighting to regain my equanimity. 'I wish we could have met in different circumstances. I'm the head's wife.'

'I know who you are,' she replied, her voice suddenly cold.

Her expression told me quite clearly that Sue's family blamed Nick for what had happened. No doubt they believed he had bullied her into ending her life. Sue's eyes stared at me from her sister's face in silent accusation. I could almost hear what she was thinking: 'Sue was perfectly happy at this school before your husband came along.'

'I'm so sorry for your loss. We're all devastated. Sue will be missed. I don't know how we're going to manage without her.'

Judy's silence reverberated in my head. She had no desire to grant me a reprieve from my misery. Without another word, I led her into Nick's office, where he was seated with a middle-aged couple who were both in tears.

'If there's anything we can do,' Nick was saying as I entered the room, 'anything at all.'

'Bring our daughter back,' the woman sobbed. 'We just want her back.'

'How could this happen?' Sue's father asked in a helpless appeal.

'There was nothing wrong with her, nothing at all,' Judy added. 'They're trying to make out she was depressed but that's an out-and-out lie. Something must have happened to make her do this. I don't know what she was even doing with those pills. She never had any trouble sleeping.'

Nick dealt with them in a masterful way, speaking soothingly, assuring the grieving family that he had grown very fond of Sue in the short time we had known her, and stressing how much he had appreciated her excellent skills and strong work ethic. Her death, he said, had come without any warning. Haltingly, her parents expressed their gratitude for his kind words, but Judy continued to glare at him as though she considered him personally responsible for her sister's death. I wondered whether Sue had told her sister about her ill-fated love affair.

After they left, I broke down in tears. Nick mistook my unrestrained weeping for an expression of grief. I could hardly explain that I was crying tears of relief that Sue's family had gone.

Later, in front of the whole school, Nick gave an impeccably worded tribute to Sue and the work she had done for Edleybury, in which he referred to the tragic illness which had ended her life. There was no mention of suicide, and no suggestion that she might have been suffering from mental illness. The staff had been instructed to remain discreet about the nature of her death, and her suicide was skilfully glossed over. So much so, that when a member of the parents' association asked me whether Sue had died of cancer, I realised no one had given me an official specific cause of her death. All I knew was that she had taken her own life, and I could hardly say that to the inquisitive woman challenging me for the truth.

Heaving a sigh, I shook my head. 'I'm not quite sure. Something like that.'

It was a clumsy response. The woman looked riled, as though I was giving her the brush off which, of course, I was. But not in the way she thought.

All the following day, I felt Judy's accusatory eyes on me, even though she and her parents had gone.

'Nick, as soon as the Gala Dinner's over, let's go away,' I suggested. 'Even if it's just for a few days. Let's go somewhere completely different.'

'That would be wonderful, but we can't book anything until we hear about the funeral.'

'Haven't you heard anything yet?'

'I spoke to her family again today, but they still haven't released the body.'

'What do you mean, they haven't released the body? Who hasn't released it?'

I had a horrible vision of Sue's body still lying on her bed, open-eyed, while her family insisted no one move her.

'The police. Apparently they're looking into the circumstances of her suicide.'

Luckily, Nick was lying back on the sofa with his eyes closed when he said that, so he didn't catch the expression of fear on my face. By the time he opened his eyes, I had recovered myself. He reached out to me with one hand.

'I could never have got through all this without you,' he said.

'I haven't done anything.'

'Come on,' he went on, shifting in his seat, 'let's go to bed.'

It was hard to sleep with a heartless monster like my husband, but my cyber bullying was far worse than anything he had done. Within the limited world of Edleybury, the power Nick's position bestowed on him had gone to his head, and he had simply indulged in a fling, as many men did when they encountered temptation. His transgression had been to sleep with the wrong woman. I should have been pleased that Sue's death hadn't broken his heart. What he had done was thoughtless, perhaps the result of a moment's weakness. I, on the other hand, had carefully planned out a series of actions that had very possibly led to her death. Of all people, I was in no position to condemn my husband for making love to her when I had helped to kill her.

Chapter 16

The day of the Gala Dinner and Ball dawned, and Nick and I were up early. Nick left the house before breakfast to eat in the school dining room and talk through the plan for the evening with the rest of the senior management team. I promised to follow him over to the school soon and offer my help to the secretarial staff. I didn't tell him I had another task to carry out first. Nick had mentioned the police were investigating the circumstances of Sue's death. While it was highly unlikely that anyone would come across Sue's diary hidden beneath my underwear, I could not risk discovery. The diary had to be destroyed. Ashes told no tales.

Stuffing the diary into the pocket of my jeans, and armed with a box of matches, I strode into the garden. No one was around to see what I was doing, but even so I went to the very end and squatted down in a small clearing in the bushes. The diary proved unexpectedly difficult to burn. When I held it by one corner and put a match to it, the flickering flame went out before the pages caught fire. Every attempt was foiled by the breeze extinguishing my lit matches. I couldn't spend too long fiddling around with it, and was worried that Nick might return.

After a few minutes, I gave up and went back inside.

Flustered, I hurriedly switched on the shredder in Nick's study, tore off the diary's cover and destroyed the pages, a few at a time. On its own, the cover was unidentifiable so I shoved that in the bin outside the front door to be reduced to pulp by the refuse collectors. The rubbish was due to be collected the following day and that would be the end of it.

Trembling with a mixture of fear and relief, I put the box of matches away and went over to the school.

For the past seven years, Sue had overseen all the practical arrangements for the Gala Dinner and Ball. It now fell to Julie, the admissions secretary, and David's secretary, Mandy, and the other staff on the administration team to pick up the many threads, and run the event without Sue. Juggling so many balls at short notice, and still suffering from shock at the news of their friend and colleague's suicide, they were under almost unbearable pressure.

The sun was beating down, and the air was already warm with the promise of a beautiful summer day, but no one was relaxing at Edleybury. On the contrary, the place was buzzing with an air of feverish activity. A huge white marquee had been erected on the grass between the cricket pitch and the built-up area of administration and teaching blocks. A procession of men in overalls were rolling round wooden tables and carrying stacks of gold-painted chairs into the marquee, followed by another tranche of delivery men laden with neatly folded white table cloths, and boxes containing gleaming cutlery, glasses, napkins and other dining paraphernalia, while a group of carefully selected sixth form pupils were in attendance to run errands and help set out chairs, ten to a table. Whistling and joking, the delivery men were cheerfully ignorant of the circumstances of Sue's death. It was hard to believe there were people in the world, living and working so close to us, who were continuing with their normal lives untouched by the tragedy that had struck the school.

The interior of the marquee resembled a scene from Dante's Inferno, with bodies manoeuvring their way around one another in an atmosphere of frantic activity. Rush matting had been laid on the grass, dense enough to protect the turf beneath from the high heels of hundreds of women dressed to impress. Even with the side flaps of the tent pinned open, the atmosphere inside was muggy and warm in the growing heat of the day, but by evening the temperature would become more comfortable in there.

Leaving the marquee, I made my way past queues of delivery men unloading from a line of vans, and went into the administration building where I found Julie in the corridor haranguing a man in a blue overall. Her voice was raised and she looked agitated.

'What do you mean there aren't any lilies?' she was asking as I joined them. 'The order distinctly specified lilies for the top table.'

'That's as may be, madam,' the man replied. 'But we can't deliver lilies if we haven't got any. Don't go blaming us. It's our supplier that let us down. We ordered lilies all right but they never sent them. So we've brought roses instead, and I've already said we're prepared to discount the price and I can't say fairer than that. We've been supplying your flowers for this event for seven years, madam, and this is the first time there's been a problem of any sort. But it's not our fault. We ordered lilies for you, just like you requested, but they sent us roses.'

'We ordered lilies. Look!' Julie brandished a printed document at him. 'It says lilies.'

'I know,' he replied stoically, 'but they sent us roses.'

This exchange was going round in circles.

'Roses are fine,' I butted in. 'As it happens, the headmaster is allergic to lilies. He'll prefer roses on the top table.'

Julie scowled but the man turned to me, all smiles now that the mishap had been smoothed over.

'It's only flowers,' I said to Julie when he had gone. 'I'm sure they're lovely roses and all the flowers are going to look just fine.'

She nodded. 'Yes, you're right of course. I don't know why I got in such a state over it.' She smiled apologetically. 'I didn't know Nick was allergic to lilies. That's the sort of thing Sue would have known. I don't know who ordered lilies for the top table.'

She broke off. Perhaps, like me, she was thinking that lilies were traditionally associated with funerals.

'I'm sorry you caught me throwing a bit of a wobbly,' she went on, sniffing back tears. 'There's so much to do and everything seems to be going wrong this morning. I miss Sue,' she added, with a catch in her voice.

'We all do, but we can pull this off without her. We have to.'

'The show must go on and all that,' she said, a trifle bitterly.

I wondered if she thought we ought to have cancelled the event, given recent circumstances. It certainly felt strange, throwing a huge party so soon after Sue's death. But it would have been impossible to pull out of the event at such short notice. Apart from the extravagant catering bill, the marquee had been booked and paid for months earlier, and dodgems were being installed while we stood there discussing flowers.

'Nick would have liked to call it off,' I said, 'but there's just too much going on, too many people relying on payment, and orders for food, and flowers, and wine, and chairs, and all the live music, and everything. It was too late to pull the plug.'

She nodded, understanding if the Gala Dinner and Ball had been cancelled, we would have had to reimburse ticket holders, but would still have had to pay for all the goods and services. In addition, cancelling the event would have drawn attention to the recent tragedy which the governors were keen to play down.

'It's a horrible thing to say,' I added, 'but we can't afford to cancel it. And it's a horrible thing to have to do, but we just have to soldier on and get through it.'

'I'm not staying for the evening,' Julie said. 'I just can't.'

I told her I would have liked to duck out as well, but the absence of the new headmaster's wife would raise too many eyebrows and I couldn't let Nick down. After a great deal of deliberation, I chose to wear a dress with a cowl neckline that seemed appropriate both for the occasion and for the recent tragedy. It was flattering, long, elegant, figure hugging, and black. Gazing around the marquee, I was glad my dress looked smart and sophisticated.

Many of the mothers of pupils at Edleybury were women with considerable disposable funds, much of it passed on from previous generations or earned by overpaid husbands holding down jobs in the city. These women had never worked in their lives, other than on their figures and their faces. Ostentatiously wealthy, pretentious and sexy, they knew how to dress for an occasion.

'What a fashion show,' Nick muttered contemptuously, as we stood at the entrance to the marquee waiting to greet guests as they arrived.

'They pay your salary,' I replied, under my breath.

He must have heard me, because he chortled. 'Yes, they certainly do. And some of these frocks probably cost more than a year's salary for a new–'

He broke off abruptly and left my side to chat to a man I didn't recognise, who looked like a governor.

'Louise, let me introduce Simon Tiverton, the chairman of the school governors. Simon, my wife Louise.'

I smiled. 'It's a pleasure to meet you, sir.'

'Oh, the pleasure is all mine, my dear. Allow me to introduce my wife, Evelyn.'

'What a lovely evening we have for the end of year festivities,' Evelyn said, smiling myopically in my direction.

Banal pleasantries completed, they drifted away, and Nick watched them go with a wistful expression.

'They've been married for forty years,' he said. 'Do you think we'll make it that far?'

'Of course we will,' I assured him.

A noisy gaggle of parents arrived, demanding our welcome, before we were swept away to the top table, and we had no more time for private conversation.

The dinner was appropriately lavish, and the music far too loud as it usually is at these events. Nick made no mention of Sue in his after dinner remarks, having paid tribute to her service to the school in the end of year assembly and also at Speech Day, and for that one evening we behaved as though his late secretary had never existed.

We got through the dinner, making polite conversation, and afterwards we danced with tipsy parents who were footing the bill. It would have been enjoyable enough, but for the strain of an invisible pall of death that hung over us, so that I was glad to finally get home and kick off my shoes.

The Gala Dinner and Ball was traditionally a fairly riotous affair, with staff carousing into the small hours after the parents left. But this year, all the teachers went home after the formal festivities, and everyone was subdued throughout the event. Nick had carried the evening with his usual aplomb, and I was possibly the only person there who could tell quite what a strain he was under.

As soon as we reached home, he collapsed on the sofa in the living room, without even stopping to remove his jacket or shoes.

'Thank God that's over,' he said. 'Talk about bad timing! Why the hell didn't she wait until the term was over? It's not been easy keeping it under wraps. You know how the staff gossip. Might as well try to stop a troupe of monkeys from chattering. By September hopefully the talk will have died down.' He loosened his tie. 'At least I've got the summer to find a replacement.'

Pained by his lack of consideration, I wasn't sure how to respond, and for a few moments neither of us spoke.

'You look tired,' I said at last, unable to bear the silence.

It was true. Now that he was no longer putting on a show for the parents, he looked pale and drawn.

'Not quite the end of year celebration we were expecting,' he replied. 'I was planning to crack open a bottle of Champagne—'

'Haven't you had enough to drink tonight?'

'I thought we'd have a little celebration of our own, after surviving our first year here, but it hardly seems appropriate to celebrate after what happened with Sue. I thought we'd need a holiday to recover from our first year, but I never thought I'd be so desperate to get away from this place.'

We went upstairs. Having returned my glittering jewellery to its case, I turned and stared at my reflection. Dressed all in black, without any adornment, I could have been going to a funeral.

Chapter 17

The next morning, at breakfast, I quizzed Nick about why the police were holding onto Sue's body for so long.

'What on earth are they doing? Surely the family want to start making arrangements for a funeral.'

Stirring his tea, he nodded thoughtfully. 'You know we'll have to attend, whenever it is, and until we know when it's going to be held, we can't book a holiday. But yes, we must go to the funeral if we possibly can, of course we must. And perhaps we'll invite the family to a memorial service here at school before the beginning of term. Something quite low key. It's probably best not to involve the whole school. I don't think we want the pupils meeting Sue's family.'

He pulled a face and pretended to shudder at the prospect.

'But we still don't have any idea when the funeral might be?' I asked, after a pause.

'I told you, they haven't released the body yet.'

'Why not?'

'How should I know? She killed herself, so I suppose they have to look into it. Just forget about it, will you. I'm trying to put all that out of my mind until we need to deal with it, and I suggest you do the same. You're not helping me, dwelling on it like this. You've no idea how tough it's been for me, keeping the situation under control. If it had happened earlier in the term, it would have been different. As it is, we were absolutely right to keep the circumstances of her death quiet. I've mentioned her untimely death in assembly and in my end of year report, and I think we need to leave it at that. Let it remain as a tragic accident for as long as possible. Even if the papers get hold of it, which they will, it's going to be old news by the time the summer's over. What we have to do now is focus on the future, get a new secretary in place and up to speed by September. I'm thinking of asking Mandy to double up as my secretary, at least in the short term, with Julie as back up. And we'll recruit a temp to help out with some of the routine administrative tasks. But for now, we have to try to get past all this as best we can and find our way back to where we were in our lives before Sue died.'

He was right. Even though what had happened was terrible, guilt wouldn't dominate my thoughts indefinitely. I knew it was a cliché, but it was true that in time the sharpest feelings would soften. I had to cling to the knowledge that I had never intended to cause so much distress. Even without knowing what I had done, Nick had been right to say that Sue must have been unhinged to take her own life.

To be fair, I had known nothing about her mental instability, so I reasoned that if she had committed suicide it could hardly be my fault. My emails might have been one of the details that had tipped her over a personal precipice, but she must already have been fighting to escape from the darkness that had threatened to engulf her, and had finally claimed her life. If I had not been the catalyst that pushed her over the edge, someone or something else would have come along. In any case, I had merely reacted to her behaviour, without initiating anything. So I tried to exonerate myself for my role in her death by imagining that it was my misfortune that this had happened to me and that, if anything, I was the victim. I wasn't really convinced, but it helped me to think about it like that.

In the meantime, Sue was dead, and there was no point in dredging up what had happened between her and my husband. We both needed to forget he had been screwing her, and concentrate on getting our marriage back on track. Nick was right about that too. Convinced that Sue had never meant much to him, I had been eager to drive her from the school so that she and Nick would never see one another again.

Without their enforced physical proximity, I had believed their relationship would quickly fizzle out. Now it had been forcibly brought to an end, in the most tragic way possible, but at least it was over. I would have preferred it to end differently. Despite what she had done, I had liked Sue, and my husband was a very persuasive man. It was an uncomfortable thought, but I doubted she had been entirely to blame for the seduction.

'You're right,' I agreed. 'We have to get back to normal, and carry on as though Sue never came into our lives.'

He nodded. 'I worked with her every day, but she hardly came into our lives. You make it sound as though she was our child. Let's not overdramatise what happened.'

Before I could respond, there was a ring at the doorbell. Putting down the breakfast dishes I was clearing away, I went to see who it was, and did my best to sustain an expression of calm interest when a tall man on the doorstep held up an identity card and introduced himself as Detective Inspector Steven Jarvis.

'What can we do for you, Detective Inspector?' I enquired. 'Shall I call my husband?'

'Perhaps I can come in?'

'Oh yes, of course. Please follow me.'

I led the way into the living room where Nick was seated at his laptop. He looked up and rose to his feet in one lithe movement as the detective inspector entered the room and introduced himself. Nick shook his hand and invited him to sit down.

'I take it this is about the recent loss of a member of my staff,' Nick said.

'We're just making a few enquiries,' the inspector explained, sitting down and gesturing to me to take a seat. 'You worked closely with Susan Ross, didn't you, sir?'

I sat quietly while Nick dealt with the inspector in a manner both slick and overtly frank. He said nothing untoward, and I appreciated having time to plan my own responses.

'And you, Mrs Kelly, how well did you know Miss Ross?'

'I wouldn't say I knew her well. We had regular discussions, of course.'

'Discussions?' the inspector echoed, a slight interrogation in his tone.

'Yes, we talked about the weekly flowers in chapel, and refreshments at school events, and arrangements for the Gala Dinner at the end of the school year, which tragically Sue couldn't attend, of course.' I lowered my head and looked sad.

'So you talked about matters relating to her work?'

'Yes, that's right.'

'Anything else?'

'No, nothing else, really. She was a lovely person, but I'm sure others who knew her better than I did have told you that.'

'Yes, they have. But I'm interested to hear your views, Mrs Kelly.'

'I don't have anything much to add to what I just told you. Sue was kind and helpful to both of us, and I have no doubt she was like that with everyone, and she was an excellent secretary to my husband. We had no idea she was suffering from depression and we're all in shock over what happened.'

The inspector did not stay long and I breathed a sigh of relief when the front door closed behind him. Suddenly, I felt the need to get out of the house. Checking that my laptop was safely hidden away, I told Nick I was going shopping. He merely grunted, without looking up from his work.

'You need to take some time off,' I told him. 'Term's over.'

'Once I've sorted out a replacement secretary, I'll relax,' he promised me.

Returning from the shops a couple of hours later, I found Nick sitting in the living room, absorbed in a printed document.

'Did you have a successful outing?' he asked without looking up from the paper he was studying.

'I got a few things for the weekend. We were out of milk. What's that?'

'Hmm? Just reading through the job description that was written last time around. It needs a bit of updating, but it's incredibly difficult without any input from the last incumbent.' He sounded exasperated. 'Julie's made a reasonable stab at it, working from the job specification when Sue was recruited, and adding in the additional responsibilities Sue took on over the years, but there's a lot more that needs to be included, and we're bound to overlook a lot of what she actually did. The list of her responsibilities is monumental. I don't know how she managed to do it all.' He frowned, making a pencil mark on the paper. 'There's no way someone new to the school will be able to do all this. And we don't want to put off any prospective candidates by making the job look impossible. Oh, and the police were here again,' he added, still staring at his document.

'What? The police? Why? What did they want?'

He raised his head, looking surprised at the urgency in my tone.

'What did they want?' I repeated.

'Oh, nothing. It was routine.'

'What was? What did they want?'

Afraid the police had discovered Nick had been having an affair with Sue, I wondered how he could remain so calm.

'They just wanted to take a look around.'

'You mean they searched our house?'

He nodded. 'They were simply doing their job.' He sounded very laid-back about it. 'They took our computers,' he added, 'but they said we'd have them back tomorrow at the latest. And don't worry. They were extremely careful not to disturb anything.'

'What? How could you let them take our things?'

'They have to go through the motions with us as well as everyone else on site. We can't be treated differently to everyone else.'

'You mean they're looking at all the computers in the school?'

'Of course. You didn't think they were only interested in us, did you? Yes, they've taken the lot. That is, they've taken the laptops. And they've got a team here checking the PCs. Thank goodness term's over. Can you imagine the furore if they'd swooped in on us like this while all the kids were here?' He gave a mirthless laugh.

I thought quickly. Obviously someone had told them about the emails that had been sent round. Maybe Nick had told them himself, not knowing he might be landing me in trouble. But I knew the police had been speaking to the academic and secretarial staff as well as to Nick, and everyone knew about the attack on Sue's reputation. Anyone could have told them. In fact, I might have been the only person who had failed to mention the emails when the police had questioned me. At least I had been prudent enough to destroy Sue's diary.

Without another word, I raced upstairs. Nothing appeared to have been moved in my study. It had not been ransacked, as I had feared. I ran to my bedroom and opened the top drawer of my chest. Relieved to see the underwear I had left covering my laptop had not been disturbed, I lifted it out. With a stab of terror, I saw that my laptop had gone.

Chapter 18

My confidence that Avenger's true identity would remain anonymous had been based on the care with which I had concealed myself from the school IT technicians. I had not reckoned on the police coming in to investigate Sue's suicide, with all the forensic powers at their disposal to back up their technological expertise. In spite of my guile, my part in the events leading up to Sue's death risked exposure, and all I could do was pray they wouldn't find anything incriminating on my laptop. If they did, I would have to lie my way out of the situation. Whatever happened, were the police to establish the authorship of those emails, Nick's position as headmaster of a leading school could be compromised. Even worse than that, our marriage might be in jeopardy.

Lying in bed that night, I wracked my brains, trying to recall every step of my email campaign. What mattered was whether any of the emails about Sue had been sent from my own laptop. Once I had gained unrestricted access to the school intranet, my emails had gone out from a fake address which I had set up directly through the main server in the IT office. Hopefully nothing could link me to those messages, other than the fact that I had been given free access to the heart of the system, and I remained cautiously confident my disguised identity would safely mask the real source of the malicious emails. The problem was that I couldn't remember whether the first email had been sent from my own laptop, before I had been given the freedom to work from the school office. I was almost certain I hadn't used my own device, but doubt niggled at the back of my mind. If the police were able to link that first email to my private laptop, my anonymity would be blown.

Not only was I worried about the authorship of those emails being discovered for my own sake, but it was devastating to think that my actions threatened to destroy Nick's career. He would never forgive me for what I had done, and it was hard to see how I could live with myself if my worst fears were realised. And then there was Sue. It was difficult to hold back my tears whenever her name came up. Once Nick was asleep I wept silently, tormented by remorse. I even considered making a full confession, but Nick was snoring gently and it seemed unkind to wake him to tell him his wife had hounded his secretary to her death.

Finally, lying in bed, wide awake, I came to the conclusion that my only sensible course of action was to do nothing. Sue was dead, and there was nothing I could do to reverse that harsh reality. It would be stupid to sacrifice my own future, and probably my husband's as well, in a vain attempt to appease my conscience. Instead, I would have to learn to bear the knowledge of my guilt in silence. That must be my only punishment. As long as no one discovered my role in the events leading up to Sue's death, the horrible experience would hopefully fade from my memory, eventually haunting me no more than a distant nightmare.

'You look tired,' Nick said at breakfast, glancing up at me from his journal with an anxious frown.

We were sitting in the dining room, with orange juice and coffee and croissants fresh from the oven. Nick liked a continental-style breakfast in the mornings at the weekend.

'I promise you this will all blow over very soon,' he went on. 'It's been an exhausting year, but we came through it with flying colours. Apart from one issue that wasn't our fault, it's gone better than we could have hoped. There's no need to look so downhearted.' He gave me an encouraging smile. 'Try not to think about poor Sue.'

'I've got a headache.'

That was true, but I didn't go on to explain the reason. Plagued by guilt, or fear, I had barely slept all night.

Nick looked worried again. 'You're not ill, are you?'

I shrugged. 'Not that I know of.'

'Lou, you would tell me if there was anything wrong, wouldn't you?'

'Yes,' I muttered.

If Nick had pressed me, I might have broken down and confessed, but he merely grunted and turned his attention back to his journal.

After clearing away the breakfast things, I left him to his work. I did some desultory cleaning, and put on the laundry, anything to keep myself occupied so I could stop thinking about what the police might find on my laptop, but I didn't feel any better by the time they arrived at our house halfway through the morning.

This time the inspector looked straight past my husband and addressed me directly.

'We'd like you to accompany us to the police station, madam. We have a few questions for you.'

I knew then that the game was up.

A tall broad-shouldered man in pristine jeans and smart sports jacket, the detective's fair hair was tinged with ginger, and the skin around his blue eyes was crinkled with laughter lines. But he wasn't smiling. While my husband carried himself with an exhibition of authority, a lion leading his pride, the inspector was a tiger, his devastating power masked by the stealth of his cunning as he stalked his prey. I was that quivering prey.

Noticing the detective was wearing a plain gold wedding ring, I wondered if his wife was strong enough to withstand the force of his character, or if she enjoyed submitting to his will. But perhaps he behaved differently at home.

Outwardly I maintained an air of dignified composure, but the inspector's cold gaze seemed to see right through me. Any interrogation would be a formality. In his eyes I was already convicted.

Ignorant of my role in the events leading to Sue's death, Nick stepped in at once to defend me. 'You can speak to her here,' he blustered.

A headmaster accustomed to getting his own way, he was rattled by the inspector's high-handed interference. But, just for an instant, I thought I saw a flicker of fear in my husband's eyes, and wondered whether he had glimpsed the truth.

'It's okay,' I assured him quickly, before turning back to the inspector. 'I'm happy to do everything I can to help. But is there a problem? We wondered why the body hasn't been released for burial yet, didn't we?'

On the short journey in the back of an unmarked police car, I reviewed the transgressions that must have been uncovered. It wasn't illegal to write a few nasty emails, although sending them anonymously was a shameful way to behave and might raise a question mark over my suitability to be a headmaster's wife. At the very least, what I had done would cause Nick a great deal of embarrassment, even if it didn't cost him his job. As for what it might mean to our marriage, I didn't dare think about that. I had risked my whole way of life: my husband's career, my home, and my marriage, for a few moments of joyful insanity. But if I had endangered our marriage, so had Nick, and his actions had kickstarted the whole ugly chain of events. I had only reacted to extreme provocation. My conscience should have been untroubled.

My best course was to deny any involvement in the emails that had been sent about Sue. Even if the police were able to trace something back to my laptop, they couldn't prove I had been responsible for sending them. In addition, I loved my husband, and not only was I aware that Sue's help had been invaluable to him, I had liked her. I had no obvious motive to have wanted to harm her.

On that terrible journey to the police station, one idea remained clear in my mind. I had to stick to my story. As the headmaster's wife, I was keen to help the police investigate the death of my husband's colleague, a woman who had been a good friend to me. Outraged by the horrible emails that had been sent round, I was shocked by the suicide which none of us had seen coming. That was all I would say. I hoped it would be enough.

Chapter 19

Even sitting down, Detective Inspector Jarvis cut an imposing figure. It wasn't only his height and his broad shoulders that gave him an air of authority, his presence seemed to fill the entire room. His expression was impassive and he spoke in a flat voice, yet he commanded attention. He would have made an excellent teacher. With his eyes half shut, I could feel the force of concentration behind his apparent indifference. He was watching me closely, alert to any modulation in my voice, any heightened colour in my face, any hint of my gaze faltering.

'It's time to tell us the truth, Mrs Kelly,' he said quietly.

A policewoman sat at his side, immobile as a waxwork, her dark eyes fixed on mine. However often I glanced at her, I never saw her blink. The inspector introduced her as Detective Sergeant Hilary Woods.

'We'd like you to tell us the truth, Mrs Kelly,' the inspector repeated. With his blank expression and flat voice, he looked and sounded bored.

'Am I being charged with anything?' I asked. 'Because if not, I'd like to go home, please.'

The inspector sighed. 'We'd all like to go home, Mrs Kelly. Now, is there a reason why you're reluctant to answer a few simple questions?'

'First tell me what I'm doing here. You could have asked me your questions at home. Why am I here?'

'We're investigating the death of Susan Ross.'

'Yes, I know that. It was a terrible loss to the school. We're all in shock over what happened.'

'Was she a particular friend of yours?' the sergeant asked suddenly, with what appeared to be a flicker of interest in her eyes. She spoke calmly, but I sensed a hint of menace behind her question.

'You could say we were friends, yes. On friendly terms, at least. But I couldn't say we were particular friends,' I replied truthfully. 'I didn't know her well, but I liked her. Sue was a very warm person. She got on well with everyone. I don't think you'll find anyone on the staff who wasn't friends with her. She was that kind of a person.'

'What kind of a person is that?' the inspector asked.

'What I mean is, she was popular. She'd been working at Edleybury for about seven years. She knows – that is, she knew everyone at school, and everyone liked her.' There was a pause, and then I stood up. 'I'd like to go home now.'

'Please sit down, Mrs Kelly.'

The words were polite, but something in the inspector's tone made me resume my seat and ask him whether I should call a lawyer. 'If I'm being kept here against my will, I would like someone to represent me,' I added.

The detective raised his eyebrows, very deliberately. 'Hardly against your will, Mrs Kelly. We merely wish to ask you a few questions about the death of your colleague and friend.'

I wondered if there was a slight sneer in his tone as he said the last word, but his face remained deadpan.

'Go on then. What is it you want to know?'

I frowned, aware that I sounded agitated. The inspector had riled me, and he knew it.

He leaned forward in his seat. 'On the eighteenth of June an email was sent to all the staff at your school describing Susan Ross as a slut. Do you have any comment to make about that?'

My mouth felt dry and it was an effort to speak. 'Shocking,' I mumbled. 'It was shocking,' I continued, forcing myself to speak up. 'We all thought it was – shocking. That's the only word for it.'

'Do you have any idea who sent that email?'

I shook my head, wondering whether he already knew the answer to his question.

The policewoman at his side stirred. 'What we really want to know is *why* it was sent. Please tell us the truth, Mrs Kelly,' she added, as though she knew I was going to lie.

For a moment no one spoke.

At last I broke the silence. 'What do you mean by asking me to tell you the truth? If you don't trust me, what's the point in my saying anything?'

'We would like you to answer our questions honestly,' the inspector said. 'Is that unreasonable?'

His even tone had begun to grate on me.

'I want to call my husband and ask him to get me a lawyer. I refuse to answer any more of your questions until then.'

The inspector nodded and leaned back in his chair. 'Make the call.'

Inspector Jarvis and Sergeant Woods disappeared, leaving me in the company of a stout female constable.

After that matters progressed slowly. First of all, it took me a while to persuade Nick to arrange for a lawyer to join me at the police station.

'What's going on?' Nick asked. 'I don't understand what they're playing at.'

'I don't know what's happening. They suggested it would be a good idea for me to have a lawyer here.'

That wasn't quite true, but I needed to convince Nick to help me.

'Why don't I come and get you?' he replied.

'There's no point. They're not going to let me go just yet.'

'Put the inspector on the phone. No, don't bother, I'll come in and speak to the superintendent, or whoever is in charge there, and sort this out.'

'Nick, please, just find a lawyer and it'll all be done with much quicker. Don't drag this out any longer than necessary.'

When he finally understood that finding a lawyer was the best means of expediting my departure from the police station, he said he would contact one of the school governors, a fairly eminent criminal barrister who would be able to recommend someone suitable. After that, I could do nothing but wait.

Another constable brought me some tea and biscuits, and escorted me to the toilets where she waited right outside my cubicle, as though she suspected I might try to make a run for it. Other than that, I was left sitting in a small room, with my police guard standing by the door. If it hadn't been so frightening it would have been funny, like being catapulted into a film. I comforted myself with the thought that they hadn't charged me with anything yet and when the truth came out, as seemed likely, all that could be proved against me was that I had sent a few stupid emails.

The most difficult part of it was going to be squaring my actions to Nick. Perhaps it might be best to claim I had a drink problem. Whatever happened, we were in for a difficult time, but this whole situation was not of my making. If my husband had kept his dick in his trousers, Sue would still be alive. He alone was to blame for everything we were going through. He had known the risk he was taking, but he had gone ahead anyway. The more I thought about what had happened, the more aggrieved I felt.

By the time my lawyer arrived, I was furious, convinced that I was an injured victim.

'None of this was my fault,' I blurted out to a tall willowy woman who entered the room and introduced herself as the solicitor who had been sent to defend me.

Ingrid Sunderland was dressed in a silvery grey jacket over a crisp white blouse and black pencil skirt that reached just below her knees. Her blond hair was pinned up in a neat swirl and her make up was flawless. It must have cost a fair amount to perfect that look of casual elegance. I wondered how much Nick was paying her to act on my behalf.

'I need you to tell me everything,' she said in a firm clipped voice. 'Remember, whatever you say to me is in complete confidence, and I'll share only what is going to help us get you out of here as soon as possible. It's not my job to judge your actions, only to defend you. Your husband has told me quite unequivocally that the police interest in you is a mistake, but I suspect they may be privy to information of which your husband is ignorant. I need to know everything, including what you haven't told anyone else, even your husband. I can't help you if you conceal the truth from me. Start at the beginning and leave nothing out.'

I nodded. My mouth felt dry. I thought quickly, wondering how much to tell her.

Chapter 20

'So you sent those emails?' Ingrid asked when I finished speaking.

Relieved that she didn't sound shocked, I burst into tears. This was the first time I had shared my secret with anyone. Without mentioning Rosie, I told Ingrid that I had discovered my husband was having an affair, and how I had reacted. My lawyer was there to help me, and it was important to be completely honest with her about those wretched emails. As she took pains to point out, if I hid any detail from her that the police later discovered, she might be unable to defend my credibility.

'I never meant this to happen,' I sobbed, shaking with a mixture of worry and relief at finally being able to share my dark secret. 'I never meant any of this to happen. How was I to know she was going to kill herself? No one knew she was going to do that. She must have been unstable to do something like that. Who does something like that? How was I supposed to know? Even her own family said they didn't have a clue about her fragile mental state.'

I had to be careful not to let slip that I had been to Sue's house and seen her body lying across the bed. My orderly life had descended into unimaginable chaos, and every move I made was fraught with peril, every word I uttered had become a potential grenade that might blow up in my face and destroy me. I would have given anything for Nick never to have gained his headship, and for us both to be transported back into the classroom, working within the constraints of a timetable that prevented us straying too far from the safe territory of an externally dictated syllabus, plagued by nothing worse than insolent pupils and poor examination grades – ordinary people, living ordinary lives, contending with ordinary fears and disappointments.

'I never meant for any of this to happen,' I repeated.

'But you meant to send those emails,' Ingrid replied, in her clipped tone. 'It's unfortunate, but we can't skirt around that fact, not after you took such pains to try to cover your tracks. Hiding your identity like that proves beyond doubt the emails were premeditated. And to make matters worse, you planned your actions very carefully to avoid detection not once, but three times, over a period of eleven days. We can't argue those emails were sent in the heat of the moment, a jealous wife losing control and not responsible for her actions. If we try to claim temporary insanity we'll be shot down.'

Her cool gaze and measured tone helped me to regain my composure. Despite the depressing impact of her words, she seemed thoughtful, not dismayed. Her clothes were unwrinkled, her hair as neat as if she had just stepped out of a salon. By contrast, my eyes must have been red and swollen from crying, and my hair a mess. Glancing down, I could see my trousers were creased, and no doubt there were damp patches under my arms. When I turned my head to the side I was aware of a faint unpleasant odour of sweat, and wondered if she could smell it too.

'It was stupid of me, I know, but I was angry. They were having an affair. I wanted to warn her off, force her to leave him alone. And yes, I wanted to punish her. She deserved to be taught a lesson. I wanted to show her up for the slag she was. But I never intended to make her that desperate. If I'd suspected for one second the emails might drive her to commit suicide, I wouldn't have done it. Believe me, I'm as horrified as anyone about what happened. More so, because it was my fault, in a way. But I never imagined that would happen. How was I supposed to know? She always seemed so calm and capable, so cheerful.'

Ingrid nodded. 'Her response was unpredictable and certainly excessive. Your emails might have triggered her death, but there's nothing to indicate that was your intention.'

'Of course it wasn't my intention! I just wanted to rattle her, make her post at Edleybury so uncomfortable she would be forced to find another job and leave us alone. I certainly hoped they would think twice about continuing their relationship once they realised someone else knew about it. But that's all it was. I was jealous. That's not a crime, is it? They were the ones who started it. I just wanted her to go away. She was hardly innocent in all this, was she? All I did was dash off a few emails. She was having an affair with my husband, trying to undermine our marriage. Surely that's a lot worse than sending a few insulting emails.'

Ingrid looked solemn. 'A jealous wife.'

'Yes, that's what it comes down to. And that's all it was.'

'Very well. I advise you to remain calm, if you can. A suicide is not going to exercise the police for long. They are going through the motions, and that's all this is. So there's no need to worry. This can all be resolved swiftly and discreetly.'

Warning me to leave the talking to her, she rose to her feet and knocked on the door.

A few moments later, we were led to another room where we sat facing Detective Inspector Jarvis and Detective Sergeant Woods across a table.

The inspector began the proceedings by asking me about the three emails I had sent. Cursing myself for ever having been stupid enough to write them, I listened to Ingrid's defence. She described my shock on discovering my husband was having an affair, and how traumatised I had been to see photographs of Nick and Sue together. Ingrid talked about my unswerving loyalty to my husband, and how I had sacrificed my own career to support him in his role as headmaster of an eminent school. Listening to her, I found myself fighting back tears of self-pity. Everything she said was true. I had given up my own career for Nick, and he had repaid me by betraying my trust in the basest way imaginable. Sending those three emails had been an understandable, if foolish, response which I now deeply regretted.

'It is perhaps conceivable that my client's actions may have contributed to Susan Ross's decision to take her own life, but in the absence of any testimony from the deceased, that has to remain a matter for supposition,' Ingrid concluded. 'What is certain is that the possibility that her victim might overreact so violently never once crossed my client's mind, and there is no reason whatsoever to suppose she should have considered so excessive a response to her provocation. There is clearly a background to this of which we have not yet been apprised, and no blame can attach to my client, who was by no means alone in her ignorance of Susan Ross's mental state.'

'Mental state?' the inspector repeated. 'What mental state was that?'

'The deceased was clearly unbalanced—'

'How was I supposed to predict that three stupid emails would drive her to take her own life?' I interrupted. Ingrid gave me a warning glare, but fear made me angry. 'I could just as easily have killed myself when I discovered they were having an affair. Would *she* have been to blame for my death if *I* were the one who had killed myself? Think about it. I had a lot more to lose. Nick's my husband. Her suicide is not down to me. All I did was retaliate when I found out about their affair—'

'She must have had a history of mental illness,' Ingrid cut me short. 'It is unreasonable to believe that my client's actions alone could have led her husband's mistress to kill herself.'

I flinched, hearing her refer to Sue as Nick's mistress.

'There must have been more leading up to this death than my client's three emails,' Ingrid insisted.

The inspector inclined his head, and when he spoke his voice sounded as casual as someone commenting on the weather. 'Oh, there is more to it. A lot more.' He turned to me, his expression blank. 'We don't investigate suicides.'

Chapter 21

My heart seemed to stop. Almost immediately, I felt throbbing in my chest that rose up to my throat and through my head like a shot of adrenaline coursing through my veins. At the same time, blood pulsed behind my eyes and I began to tremble. For a moment, everything went black, but no one appeared to notice my distress. Seated at my side, Ingrid had probably not seen the expression on my face change, and the detectives must have been accustomed to maintaining an almost inhuman impassivity when they observed people react in extreme ways. But my shocked reaction was no admission of guilt. Having known Sue, obviously I would be horrified to hear that the police did not believe her death had been suicide.

The detective inspector looked back at me and blinked very slowly. His features were not unattractive but his cold reptilian eyes made me shudder. In that moment he seemed inhuman, pitiless. Yet of the two of us, I was the one suspected of murder. The inspector was just doing his job to punish the guilty and protect the innocent. Like Sue, he was not a bad person, yet, like her, he was my enemy. In that moment, it seemed to me that the problem lay with my own moral compass. After all, what was it that made anyone righteous, if we were all capable of committing an evil act in a moment of thoughtlessness?

Gazing into the inspector's eyes, I was paralysed by the conundrum. My husband was held up as an example of a man of integrity, the morally upright headmaster of a school, yet he had strayed into deceit and betrayal, while I was considered as good as a murderer – or as bad. And the detective, who demonstrated not so much as an iota of humanity, was a champion for justice and virtue. None of it made any sense.

I longed to ask him if he had never done anything he deeply regretted but, just in time, I remembered that Ingrid had told me to leave the talking to her, and some instinct of self-preservation held me back. Ingrid remained motionless at my side, looking as cool as ever, but she wasn't the one under threat. When the interview was over, she would return to her smart office, or perhaps go out to a fashionable restaurant, while I languished in a cell awaiting trial for murder. Chatting over an expensive dinner later that evening, she might mention that she was defending a client suspected of murdering her husband's mistress, before the conversation drifted onto other subjects.

For her, I was no more than a topic of conversation at the dinner table. For me, what happened in this small room would determine my future. And the contrast between my potential prospects was stark. In place of my present luxurious life style, I faced the possibility of life in prison, locked in a cell smaller than the room in which we were sitting.

The inspector was watching me, impervious to my terror.

'What do you mean? What exactly do you mean by that?' I asked.

Despite my efforts to remain calm, my voice rose as I repeated the question, because the implication of his words had been clear.

'Are you really asking me to spell this out for you?' He leaned forward slightly in his chair and his eyes, previously so blank, seemed to glitter with intensity. 'Susan Ross was murdered. But of course you already knew that, didn't you, Louise.'

'You can't think I did it!'

'Where were you on Tuesday the twenty-sixth of June between six and eight o'clock?'

It was hard to believe anyone could remain so unruffled when the whole world was spinning out of control.

'Where were you on the twenty-sixth of June between six and eight?' he repeated in his quiet voice.

'At six o'clock? I would have been at home, preparing supper.'

'Can anyone vouch for you?'

'What?'

'Are there any witnesses who can confirm that?'

'My husband, but please, you can't tell him what I did. The emails, I mean. That's all I did. You have to believe me. You can't tell him. You can't.'

'Your husband was having dinner with the chairman of the governors that evening,' the inspector informed me coldly. 'That has already been established.'

The rest of his words flew around me unheard after which, numb with shock, I was led to a cell. All I could think was that this couldn't be happening. It was too terrible. Nick was going to find out what I had done and know that I had discovered his affair. I almost envied Sue. At least she was free of any more torment. Given the means, I might have ended my own life right there in that bare white cell. While I was lying on the hard bunk, trying to come to terms with what the inspector had told me, and wondering what was going to happen to me, the door to my cell opened and I was summoned.

'What now?'

'Your husband's here to take you home.'

Following the constable along the corridor, I tried to smooth down my matted hair. I must have looked terrible.

Nick was waiting for me, seated at a table. He leaped to his feet when he saw me.

'Louise! You poor thing! What the hell are they doing to you? Come on, let's go.'

Taking me by the arm, he led me out to the car, and we drove home in silence.

'Now,' Nick said, when we were seated in our living room, a pot of tea on the table between us. 'Tell me what that was all about.'

'They think I killed her,' I said flatly.

He frowned at me and lowered his voice. 'Did you?'

'What? No, of course not! How could you think that?'

'I never believed it, not for a second.'

There was no point in trying to hide what I *had* done. 'All I did was send those emails.'

'What?'

'Those emails accusing her of being a slut. I sent them.'

'What? Why would you do that?'

I stared into his eyes. 'I know about the affair,' I said softly.

'What affair?'

Nick looked so puzzled, I almost believed he had no idea what I was talking about.

'Oh, you're good,' I said, remembering how he had told me he was an expert liar. 'You're very convincing. You almost had me fooled.'

'Louise, what the hell are you talking about?'

He was almost in tears.

'I'm talking about Derby. And the rest of it.'

'Derby? What about Derby?'

'Your weekend away with her.'

He frowned. 'Sue? Me and Sue? You– surely you don't think there was anything going on between us?'

'Nick, you can stop this pretence, because I know.'

'Whatever it is you think you know, you're wrong. You're completely wrong.'

'Stop lying to me.'

'Louise, this is madness. You've got it all wrong.'

'I'm not wrong,' I replied, remembering how Rosie had said those same words to me.

'Louise, we need you to see a doctor, you're not well–'

'Stop lying to me! Please, just tell me the truth. Did you love her?'

'You need help, Louise. This is a fantasy–'

'So you keep saying. Is this the defence Ingrid has cooked up? Is she putting you up to this, to say I'm sick and that's why I did it? That would suit you, wouldn't it. The poor headmaster with his crazy wife. That way you could put me away and maybe even still keep your job, with your reputation untouched. Is that what this is all about? Covering up what you did. And what then? Divorce after a decent interval, to pave the way for another wife? Is that the plan?'

My voice had risen until I was yelling at him, shaking, lost in a fit of rage.

'Louise, calm down, please. You're talking complete nonsense. Can you hear me? Do you understand me? What you're saying makes no sense. Listen to me. Listen. I wasn't having an affair with Sue, if that's what you're thinking. I wasn't having an affair with anyone. It's always been you and me, ever since we first met. You're my wife, Louise, and I love you. There's no one else, and there never has been. Whatever you've done, I don't want you to worry. I'm going to look after you. We'll get you the help you need and you're going to get better, and we'll be together just like before–'

I shook my head, wishing he was right and he could make all this go away.

'Listen to me. The police don't think you killed Sue because you suspected I was being unfaithful. That's just your overactive imagination talking. And anyway, we both know it's not true. It can't be true. It's crazy. If you really suspected I was being unfaithful, you would have challenged me about it. You wouldn't have done this. What? Killed someone? You would never have done it. Never. I know you, Louise, and I know you would never have done something like that. And the police don't believe it either. They've just questioned you because you said you sent those emails. Let's hear no more about you being suspected of murder, for Christ's sake. Please. I know you didn't kill her. You couldn't have.'

'Of course I didn't kill her. But I did send those emails because– because–' I heaved a sigh that was broken by a sob. 'I was so angry. More than angry. I wanted you both to know that your affair was no longer a secret. I wanted everyone to know about it so that it would stop. I couldn't bear it, Nick. I couldn't bear it. And I wanted her to go away. I thought that threatening to expose you would make it stop. But I didn't mean to kill her.'

'It's all in your head, Louise. This alleged affair I was having, it's some kind of fantasy you're suffering. It's not true.'

'I saw the photos,' I said.

'What photos?'

'Photos of you and her. I saw them.'

'There were no photos because there was no me and her.'

'I saw the photos,' I repeated, but suspicion had begun to undermine my conviction.

If Nick was right, and I had imagined seeing him with Sue in the photos Rosie had shown me, I might also be deluded in believing that I hadn't killed her. Or perhaps the image of her dead body had been a delusion too. I was no longer even sure I had been there, at her house, when it happened.

The one certainty in all this was that Sue had been murdered.

Chapter 22

I thought about everything that had happened. In a way the details of my husband's relationship with Sue were no longer important now that she was dead. Even the truth about her death ceased to matter, although I still wanted to know about the affair. Assuming I wasn't completely crazy, then someone must be lying. The simplest explanation was usually the right one, and the obvious conclusion was that my husband had been unfaithful.

Determined to maintain the appearance of rectitude which his position required, of course he would deny that he had been having an affair and, according to the police, Nick had been having dinner with the chairman of the governors on the evening Sue was killed. Yet there was no doubt that Sue's death helped to protect Nick. Perhaps she had threatened to expose the truth and he had killed her himself to shut her up, believing that no one else knew about their affair. But he hadn't known about the photos Rosie had shown me.

Assuming I hadn't been hallucinating, the other possibility was that Rosie had fabricated the story of Nick's affair with Sue. If she had been lying all along, and the photos were fake, she was hardly likely to own up. Recalling how she had offered to give me copies of the photos led me to believe they were genuine, but I needed to be sure. There was nothing to be gained from tackling Rosie head on. That would only arouse her suspicion. I needed another ally, someone who wasn't directly involved in the situation and, ideally, someone with the power to investigate the role Rosie had played in the circumstances leading up to Sue's death. In desperation, I decided to approach Detective Inspector Jarvis for help.

Nick wasn't keen on my returning to the police station. Realising I was adamant, he insisted on driving me there and waiting for me in the entrance hall.

'You have something to tell me?' the inspector asked, as he entered the room. 'I'm ready to listen, but wouldn't you like your solicitor to be present?'

I shook my head. 'I've already told you everything I did. There's nothing to add to my statement. But there is something else.'

He must have been annoyed at my equivocation, but his expression gave nothing away. 'Go on,' he said, sitting down.

Having explained my suspicions of Rosie, I urged him to find the photos she had shown me.

'She had them on her phone,' I said. 'Even if she's deleted them, you can restore them, can't you? I know nothing is permanently wiped out, and there would be a record of her tampering with them if they were photoshopped. And if they were genuine... at least that would prove they were having an affair. At least we'd know for sure what was going on with Nick and Sue.'

'We're not concerned to establish whether or not your husband was conducting an extramarital affair,' the inspector replied, rising to his feet and towering over me. 'What is of interest to us is that you believed he was unfaithful at the time his mistress, alleged or otherwise, was killed.' He stared at me as though he was trying to read my mind. 'Please think very carefully about the statement you gave us, Louise. Would you like to change it?'

'No. I've already told you the truth.'

Without another word, the inspector nodded and strode out of the room. It was clear he had no intention of pursuing my enquiry, so my only other option was to suggest to Nick that he get hold of Rosie's phone. By now she had no doubt deleted any photos she had taken or created, but Nick would be able to find someone who could restore them. It would be best to ask someone independent to work on the phone. Even if I could find the deleted photos myself, my testimony was hardy likely to be believed. I planned what to say to him as I was escorted back to the entrance of the police station. Nick wasn't there.

'Your husband is speaking to the DI,' the constable who had accompanied me informed me. 'He said he won't be long and you should wait for him here.'

I waited for Nick as patiently as I could and at last he appeared, looking tired and irascible.

'Come on, let's get out of here,' he muttered.

Once we were in the car and driving away, he burst out, 'I've tried to tell that bloody detective he's got the wrong end of the stick, but he seems convinced they have some sort of case against you. Damn it, why did you do it?'

He glanced at me, his blue eyes frantic with worry.

'I didn't– I mean I did send those messages, but that was all,' I stammered. 'You have to believe me. I thought you were having an affair and I was jealous. I went crazy.'

'You are crazy. Why on earth would you think that?'

'Listen, Nick, it was that reporter, Rosie. Do you remember her?'

'The one writing a feature on us?' He laughed bitterly. 'About the ideal couple to be put in charge of training impressionable young minds. The perfect role models, aren't we.'

'That reporter told me point blank you were having an affair. And she showed me photos of you and Sue on her phone. You have to get hold of that phone. I don't care how you do it, but you have to look at her photos. She had photos of you and Sue–'

Nick shook his head. 'No. No more of this, Louise. Listen, I've spoken to Ingrid, and she's confident she can get you off with a caution for sending those emails, on the basis of diminished responsibility, and your previously unblemished record. And they can't charge you with some trumped up murder charge simply because they think you may have a motive. That's not going to happen. They don't have a leg to stand on, and they know it. Ingrid will come and see us first thing this afternoon, and make sure all this gets sorted out as quickly as possible. You're not even a suspect, because although they think you had a motive, they have no evidence placing you at Sue's property on the evening she was killed. Ingrid is quite clear that just because they can prove you had a grudge against Sue doesn't mean they can charge you with her murder. And once it's over, we'll talk about everything that's happened. Whatever the outcome, I'm going to look after you.'

'I don't need looking after,' I muttered ungratefully. 'I'm not an invalid.'

'No, but you're not well. I've arranged for you to see someone.' He hesitated.

'Someone?'

'I've spoken to Ingrid. We've discussed this and we both agree it's the best thing, for your defence, and for your future health.'

'My health? You mean my mental health, don't you? You think I'm crazy. You want to get me committed. That would suit you, wouldn't it. You don't want to live with a head case.'

'I'm not going to argue with you about it,' Nick said wearily. 'Please, Louise, do this for me. I just want you to get well.'

'I am well. I'm perfectly lucid.'

In the end, I agreed to talk to a psychiatrist if Nick went to see Rosie.

'I'm not making a deal here,' he replied, growing testy.

'I'm not talking to anyone unless you go and see her and get hold of her phone,' I insisted.

'Don't be ridiculous. I'm not going to steal her phone.'

'You're just borrowing it, Nick. Or don't you want anyone to know what's on it?'

Pulling up in the drive, he threw me a helpless look. 'Come on, let's get inside and then we can talk.'

Watching him walk to the front door, slightly bowed like a man beaten down by years of hardship, I wondered what effect my sleepless nights were having on me. As though he could read my mind, he turned in the doorway.

'You look dreadful. But don't worry, we're going to get through this together. One day we'll look back on all this...'

He turned away. I knew what he had stopped himself from saying; there was no way we were ever going to laugh about any of this.

Chapter 23

'I went to see Rosie,' Nick told me the following evening.

'And? Why didn't you say so at once? When did you see her?'

'This morning. I went to see her while you were still in bed.'

'Why didn't you wake me?'

'I wanted you to stay in bed for as long as possible. You needed the rest.'

He was right about that. After a disturbed night, I hadn't woken up until after midday and felt much better for my lie in.

'You asked me to speak to her so I did.'

'And? What did she say? Did she tell you exactly what she told me? Tell me what she said! Tell me!'

'Louise, I want you to calm down.'

'I'm calm, I'm calm!' I replied, infuriated by his composure. 'What did she say?'

'She said she didn't know anything about any alleged affair between me and Sue.'

'But she was the one who told me about it in the first place. She showed me photos of the two of you, kissing and– there was more–'

'She flatly denied having said anything of the sort to you, and she claimed she didn't know anything about the photos you say she showed you.'

'She would deny it, wouldn't she. But did you manage to get hold of her phone?'

'Yes, yes, I looked at her phone. Rosie offered to accompany me to the police station so we could get it checked.'

I frowned. 'Do you mean she went with you?'

'Yes. She volunteered to go to the police station with me to get her phone checked out. It was her idea.'

'And?' I pressed him. 'Did you find the photos of you and Sue?'

'No, no one could find them. They never existed. There were no photos of me on it anywhere.'

'She must have another phone. Go back and get it and show it to the police. They'll be able to find whatever she's hidden.'

'I just told you, I already did. Rosie and I went to the police station together and waited while they checked her work phone and her private phone. They found nothing on either of them. Louise, what you're saying, it didn't happen. You imagined it.'

'I didn't. Rosie told me about your affair and she showed me photos of you and Sue, together.' Just the memory of those images made me shudder. 'How was I supposed to react?'

'Not by sending anonymous emails. Why didn't you speak to me? Ask me about it? I would have put your mind at rest.'

'Speak to you? As if you were going to come clean about it.'

'Come clean about what? How many times do I have to tell you? It's not true. Louise, surely you can see that nothing you're saying makes any sense.'

The more he talked, the more I questioned my memory of what had happened. Even the police had been unable to find any evidence of the photos I had seen on Rosie's phone. Gazing into my husband's eyes and seeing how genuinely troubled he was, I started to doubt my own sanity.

'Do you really think I imagined it all?' I whispered.

'I don't know what to say to you, if you keep insisting this fantasy is true.'

'But what do *you* think? Am I going mad?'

In that moment, I really thought I must have lost my grip on reality.

Nick shrugged. 'That's what we're going to find out. Whatever's going on, we're going to get you through this, I promise, however long it takes.'

The psychiatrist who had been recommended to Nick, in confidence, by a school governor, was based in central London.

'I said it was for the wife of an old friend of mine,' he explained, confirming my suspicions that he wanted to keep this as quiet as possible.

Of course if my case went to court, we would be unable to keep it completely under wraps, but Nick was optimistic that we could avoid that.

'Do we really have to go into London?' I asked, when Nick told me where we were going. 'Surely there's someone closer to us?'

'It's less than an hour on the train. Come on, get your coat. It looks like it might rain.'

'I wasn't planning on going out without a coat,' I muttered, hating the way he had been treating me like a child ever since we had left the police station.

Already at the car, Nick didn't appear to hear me.

'Come on,' he called out, 'we don't want to miss the train.'

I had no idea how much this jaunt was going to cost us, but didn't dare ask. I knew what Nick's answer would be. Somehow I doubted he would use our medical insurance to pay the bill, because he was keen to hush up what he was calling "a psychotic episode" brought on by overwork. That was probably why he was dragging me all the way to London to see a psychiatrist. We were less likely to be recognised there.

'We're going to get you better and put this behind us,' he told me several times. 'And we're going to get you more help around the house. You've been overdoing it, and I've been neglecting you shamefully. Next year won't be nearly as stressful, I promise. I'm going to make sure of that.'

I laughed. 'Overdoing it? All I've done is sit around for a year while you've been running the school. This is nothing to do with working or not working. This is... I don't know what it is. What's happening to me, Nick?'

He nodded. 'Hold on, love. We're going to get you the best treatment money can buy, and you're going to get better. You have to get better.'

Hearing the desperation in his voice, I struggled to hold back my tears. 'I'm sorry. I'm so sorry. You're the one who needs support, not me. I should be here for you, not the other way round.'

'None of this is your fault,' he replied firmly, but I knew he must blame me for sending those crazy emails.

I would have given anything to be able to travel back in time and delete the emails without sending them. It had taken less than a minute to risk destroying my marriage, and our happiness, not to mention Sue's life. 'I wish I could turn the clock back,' I said.

Nick didn't answer and we travelled the rest of the way without speaking, maintaining our silence as we waited in the reception area of the smart block where the psychiatrist worked.

'I'll be here when you come out,' Nick told me, when I was finally summoned to enter the consulting room, as though I was in need of his reassurance.

'You don't have to stay. I can find my own way home.'

But we both knew he would wait for me.

The psychiatrist was nothing like I had expected. In place of the distinguished grey-haired gentleman I had prepared to meet, I was introduced to a snappily dressed woman of about my age. Her shoes were pointed, with fairly high heels, and she wore a well-fitting navy trouser suit with a white shirt open at the neck.

'Hello, Louise.' She greeted me with a smile as firm as her handshake.

Ushering me into her consulting room, she closed the door on Nick without even glancing at him. She was making it clear that this meeting was for me, and no one else.

Despite the circumstances of our meeting, I liked Dr Scott and felt confident in her ability to dismiss the question mark that had been raised over the state of my mind. I was further reassured when instead of inviting me to lie down on a couch, she offered me a chair. Seated opposite one another, we exchanged a smile.

'Would you like to tell me why you're here?' she suggested. 'You don't mind if I take notes?'

'Please, go ahead.'

She smiled again. 'So, Louise, why have you come to see me?'

'It was my husband's idea, and my lawyer's—'

She nodded. 'Please, start right at the beginning.'

So I did. No longer smiling, Dr Scott listened gravely as I told her about Nick's new job, and how happy we both were, and how pleased I had been to play a supportive role in his career move.

When I reached the part about the interview with Rosie, and her revelation that Nick was unfaithful, the psychiatrist's expression didn't alter. She continued making notes, looking up at me as she scribbled, no doubt trying to gauge my own response to my story. I did my best to keep my face impassive, but as I talked about the images Rosie had shown me on her phone, my eyes filled with tears and I felt myself shaking, caught off guard by the pain of reliving the moment when my life had fallen apart.

'The thing is, I really believed it was true. I mean, I believed he was having an affair. But Nick went to see Rosie and she denied it all. She said she never told me anything like that. He had her phone checked by the police and there was nothing on it. Nothing about Nick and Sue. I— I must have imagined it all. Yet I saw the photos of the two of them together, I know I did. It wasn't a dream, although it felt as though it was at the time. But the photos don't exist.'

The psychiatrist nodded. 'You're doing very well.'

'What do you mean?'

'You recognise you suffered from a temporary delusion, probably brought on by the stress of your new situation. You mentioned you felt your life had taken on almost a dreamlike quality. What did you mean by that?'

'Dreamlike? Yes, in the sense that I'd given up my home, and my work, and moved to a different area, leaving behind everything that had previously defined me as a person. Reality felt different. But I had only moved on to face a new challenge. Doesn't that happen to anyone who moves area for a new job? It's not exactly unusual.'

She nodded but didn't answer my question.

I was very quiet on the train home, thinking about everything the psychiatrist had said. As soon as Nick went out, I googled schizophrenia.

"Schizophrenia is a mental disorder characterised by abnormal social behaviour and failure to understand reality. Common symptoms include false beliefs, unclear or confused thinking, hearing voices that others do not, reduced social engagement and emotional expression, and a lack of motivation."

With a thrill of terror, I understood what must be happening to me. My mental disorder had cost Sue her happiness, and possibly her life. I wondered whether Nick would still remain committed to getting through this together once he knew his wife was mentally disturbed.

Chapter 24

For the next couple of days, I kept to the house, only venturing outside to sit in the garden. It was a pleasure to sit on the patio that lovely summer, looking at roses and dahlias, wallflowers, delphiniums and fuchsias, begonias and lobelia, in a profusion of bright colours. Nick was out a lot of the time, supervising maintenance and improvements around the site, but he returned home at regular intervals. When I told him it felt as though he was checking up on me, he gave an embarrassed laugh.

'If you mean do I feel bad about leaving you on your own so much of the time, yes, of course I do. It's the holidays and I want to spend time with you, but there's just so much to do while the pupils are off for the summer.'

'It's fine,' I assured him. 'You crack on. I'm very happy pottering around here by myself.'

'Why don't you see some of the others? I know a lot of the staff are away, but Angela's around for the next few weeks and she'd love it if you asked her for a game of tennis. I'm sure some exercise in the fresh air would make you feel better. And the administrative staff are around, on and off, all summer. They're up to their ears in work right now and would appreciate some help. You could help out with vetting the overseas entry papers if you want something useful to do.'

'Thank you,' I replied in as frosty a tone as I could muster, 'but I've got plenty to do here to keep me usefully occupied. We still haven't finished unpacking all the books, for a start, and the whole house could do with a spring clean.'

'I can send Verity over, in fact she can organise a team of cleaners to–'

'No, thank you. I know you're trying to be helpful, but that won't be necessary. I've got Verity's number if I want to call her, but I really don't want a team of cleaners to come over and sort the place out. I want to do it myself. Please, leave the house to me.'

I just wanted to be left alone to fill my head with plans for cleaning and laundering, dusting and polishing, wearing myself out with physical work so that I would fall into bed too exhausted to stay awake, and too tired to dream. The only alternative was to go to the doctor and ask for a prescription for sleeping pills. I was reluctant to go down that route, yet I had to find a way to rest. Alcohol didn't help. Although I was drinking more than ever, my sleep remained disturbed, and my nightmares were growing increasingly vivid and violent. When my dreams didn't wake me, Nick sometimes roused me in the middle of the night, calling my name and seizing my shoulders and shaking me out of my sleep.

'Louise, Louise, wake up. Wake up!'

'What? What is it?' I would enquire drowsily.

Sometimes I snapped awake at once, still shivering with shock at my nightmare. The scenario differed from dream to dream, but the ghastly figure lying on the bed appeared in them all. Sometimes her dead face spoke to me. 'Why did you do it? Why? Why?' And my dreaming self could only shudder and back away in horror from the knowledge of my guilt. 'I have sinned, I have sinned,' I told the ghastly effigy that haunted my dreams. 'Mea culpa, mea culpa, forgive me, oh forgive me so that I may forgive myself.'

Every morning I gazed at myself in the mirror, hardly recognising the wan features staring back at me. Concerned at my physical deterioration, Nick insisted I see the doctor, and I was too worn out to resist his exhortations. First I had seen a psychiatrist, now I was consulting the GP, but no one could cure me of my guilt at having hounded an innocent woman to her death. It was hard to believe, but if Rosie was honestly denying my allegations, then I must have been mistaken, or deluded, or dreaming, and Sue hadn't been having an affair with my husband. All I wanted to do was apologise to her, but of course that was never going to happen. Death was absolute. There was no going back. Somehow I had to live with the truth that there had been no grounds for the jealousy that had driven me to send those emails. In short, it had been insane of me to send them.

The psychiatrist's report arrived after a couple of days, and I read it with growing disbelief. Dr Scott didn't think I was suffering from schizophrenia. On the contrary, she judged me to be self-aware and in touch with reality, and in no way mentally disturbed. According to her report, I had experienced a temporary fit of jealousy brought on by a misunderstanding, the kind of upset that could happen to anyone at a difficult time of their life. She concluded that such an episode was unlikely to happen again, but my husband should keep a watchful eye out for any signs of a recurrence, and I should avoid stressful situations as far as possible.

She suggested my belief in my husband's affair had more to do with my insecurity about his job causing him to lose interest in me than with any genuine suspicion that he was being unfaithful with another woman, along with some mention of unresolved abandonment issues that had never been addressed when my mother died. Everything in the report made sense, in a clever analytical kind of way, but I felt Dr Scott had missed the mark in finding me blameless.

In a way, the psychiatric report placed me a worse situation than before. Ingrid, my solicitor, came over to visit me and, while I was in the kitchen making tea, I overheard her talking to Nick. She sounded grave.

'We could try another mental health specialist. This report is worse than useless.'

'She's an eminent psychiatrist,' Nick replied, as though he felt the need to defend his choice.

'Oh, I don't doubt that,' Ingrid said, 'but you understand the difficulty. If the police decide to charge Louise, we can hardly plead temporary insanity, with a report like that. And if the prosecution get hold of it, they'll go to town with it.'

'She's really thrown us a curve ball, hasn't she? But surely they're going to have to stop regarding her as a suspect. It's not as if they have any evidence.'

They carried on talking and plotting while I prepared the tea, absorbed in my own thoughts. Despite Ingrid's dismay, to my mind the report seemed really positive, because an expert psychiatrist judged me to be sane. Reading that one, fairly brief, report made me feel like a completely different person. Energy flowed through my veins, like a drug, and I set about considering my situation with rediscovered optimism. Only someone who has been led to believe they are mad and then learns they are sane after all, could appreciate my elation. My mind seemed to swell with joy.

'So what do you suggest now?' I heard Nick say. 'Where do we go from here, after this disappointing report?'

'How was it disappointing?' I blurted out as I joined them. 'Dr Scott thinks I'm not crazy. Surely that's a good thing?'

'Was sending those emails the action of a sane person?' he replied, with a trace of irritation in his voice. 'How on earth are we supposed to put up a defence, once everyone knows what you did? We can't hide it forever.'

I frowned. 'Look, what I did was stupid, I admit that. I ought never to have sent those emails. But that's all I did, and no one can prove anything else, because I didn't do anything else.'

'Sending those emails establishes you had a motive,' Ingrid said.

'A motive for what, exactly?'

She didn't answer, but we all knew what she meant.

'I know it was stupid to send those emails. It was a ridiculous thing to do and I regret it, sincerely. I'll regret it to the day I die. But that's all I did. I sent three stupid emails. It's hardly a crime. If a pupil had admitted doing it, he wouldn't even have been expelled. David said if the culprit owned up he'd be suspended. If Sue were still alive, I'd confess to her and apologise, and do whatever I could to make it up to her, but I wouldn't be in trouble with the police.'

'But she's not alive,' Ingrid replied. 'Someone murdered her after you sent those emails and, as far as we can tell, the police have no other suspects.'

'That doesn't mean I killed her! And it doesn't mean her death was my fault.'

Ingrid sighed. 'Of course it doesn't. But if you end up being charged, is a jury going to take your word for it?'

Gazing from her solemn face to Nick's anxious eyes, I understood that my relief had been premature. My troubles were not yet over.

Chapter 25

L ying in bed that night, unable to sleep, I reviewed my conversation with Ingrid and Nick. Both of them had expressed bitter disappointment at the psychiatrist's conclusion that I was sane. Even though I appreciated their reasoning was to keep me out of jail, their attitude was disconcerting, to say the least. I was more interested in proving my innocence than in finding a way to reduce my sentence. Working out how to get myself put away in a mental institution rather than a conventional prison didn't interest me. But if I wasn't mad, then it all came back to the same problem: either Rosie had lied to Nick, or else he had lied to me. With that in mind, I resolved to go and confront Rosie in the morning and try to get to the truth. Having reached that decision, I slept through the night for the first time in weeks.

The offices of the Hertfordshire Style magazine were located in the town of Watford. The following morning I drove out there and cruised up and down looking for the building where Rosie worked. It was impossible to spot it from the car, so I drove to a car park and walked back along the street, checking for numbers and names on the buildings. Just as I was on the point of asking a passer-by, the name: "Hertfordshire Style" appeared in front of me, displayed in elaborate gold lettering above a large window. It was hard to see how I could have missed it. The foyer was less imposing than the frontage of the building and looked surprisingly rundown. I went straight up to the receptionist and asked to see Rosie. The girl behind the desk gave me an appraising glance and asked for my name.

'Is she expecting you?'

'Probably,' I lied, determined to do everything I could to make sure the meeting took place. 'Yes, she should be. Can you call her for me please? I– I may have a story for her,' I added lamely.

'Just one moment, please,' the girl replied, checking a list on her screen. 'What did you say your name was?'

She picked up her phone and muttered to someone at the other end. After listening for a moment, she hung up.

'I'm sorry, Rosie's busy right now. You can email your story to the news desk, or call and make an appointment to speak to someone.' She handed me a card. 'Here you are. It's best if you send us an email and someone will get back to you if we're interested in your story. There's a form on the website that tells you all you need to know.'

Clearly I was getting nowhere. 'It doesn't matter,' I said haughtily. 'I'll take my story elsewhere.'

The receptionist was already looking at her screen and didn't even glance up as I made my way to the door.

There was a café along the road from the office on the opposite side of the street. I bought a drink and a pastry and took a seat in the window, looking out. Nursing my mug of coffee, I munched on my pastry and waited for Rosie to take her lunch break, but one o'clock passed and there was no sign of her. With nothing else to do I stayed, waiting, never taking my eyes from the building where Rosie worked. After a while, I grew hungry and ordered a sandwich. Each time I ordered, I kept my eyes on the window and resumed my seat as quickly as I could, afraid of missing Rosie if she left her office.

At last I saw her emerge from the building on the opposite side of the street. I still hadn't made up my mind whether to accost her or follow her and find out where she lived, but I knew I didn't want to lose her. Abandoning my half-eaten sandwich, I ran out into the street. Before I had reached a decision about what to do, she turned and caught sight of me dashing across the road to join her on the pavement.

'You!' she said, looking surprised.

'Hello.' I smiled. 'Yes, it's me. How are you?'

I still had no idea how I was going to play this, or what I was going to say to her.

'Was it you asking for me at reception earlier today?'

'What? No. I'm just on my way home.'

Somehow I seemed to have developed a habit of lying, but only in response to the deception other people were practising against me.

'I've been shopping,' I explained, adding, 'I take it you've been at work today.'

She grunted.

'So, how are you?' I asked again.

She frowned and I thought she looked unsettled by my cheery greeting, although it was difficult to be sure. She was wearing a grey beret that pushed her fringe downwards so that her eyes were half hidden, their expression inscrutable through a veil of fine dark hair.

'Me? I'm fine,' she replied.

'That's good. Do you fancy going for a coffee?' I suggested, as though the idea had only just occurred to me.

She hesitated.

'There's a café over the road,' I went on quickly, before she could turn me down. 'It's not far, a minute's walk. You can see it from here.'

'I know it.'

'Come on then, and I'll tell you what's been happening.'

She took a step away from me.

'Or we could go for a drink, if you prefer,' I went on. 'There's a pub round the corner. It's very nice inside, and I'm buying. I may have an interesting story for you,' I added.

Actually, I had never been inside that pub, but had noticed it earlier, a large red brick building that looked as though it had stood there for a century or more. I hoped she would be unable to resist the lure of a story, or perhaps the offer of a free drink would entice her, but she shook her head.

'Just the one?' I wheedled, kicking myself for sounding desperate.

As a reporter, she should have been eager to interview me, a suspected murderer, but instead she was backing away from me.

'So, what's this about?' she asked.

I took a step towards her, encouraged by her faint flicker of interest. 'I think you know better than anyone what this is about,' I murmured. 'It's time for you to give me some answers.'

Her eyes widened, but not in fear or surprise. On the contrary, her red lips stretched in a sudden grin.

'You want answers from me? That's a bit rich, coming from you. And what are you doing here anyway? This is no coincidence, our meeting like this.'

'I told you, I've been shopping.'

'Shopping? Shouldn't you be in custody somewhere?'

To my dismay, she turned to leave. The conversation was rapidly going downhill and unless I could salvage it quickly, the opportunity to question her would slip away from me.

Aware that I might never have another chance to quiz her about Nick and Sue, I reached out and grabbed her by the elbow. 'Wait! Please! You have to talk to me.'

'Let go of my arm right this minute or I'll scream!' she hissed, glaring viciously at me.

I believed she would do it. Her eyes narrowed, calculating. This would be a story for her. I could just imagine the headline: *Reporter Assaulted by Murder Suspect*, or some equally sensational caption. A couple of women were approaching us from different directions, and a van drove by.

Rosie knew as well as I did that I couldn't afford to cause a scene in public. With a curse, I released her arm and she hurried away, glancing over her shoulder several times to check whether I was following her. But I was neither that desperate, nor that stupid.

Defeated, I made my way back to my car and drove home, wondering what to do next.

Chapter 26

'I came as soon as I heard,' Jen said as she leapt out of the taxi. She flung her arms around me and gripped so tightly, I squealed in mock alarm. Breathing in the familiar scent of her shampoo, I was fleetingly transported back to the comfort of a childhood embrace and began to relax, in spite of myself.

She released her hold and took a step back to stare at me. 'Now, I want to know everything. And I mean everything. And this time, don't leave anything out.'

Her words reminded me of Ingrid's first instructions, and I shivered. Leaning towards me, Jen held my face in her hands and peered at me, as though she was trying to decipher an intricate code written in my eyes. She had been like a mother to me, only closer, since we were virtually the same generation, and she had always been there for me, a comforting presence in my life for as long as I could remember. In addition to that, she was fiercely intelligent and I had learned there was little point in trying to pull the wool over her eyes. She had always been able to see right through my childhood fibs and in any case, as we grew up, too much trust had built up between us for any deceit.

This was the first time I could remember contemplating deliberately lying to her about something more serious than a surprise birthday party or a Christmas gift. I had to conceal from her not only that I had been to Sue's house, but that I had actually seen her dead body sprawled on her bed. The secret blazed inside my brain, bursting to explode into words, but I had to keep it to myself. Doing my best to sound nonchalant, I asked Jen what she had heard that had brought her hurrying to see me in such a panic.

'Only that you've been in trouble with the police,' she replied, answering my clumsy endeavour to sound casual with an equally crass attempt of her own. 'Nick was incredibly circumspect in what he was prepared to tell me over the phone and refused to answer any of my questions. He kept saying I had to ask you. Now I'm here, and I'm asking you. I want to know all about it. Tell me what's going on.'

Avoiding looking directly at her anxious face, I put the kettle on and bustled around, arranging biscuits on a plate.

'If I'd known you were coming I would have made a cake.'

'I'm not here for cake.'

Over a cup of tea, I explained to Jen that there had been a rumour Nick was having an affair with his secretary. It was difficult to talk about, partly because it was upsetting, but there was also the practical problem that I didn't want to mention the photos Rosie had shown me.

'I don't understand what made you believe the rumour,' Jen said. 'Had you seen anything to convince you it was true?'

It was a fair enough question. I would have asked her the same thing had our positions been reversed.

'I don't know. I just don't know. She seemed so certain.'

'She? Who's "she"?'

'The reporter I told you about. She was the one who told me about Nick's alleged affair, and there was no reason for her to invent a story like that, but she must have been mistaken, or crazy. Anyway, she was so certain he was being unfaithful, she managed to convince me and so–' I broke off. 'This is so hard, and don't ask me why I did it because I can't explain. It was incredibly stupid. All I can say is that I really regret it now.'

In a trembling voice, I told my sister about the three emails I had sent. To my surprise, she burst out laughing.

'You never,' she spluttered, putting down her teacup. 'Really, Louise, how could you? My God, you're not ten!' She giggled.

'I know,' I said, shamefaced but enormously relieved that she wasn't appalled at my behaviour. 'I know it was daft. It was worse than daft, it was stupid. Really stupid. I don't know why I did it. But anyway, after that all sorts of shit kicked off.'

When I told her that Nick's secretary had committed suicide, Jen replied without hesitation that my emails couldn't possibly have had anything to do with Sue's death.

'At most, the emails you sent might have been a tiny contributory factor,' she said. 'But the woman must already have been depressed. No one tops themselves because of a few offensive emails. And what you wrote wasn't that bad, anyway, was it. I'm guessing you were trying to sound like a kid when you composed your elegant messages.' She sniggered, clearly amused. 'I'm sorry, I shouldn't laugh,' she went on, controlling her amusement. 'The poor woman killed herself and that's terribly sad. I'm sorry. But it's not your fault. God, Lou, the woman was unhinged. Surely Nick wasn't really seeing her on the side. I'd have credited him with better judgement than that. I didn't have him down as a complete moron.'

I was surprised and pleased that Jen was taking this all so lightly, but of course she didn't yet know that Sue had been murdered.

'That's not all,' I muttered.

'There's more?' Jen raised her eyebrows. 'Tell me. What else?'

When I explained that the police had subsequently established that Sue hadn't actually taken her own life but had been murdered, Jen's expression grew serious.

'Surely they don't think you had anything to do with it. Louise? Do they?'

I shrugged miserably. 'They say I have a motive.'

'A motive for emailing a few insults, perhaps, but that's hardly the same as committing murder, is it?'

'No, of course it isn't. But try telling the police that. They suspect I was involved in what happened.'

'You didn't do it, so they can't possibly find any proof that you did.'

'They don't have any other suspects.'

'So?' She smiled pityingly at me. 'My poor little sister, sending your daft emails. You always were a goose. But that doesn't make you a bad person, just a silly one. And it certainly doesn't make you a murderer. The police will have to keep on looking for the real killer. And don't look so worried. They can't charge you without any evidence. And they won't find any evidence of something that never happened.'

'Someone killed her.'

'That's got nothing to do with you.'

As I was thanking her for her support and she was telling me there was no need for me to thank her, the doorbell rang. We heard a muted buzz of voices in the hall before Nick opened the door to the living room. Looking up, I was dismayed to see the detective inspector standing in the doorway.

'Louise,' Nick said, 'the inspector would like another word with you.'

'Can't this wait?' I asked. 'This isn't a good time, Inspector. My sister's here and she doesn't visit us very often.'

'No, I'm afraid it can't,' the detective replied.

His voice gave nothing away, but I thought his expression looked even more severe than usual.

Meanwhile, Jen had risen to her feet. 'I was about to go,' she said, obliging as always. 'My train's due soon.'

'Come on, then,' Nick said. 'I'll give you a lift to the station.'

Jen turned to me. 'Take care, Louise, and call me any time. And I mean, any time. Make sure you let me know what happens. And don't worry. You've done nothing wrong.'

She gave me a searching look. I nodded, thanked her profusely, and saw her to the door. An unmarked police car was parked outside with a uniformed driver waiting at the wheel. Somehow I had a feeling I was going to need more than the support that Jen could offer, in the coming weeks. I stood in the doorway for a moment, watching her beloved figure walking away and climbing into the car beside Nick. I almost called out to her to beg her not to go. I wanted to be a child again, and stay at home and be looked after. With a shiver, I wondered what my circumstances might be the next time I saw her, and whether I would still be at liberty, living in my own house and sleeping in my own bed.

Chapter 27

Detective Inspector Jarvis sat on the sofa and stared at me without saying a word. I waited, hoping he would find the silence uncomfortable, but he continued to gaze at me with the cold detachment I had learned to expect from him.

'What do you want with me this time?' I asked at last, unable to bear the silence any longer.

'We have uncovered some new evidence.' He spoke so softly I had to strain to hear what he was saying.

I waited for him to explain, but he said nothing else. I did my best to hold my nerve, but eventually I broke. As a detective inspector, he was more experienced in this kind of battle of wills than a woman whose only previous confrontations had been with insolent teenagers.

'What new evidence is that?' I asked. 'And what do you want from me?' I continued, losing my grip on the vestiges of my composure. 'I'm not prepared to speak to you again without my lawyer present.'

The inspector sighed. Sounding almost sorry, he said, 'We'd like you to clarify a few things for us.'

'I've already answered your questions,' I replied, abandoning any attempt to keep my voice steady. But I knew I had no choice. 'At least wait until my husband gets back. He won't be long.'

As the inspector glanced at his watch, we heard the front door open then close, and Nick came into the living room. He seemed surprised to see us sitting there in silence.

'I thought you'd be done by now,' he said. 'Hasn't Louise offered you anything? A cup of tea? Or maybe something stronger?'

He smiled affably, slipping into his customary bonhomie and treating the detective like a parent of a pupil attending the school.

'We'd like your wife to accompany us to the police station to answer a few more questions,' the inspector replied.

'Please,' Nick waved his arm in an expansive gesture, 'you can speak to her here.'

'I'm afraid that won't be possible.' The inspector rose to his feet in one lithe movement. 'The car's waiting. I'd like Mrs Kelly to come with me. Let's not waste any more time.'

An expression of irritation flitted across Nick's face, but he acquiesced with a nod. For my part, I was peeved at the way they both talked over my head as though the conversation had nothing to do with me. But I had no option other than to follow the inspector out to the police car.

'See you later,' I cried out to Nick as I climbed into the car.

'I'm phoning Ingrid,' he called back. 'She'll be with you in no time. Wait for her. And don't say anything until she gets there.'

He yelled something else about the police tying people up in knots, but the car door slammed and I could no longer hear him above the noise of the engine. He had followed us out onto the drive and, as we drove away, I caught a glimpse of him talking animatedly into his phone.

When we reached the low red brick police station, the inspector marched me inside with a uniformed constable escorting us as though I was a criminal who might try to make a run for it. The experience was both laughable and terrifying. Once inside, I had to wait for Ingrid.

She arrived within an hour, although it felt a lot longer. This time she was wearing a silver-grey trouser suit with a navy blouse, her blond hair hung loosely to her shoulders and, as before, her make-up was impeccable. In my jeans and plain white T-shirt, I felt under-dressed sitting beside her.

'What's this about?' she asked me.

'I've no idea,' I answered honestly. 'According to the inspector they've found some new evidence, but I don't know what it is. He didn't say.'

'Very well, let me do the talking. We'll make no response until we've discovered what this is about and we've had a chance to discuss it together, in private, just the two of us. And in the meantime, don't reply to anything they say.'

I nodded.

'Before we start, is there anything you haven't told me?' Her sharp eyes focused on my face, staring at me, making me feel distinctly awkward.

I hesitated. So far I had told no one that I had been to Sue's house, but unless my car had been spotted driving past and parking further up the hill, there was little chance anyone would know about my visit. If they did, I would deny having seen her. This was all becoming hopelessly complicated.

'No,' I answered. 'There's nothing else. I've told you everything there is to tell.'

'Very well then,' she said, as though she realised I was being evasive. 'If you're sure that's all you want to tell me.'

I had no choice but to cling to my lie. 'It's all there is.'

We went to the interview room, where it didn't escape my attention that the tape was switched on before the inspector began to question me. He was accompanied by the same dark-haired detective sergeant I had seen with him before. She gazed coolly at me with expressionless black eyes that made my skin prickle. I didn't imagine much would escape her attention.

'Did you go to Sue's house on the twenty-sixth of June?' the inspector asked me.

As he mentioned a date, Ingrid glanced at me and nodded.

'No,' I replied without hesitation. It was best to appear confident in my answers. If I appeared to flounder, they might suspect I was lying. 'No, I didn't.'

The inspector leaned forward slightly in his chair.

'We found an unopened bottle of wine in Sue's kitchen,' he said softly.

Ingrid looked at me, and I could tell she was puzzled.

'An unopened bottle of wine?' she repeated. 'What does that have to do with my client?'

'Did you take a bottle of wine to Sue's house?' the inspector asked me, ignoring my lawyer's question.

'My client has already told you she didn't go to the house–'

'I have been there, to her house,' I interrupted Ingrid, realising the police must have found my fingerprints on the door handles, as well as on the bottle. 'I don't deny I've been there. But I haven't been there since before half term. We've all been running around, busy with the end-of-term arrangements, this half term. And Sue was involved in the arrangements more than anyone. I went to see her, oh, maybe six weeks ago. I'm sorry, I can't remember exactly when. It was an informal visit, you know, near the beginning of term. I could check my diary but I don't suppose I even made a note of it. She just asked me one day if I was free that evening, and I said I was and went over there. It wasn't planned or anything.'

Now it was Ingrid who interrupted me, perhaps because I was talking too much. 'My client has answered your question. Is there anything else? Because I'd like to take a break and confer with my client.'

'Can you explain why there was a bottle of white wine with your fingerprints on it in Sue's kitchen?'

'I just told you, I went to see her that one time. I might have taken a bottle of wine. I honestly can't remember, but it's certainly the kind of thing I would do. I can't believe I would have gone round there empty handed.'

'So you took bottle of wine with you when you visited her, but you didn't drink it?'

I nodded. My mouth was feeling dry and I had to force myself to speak. 'That's right. I remember now, I didn't want to drink much because I was driving, and she had an opened bottle in the fridge, so we drank that.'

'There were two other bottles of white wine in the fridge. Can you explain why the one with your prints on it was out on the worktop?'

'I suppose she was planning to drink it.' I shrugged. 'Perhaps she was expecting a visitor. I've no idea. How should I know why she'd taken a bottle of wine out of the fridge and then not opened it.' I frowned, trying to look as though I was baffled by the question.

Ingrid stepped in. 'My client is not responsible for explaining the actions of the woman whose death you are investigating,' she said coolly. 'And now, I think she'd like to go home.' She stood up. 'Come on, Louise, we're done here.' She turned back to the inspector. 'I suggest you dedicate your resources to looking for your killer, and stop wasting my client's time.'

'Wait,' I said. 'There's something else I want to mention.'

Ingrid frowned at me and sat down. 'Do you want to talk to me first?' she hissed.

I shook my head at her.

The inspector fixed his unwavering gaze on me. 'I'm listening.'

'That journalist, Rosie, *did* have the photos I told you about. I've been thinking about it, and I'm sure she did.'

I didn't add that Rosie was avoiding seeing me, and had seemed uncomfortable when we met outside her office.

The inspector frowned. 'I'm not sure I understand.'

'My husband spoke to you about the photos I saw on Rosie's phone, didn't he?'

'She brought two phones here, and we checked them both. We found no traces of any such images, and none had been deleted.' I thought he sounded slightly smug.

'You need to look again. The photos were there.'

'I think we've been through this already.'

'My client would like to go home now,' Ingrid said, standing up.

'Yes.' The inspector inclined his head. 'You can go home but don't go anywhere, and stay in the area. You can expect to come and see us again shortly.'

I scowled at him.

'My client has told you everything she can about what happened,' Ingrid said.

'Maybe she has,' he replied. 'And maybe she hasn't.'

'I have,' I said petulantly.

Cursing the inspector's scepticism, I went home.

Chapter 28

Nick was confident the police would take no further action against me, but the reality was they might pursue me and, if I was charged, there was even a danger that I might be convicted. Everything Nick and I had worked so hard to achieve would be destroyed, as I waited behind bars, perhaps for years. Of course I would appeal against any custodial sentence, but months could go by while I languished in a cell and, in the meantime, Nick's career would be over. It was probably only because my husband was such a well-respected member of the community, and no one viewed me as a dangerous individual, that I was allowed to remain at liberty at all while the police continued their investigation.

The only way to deflect the cloud of suspicion hovering over my name would be to discover who else could be responsible for Sue's death. I decided to look into Rosie's background, and question people who had known Sue, in an attempt to find a feasible explanation for what had happened. Although Nick still had to go out during the day, he was at home in the evenings, partly, I thought, so he could keep an eye on me. That evening I planned to tackle him, as someone who had worked closely with the murdered woman. I opened a bottle of his favourite Chianti to go with homemade spaghetti carbonara, and waited until he was half way through his meal before I began.

'You know about those emails?'

He grunted, seemingly preoccupied with his own thoughts.

'I sent a few emails. Three, to be precise. And that was all. You believe me, don't you?'

He glanced up, frowning. 'What do you mean, that was all?'

'I'm talking about what I did. That was the worst of it. I mean, that was all. You do believe me, don't you?'

'Yes, of course I believe you.'

'Given that the police seem to suspect I killed Sue, the only way we can really clear my name and get the police off my back is if we can find out who did do it.'

Swallowing, he put down his knife and fork and looked at me. 'Do you know anything about her murder? Is there something you haven't told me? Because if there is, you'd better tell me now.'

It was the question Ingrid had asked me the last time we had spoken. I gave Nick the same answer I had given her.

'Of course there isn't. How can you even ask me that?'

'I'm asking.'

'I swear on my mother's life I know nothing about her death. Nothing. I admit I sent those emails, and yes, I did my best to cover that up, but you can't honestly say you believe me capable of murder.'

'I wouldn't have believed you were capable of sending those emails, but you did. It's like I don't know you anymore, Louise.'

'But murder? Are you serious?' I was shaking. 'You must know me better than that. You've known me for twenty years. Nick, look at me!'

'What do you expect me to say? Honestly, Louise, tell me, what am I supposed to think?'

'I need you to help me find out who killed her.'

'Leave that to the police. It's not your job and it's nothing to do with you anymore, unless you know something you're not telling me.'

'What if the police end up thinking it was me? They don't know me. Who knows what they're thinking.'

Nick shook his head. 'Of course they don't think it was you. You'd be behind bars by now if they did. But listen, Louise, I've been meaning to speak to you.'

I held my breath, wondering if he was about to confess to his affair with Sue. Certainly he looked grave enough.

'Don't take this the wrong way,' he said, 'but it would be better if you made more of an effort to show yourself around school at the moment.'

'What? You want me to go into school as though nothing has happened? How can you even say such a thing?'

'It's only what you would do if you had done nothing wrong,' he replied testily. 'And it would be best for you in the long run.'

'If I had done nothing wrong?' I repeated indignantly. 'You said yourself I'm innocent. Don't you believe me? Listen, I haven't done anything wrong.'

'It's a pity you sent those emails,' he replied curtly. 'The longer you hide yourself away here, like a criminal, the more tongues are going to wag. You know I'm right. You know what staffrooms are like for tittle-tattle,' he concluded, before turning his attention back to his dinner, as though signalling to me that the conversation was over. But as far as I was concerned we had barely started.

'So you're saying the whole school is talking about how I sent those emails.'

'What do you think?'

We were a week into the summer holiday and many of the staff had left the school to visit their families, or go travelling. Considering only a few remained on site, it seemed unlikely I was being talked about much.

'How do they know it was me, anyway? Who told them?'

'It wasn't me, if that's what you're implying.'

'Who was it then?'

'I don't know. But people talk. They must know you were held at the police station for questioning, and you're an expert in IT. Other people can put two and two together. Anyway, Louise, apart from all of that, we could do with some secretarial assistance and it's not doing you any good, hiding yourself away like this. The longer it goes on, the harder it's going to be for you when you finally decide to come back to school. Julie is struggling to cope, processing admissions and covering Sue's job at the same time. If Julie carries on like this she's going to have a breakdown and then there'll be no one left to keep things going.'

'What about David's secretary?'

'Mandy's away for a fortnight.'

'Oh. I thought you had a temp in to help.'

'Yes, but she doesn't know the school, and she doesn't understand how we do things. She needs direction. Please, Louise, I wouldn't ask if it wasn't in your own interest to go out and talk to people here as though–'

'I know, as though I'd done nothing wrong,' I interrupted him bitterly.

'I was going to say as though nothing had happened.'

The conversation was going so badly, I had little to lose by challenging him to explain his part in what had occurred.

'Tell me about Sue,' I said.

His eyebrows shot up. 'What about her?'

'What was she like?'

For an instant, an expression of such pain flitted across his face that I wanted to put my arms round him and comfort him. Her death had been a loss for him too. But the thought that I might never know how much of a loss hardened me against him.

'You know perfectly well what she was like,' he replied. 'At the risk of repeating the eulogy I gave at the end of term, she was popular, efficient and kind to a fault. I never once saw her lose her composure, and everyone liked her, without exception.' He gave me a strange glance. 'The whole school will miss her warm smile, and her readiness to help regardless of the circumstances and whatever the problem.'

His response was lifted, more or less word for word, from his end-of-term speech.

'Now, can we stop talking about her, please,' he said. 'It's not helping either of us to dwell on what happened. We have a meeting with Ingrid next week and, until then, can we please try to assume some semblance of normality. And now I'd like to eat my dinner in peace. It's a good carbonara, by the way.'

I stared at my plate miserably, wondering how he could sit there calmly eating, when the life we had worked so hard to build seemed to be in danger of collapsing around us.

'Are you really going to do nothing to help me?'

'I'm paying the best criminal lawyer money can buy,' he replied, genuinely surprised. 'What else do you want me to do?'

My disappointment at Nick's refusal to do anything more to help me was a bitter blow. Had our situations been reversed, I would have worked night and day to clear his name, and would never have doubted his word, not for an instant.

'If you were in trouble, I'd support you,' I said reproachfully. 'Even if the whole world was against you.'

'Listen, if there was anything I could do to make this go away, anything at all, believe me, I would do it, whatever the cost. But we have to let the justice system run its course. If you're innocent – which I don't doubt for one minute, so please don't start up again – given you're innocent, they won't find any evidence to convict you. And in the meantime, I'm sure the police are still looking into all this, and they must be following up other leads. They wouldn't have let you come home if they really thought you were guilty. So, unless you have something new to say, let's not talk about it again until we see Ingrid.'

He finished his supper in silence.

'That was delicious,' he said as he put down his fork.

Nick wasn't prepared to discuss Sue, and clearly it wasn't going to be easy questioning the staff at school. In desperation, I started to make plans to go and see Rosie again and force her to tell me what she knew. I said nothing to Nick about my intended visit, and resolved to be careful as well as discreet. The last thing I wanted was for a misquoted interview with me to appear in the paper after I spoke to Rosie. She was, after all, a journalist, and probably the last person to be trusted. But I couldn't just sit around at home, waiting and doing nothing to prove my innocence when no one else wanted to do it for me.

That night I hardly slept, thinking about my plans. This meeting could be crucial to my future, but I had no idea what I was going to say to Rosie, if she would even agree to see me.

Chapter 29

We were expecting Jen and her family for Sunday lunch and I spent the morning preparing a roast, peeling and chopping different-coloured root vegetables to go with the potatoes: butternut squash, parsnips, and carrots, as well as a selection of vegetables: broccoli, sweet corn and red peppers, in addition to all the trimmings.

Nick smiled at me as he walked through the kitchen. 'It looks like you're getting ready to feed an army.'

I laughed. 'You're not far wrong.'

Jen turned up mid-morning, as expected, accompanied by her family, en route to a holiday home in Wales. In an instant, the house erupted in a cacophony of lively chatter, with everyone talking at once.

'How are you?'

'It's so great to see you!'

'Take your things off and come out in the garden.'

'I'll crack open a bottle,' Nick called out.

'Where's the loo, Aunty Lou?'

My niece burst into the fit of giggles that question always prompted.

Forced to temporarily shelve my own thoughts, any speculation about how to force Rosie to speak to me was driven out by the noise. A talkative family, they were all enthusiastic about their holiday in Wales, and their break from work and studies. Listening to them was like a gust of wind from another planet where life was lively and cheerful and brimming over with interest and optimism.

Until their arrival, I had not realised how far my own life had fallen down a dark and insular tunnel, with no end in sight.

'It's the first time we've all been away together for years and years,' one of my nieces told me, buzzing with excitement. 'The whole family together.'

'Five years, to be exact,' Jen said.

'A week stuck with this lot,' my youngest nephew, Zac, groaned. 'How am I going to survive?'

His father gave him a playful cuff on the ear.

'You show some respect,' he said with mock severity, and my nephew flung himself on the floor, rolling around and complaining of parental brutality.

'Should have been a footballer,' his father chuckled.

Nick popped open a bottle of bubbly and we went outside to have a drink on the patio.

'We're going to need more than one bottle,' I told Nick.

He scurried off and returned a moment later with another two.

'Plenty more where that came from,' he said with a broad smile.

It was a bright day, sunny but not too hot thanks to a pleasant breeze, and the youngsters were soon kicking a football around on the lawn.

'Mind the roses,' Jen called out, but no one took any notice of her.

Before long before Nick and Tony joined in the noisy game.

'Make two teams,' the oldest girl shouted out. 'Uncle Nick, you come over here. Annie, stay where you are!'

'Kimberley's so bossy,' Jen complained, with a complacent smile.

'Perhaps she'll be a teacher,' I suggested.

'I don't think a classroom would satisfy her monstrous ambition. I rather think she's set her sights on running the country,' Jen replied, 'if not the world. She wants to go into politics but I'm not sure she's got the killer instinct. It's a tough game, politics.'

'The killer instinct,' I repeated softly, and laughed to cover my momentary awkwardness. 'I'd better go in and see to the dinner.'

'I'll come with you,' Jen said.

'No, there's nothing to do, honestly. You sit here and put your feet up.'

'I'm coming with you,' she repeated in a voice that brooked no opposition.

Once Jen had cornered me in the kitchen, she set about questioning me, but this time I was ready.

'If you ever need anything, you just have to ask,' she told me, gazing at me earnestly. 'You're looking tired. I can give you something to help you sleep, if you need it. You can come to me in confidence, like you did when you first moved here. I know you and Nick have to be careful to protect your reputation for being morally and mentally flawless.' She smiled.

I did not tell her that Nick had discreetly taken me to see a psychiatrist.

'Oh, the trouble we were having is all over,' I assured her cheerfully. 'The police haven't bothered us again. It was all pretty unpleasant at the time, but we've put it behind us. The problem is that Nick's got to find himself another secretary. There's no one here who can do the job so he's looking for an outside candidate, but that brings its own problems. They have a certain way of doing things here—'

'The Edleybury tradition.' Jen laughed. 'You've mentioned that before, but I thought you said Nick was changing the place, bringing it up to date.'

'He's introducing changes, yes, and all long overdue. Honestly, it's like living in the dark ages here in some ways. Do you know how the staff get their tea and coffee at break time?'

'Surprise me.'

I knew she was laughing at me, but I carried on anyway. All the time we were talking I was busy, carving the joint, stirring gravy, and checking the vegetables.

'One of the women from the kitchen – who must be sixty if she's a day – wheels a trolley loaded up with pots and jugs and biscuits all the way from the kitchen to the staff room. I'm talking about a heavy trolley which she pushes across the school, and some of it is uphill. Then when she finally reaches the staff room and gets the trolley over the doorstep, she has to carry all the pots and jugs and plates of biscuits, by hand, up the stairs to the social area in the staff room. Seriously, up and down the stairs with trays of pots and jugs.'

'And plates of biscuits,' Jen added. 'Don't forget the plates of biscuits.'

'Oh no, it's more than her job's worth to forget to bring the teachers their morning biscuits. It's a good five-minute walk from the kitchen to the staff room at the best of times, and it takes her about fifteen minutes, pushing the bloody trolley. By the time she gets there, the coffee's barely warm. And then, when break is over, she carts the whole lot down the stairs again and loads up her trolley and pushes it back to the kitchen. She's been doing it for God knows how many years – probably all her working life. No one ever questions her completely batty routine, and do you know why? Because that's how it's always been done. Can you believe it?'

Jen shook her head. 'Why don't they get a coffee machine for the staff room?'

'That's exactly what I said. It's what anyone with half a grain of sense would say.'

We both laughed.

Just then Kimberley came in from the garden. 'Everyone wants to know when we're going to have lunch,' she said.

'It's ready now. Tell them all to come in and sit down.'

She ran off and a few minutes later Nick and Tony came in from the garden, laughing and joking, followed by the four youngsters.

'Something smells good,' Tony said, prompting a string of insults between the younger siblings starting with which of them had the smelliest feet, and moving up through their various body parts.

'That's enough,' Jen said sharply. 'You're not at home now. Go and wash your hands, kids, and let's eat. I'm starving and this all looks wonderful, Lou.'

'Yes, Aunty Lou,' Kimberley said.

'It looks yummy,' Zac agreed.

'Good enough to eat,' Nick agreed, putting his arm round my waist and planting a kiss on my cheek.

Jen smiled, and I relaxed for the first time since her arrival, seeing she was convinced that everything had returned to normal. I wished I could convince myself as easily.

Chapter 30

Nick had taken to bringing me breakfast in bed. Since my encounter with the police, his solicitude had increased until my gratitude had turned to irritation.

'I'm not an invalid,' I protested when he told me he wanted to look after me.

It wasn't to spite him that I started getting up early, although that might have seemed to be the reason. The truth was I had people to see and errands to run.

By ten to nine on Monday morning I was waiting outside the office in Watford where Rosie worked. Pretending to be looking at my phone, I loitered on the pavement trying not to look as though I was waiting for someone. Several people went into the building, including the receptionist I had spoken to the previous week, but I kept my head down and she didn't notice me. When Rosie finally arrived, scurrying along the pavement with her grey beret pulled right down to her eyes, I stepped forward to block her path and prevent her from entering the building.

'You again,' she muttered. 'What are you doing here? Shopping again?'

'I need to speak to you. I won't be put off this time.'

A man approached and she called out to him. As he paused in his stride and looked round, she dodged past me to join him and they went inside together. There was no point in hanging around all day so I went home for a couple of hours.

Returning at midday, I waited for her again until she emerged at one.

'You have to stop doing this,' she told me as she strode along the pavement with me hurrying at her heels.

'Doing what?'

'Stalking me. It was no coincidence, you being here last week. Go away.'

'One drink and then I'll leave you alone, I promise.'

She stopped and glared at me, and I could have sworn I saw fear in her eyes.

'One drink,' she agreed reluctantly. 'And after that I never want to see you again.'

So far so good. At least I had persuaded her to talk to me. We didn't exchange another word or a single glance as we walked along the road until we reached the nearby pub.

Inside, subdued lighting, a dark wooden bar and maroon carpets contributed to the dingy atmosphere, the gloom disturbed only by intermittent flashing from a fruit machine winking its neon lights in a hideous assault of clashing colours.

'What'll you have?' I asked.

'A glass of red wine.'

I ordered two glasses from the young girl behind the bar.

'Make them as large as you like,' I told her recklessly.

Rosie was seated at a corner table, watching my approach. She took a gulp of wine and then another, evidently keen to knock her drink back as quickly as possible. I didn't mind. If I could get her tipsy, so much the better. She sat gazing steadily at me over the rim of her glass, waiting for me to speak, the brightness of her eyes accentuated by heavy black eyeliner. With no clear idea of what to say to her, I nodded and took a sip of my wine, playing for time. Beyond discovering whether she had lied to me about Nick and Sue I had no plans, and could think of no easy way to coax the truth out of her.

'The affair between my husband and Sue,' I said finally, putting my glass down on the table.

She frowned and said nothing.

'It was very clever, what you did,' I went on, hoping to provoke a response. 'You really had me fooled. What I don't understand, is why you did it. What was it between you and Nick? How long have you known him?'

She had removed her beret when she sat down, and she pushed her fringe off her face so that I could see her eyes as she stared at me with a mixture of perplexity and hostility.

'What the fuck are you talking about?' she asked in a low voice.

'I thought that was perfectly clear. I want you to tell me how long you've known my husband.'

'I don't know your husband. I met him for the first time when I interviewed him for the local paper, and again when I returned with a photographer. Apart from those two occasions, I've never seen him in my life.'

'And you'd really never met him before you came to our house to interview us?'

'Isn't that what I just said? I've never met him apart from those occasions, either before or since. Is that all?'

'The photos you showed me–'

'What photos?' She interrupted me, putting her glass down on the table with a gesture of finality.

'Okay, I need you to be honest with me.'

I smiled to show that she hadn't riled me in the slightest. If anything, she was the one who seemed wary and I was concerned to keep her on the back foot.

'You know,' I went on, 'I still can't work out how you did it. Some kind of photoshopping, but it was brilliantly done. You have a real talent for–' I almost said 'for lying', but I stopped myself just in time, 'for manipulating digital images. We should get you to take some photos of the school.' I laughed, inviting her confidence. 'Tell me something. We both know you did it, but what I want to know is, why did you go to all that bother? Come on, you can be frank with me. I promise I won't tell anyone but, just for my own peace of mind, I really need to know those photos were fake. One woman to another. Please, I just want to know if my husband's been playing away from home. You can understand that, can't you?'

I was reduced to begging again.

She must have realised that she had somehow regained the upper hand, because she shook her head and drank some more of her wine. 'I'm sorry, but I really have no idea what you're talking about. Not the foggiest.'

'Do you deny you came to see me at my house?'

'No, why would I deny it, to you of all people? You were there, weren't you?'

I frowned at her. 'And is it still your contention that those photos of Nick and Sue were genuine? Because unless you can convince me they were authentic, then everything you've told me is one big lie from start to finish.'

'What photos?' She leaned forward. 'You know, your husband came to see me, banging on about some photos you told him about. I take it you're pestering me about the same thing. But I'll tell you exactly what I told him.' She paused to take another gulp of her wine, draining her glass. 'I have absolutely no idea what you're talking about, and I don't know what you're playing at.'

Her words were defiant, but beneath her aggression I thought she looked nervous. Yet I could tell she wasn't really worried. I had seen exactly the same expression on the faces of pupils when they were handing over their mobile phones in class. It was futile confiscating their phones because the kids always had another one on them, and merely handed over a decoy. In that instant I realised how stupid I had been to assume that Rosie only had two mobile phones, one for work and one for her personal use. Of course she had volunteered to take them to the police station in Watford to be checked, knowing there was nothing incriminating in the memories. She must have taken the photos, and stored them, on another phone.

'I guess I was mistaken,' I said. 'I'd better be on my way. Thanks for your time. It's been very interesting chatting to you.'

She looked surprised when I stood up, but I didn't wait around to hear any more from her. Somehow the police had to be persuaded to search her house for her other phone, and then they would find the missing photos. I still didn't understand what motive she could have possibly had for taking so much trouble to convince me that Nick was unfaithful. The truth must lie somewhere in the past, in a meeting between Rosie and Nick. Maybe they had once had a fling, or perhaps she suffered from Stockholm syndrome, that strange mental condition in which people believed they had a relationship with a stranger. Whatever the truth, the key to the mystery lay with Rosie. I was going to get to the bottom of her interest in my husband, but lacked the resources do so on my own.

On leaving the pub, I went directly to the police station and asked for DI Jarvis. The inspector kept me waiting for a long time, but at last a constable escorted me to a small room and a few moments later the detective appeared, accompanied by his dark-haired sergeant.

The inspector stared at me with his cold hard eyes. 'You asked to see me?'

'I had a thought.'

Although his features didn't alter, a frown seemed to flit across his face, faint as a shadow cast by a passing cloud. I could almost hear his thoughts: *Stop wasting my valuable time with your nonsense*, but he nodded politely and invited me to continue.

'Rosie had another phone,' I blurted out.

'Excuse me?'

His expression remained fixed, but his voice conveyed his impatience.

'Do you remember the reporter, the one who showed me photos of my husband with Sue?'

'Rosie White, yes, the woman you alleged showed you some images on her phone.'

This time his voice sounded smug, as though he wished to convince me he remembered everything. The man wasn't a machine; he had an ego.

'The reason you didn't find those photos on either of her phones was that she's got another one. She must have!' I paused, aware that I was shouting in my excitement.

The inspector watched me, unmoved. At his side, the sergeant sat, equally impassive.

'Don't you understand what I'm telling you? The fact that you were unable to find the photos she showed me on her phone proves nothing. She took them on a different phone!'

'You think she had another phone? A third one?'

I couldn't have said why, but I had the impression the detective was toying with me.

'Yes, that's exactly what I'm saying. We need to find her other phone.'

The inspector gave an icy smile. 'Yes, you're quite right. She did have another phone, one for work and a second one for her own personal use. A lot of people do.'

I fought off my disappointment that he had deliberately misunderstood me. 'I mean,' I stuttered, 'I mean there must be another one.'

'The thought occurred to us too, yes.' He paused. 'We checked both phones, of course, but we found nothing.'

'No, I mean there was another phone...' I faltered, 'a third one...'

The inspector stood up and his sergeant followed suit. 'Is that everything, Mrs Kelly?' he enquired politely.

'It's just that, if I was storing something controversial, I'd get hold of a secret phone—'

'A secret phone?' he repeated, raising one eyebrow.

It did sound silly on his lips but I nodded, trying to look as though what we were talking about was a perfectly sensible idea. The inspector was wrong to dismiss it so swiftly anyway.

'People can own more than one phone,' I said. 'More than two…'

But the inspector was already moving towards the door and either didn't hear what I said, or else chose to ignore me. I was on my own with my suspicions.

Chapter 31

The police had left me no choice but to investigate what had happened for myself. Somewhere in Rosie's flat lay the answer to my question, because only an examination of her private third phone would confirm whether or not the photos she had shown me were genuine. I could live without the truth about Sue's death ever coming to light, but I couldn't spend the rest of my life in my current uncertainty, wondering whether my husband had been unfaithful.

It was half past three, which gave me enough time to drive to the magazine office and sit in the car waiting for Rosie to appear. While I waited, I googled how to pick a lock. It required specialist tools which I didn't possess, but I was able to grasp the principles. Basically, a lock comprised a series of wards that had to be aligned before a key would turn. The notches on the key had to match the position of the wards when the door was locked. From watching films, I was under the impression that it was possible to open a locked door using only a thin metal spike, but of course something that appeared plausible in fiction might not be practicable in the real world. After all, if it was easy to break into a house using only a hairpin, or something similar, locks wouldn't be much use.

It might be possible to obtain a set of tools specifically designed to pick locks, but such a purchase was bound to leave a trace and I was already in enough trouble with the police without adding to my problems. I would have to make do with a seemingly innocent tool, like a hairpin or a very thin crochet hook. It was four o'clock. There was enough time to check out the shops and see what I could get hold of and still be back in position outside the Hertfordshire Style offices before Rosie left for the day.

By five I was back, armed with several long nails, a set of luridly coloured metal crochet hooks, a packet of hairpins, and several pairs of rubber gloves.

The day was overcast and threatening rain as I drew into the kerb near Rosie's office block, just in time to see her walking out of the building. Easing my foot off the brake, I drew out into the slow-moving traffic as she reached the corner where she halted at a bus stop. Cursing my lack of foresight, I drove past and parked half on the pavement to avoid blocking the road. Keeping my eyes on my rear view mirror, I watched Rosie board a bus. Driving behind it, I waited as it pulled in at stops, or else drove further on and drew into the kerb when I could, to wait for it to pass me again. It was a tricky pursuit.

Without my sat nav to direct me home again, I wouldn't have travelled so far out of my way, up and down side streets, through small parades of shops, traversing residential estates, where the bus stopped frequently to lose and gain passengers. Some of the stops were busier than others. The bus travelled across the town, on a route that twisted and turned until I no longer knew in which direction we were heading, or where I was going. At each stop, I watched for the grey beret and finally saw Rosie step down from the bus.

Following her proved even more difficult. Eventually I parked the car and continued the journey on foot, staying as close behind her as I dared. We probably only walked a few hundred yards, but it felt like miles. Had I not been able to find my way back to the car, I would have really been in trouble searching around for it later on in the gathering dusk, but fortunately for me Rosie kept on the same road. At last she vanished into a block of flats on the outskirts of the town. I waited for about fifteen minutes, wondering what to do, before I turned and retraced my steps back to the car, planning to return the next day when Rosie was at work. Somehow I would gain access to her flat and search for her missing phone.

As I was setting my sat nav to direct me back to Edleybury, I glanced up and caught a glimpse of Rosie speeding past me in the passenger seat of a car. I had no time to see who was driving, but that didn't matter. My luck was turning. It was likely her neighbours would enter the block of flats at around that time, coming home from work. I couldn't afford to let this chance slip. Not stopping to think what I was doing, I drove off and pulled up right outside the block where Rosie lived. I didn't have long to wait before a man strode up the path and entered the building, barely noticing me as I slipped through the street door behind him, my tools concealed in my bag.

Once again, luck was with me. There was a row of metal mailboxes fixed to one wall in the communal hall. I studied them and found R White printed on the label of box number 17. Assuming the numbers on the mailboxes tallied with the numbers of the flats, I had identified where Rosie lived.

Number 17 was on the third floor. I took the stairs and found the corridor on the top floor empty. I wanted to enter the flat without leaving a trace, but was desperate enough to break the lock if that was the only way to gain access to her apartment. There was no one around, but I didn't know how long Rosie would be away. I could only hope she was out for the evening.

Working as quickly as I could, it still took me over an hour to open the door. At one point, I was interrupted by the arrival of a neighbour. I turned aside and pretended to be talking on my phone and the man entered his own flat without giving me a second look. With a sigh of relief, I resumed fiddling with the lock, twisting a crochet hook, then a hairpin, pushing and stroking the inner workings, and cursing whoever had invented keys. But at last there was a click, and I was in.

Praying that Rosie didn't have a burglar alarm, I pushed the door gingerly. At the first sound of an alarm, I would shut the door and flee. As long as the door was closed, and I remained on the outside, hopefully there would be no evidence of my attempted break in. Burglar alarms sometimes went off in error. The flight of an insect could set off a sensor, or even a sudden change in temperature could disturb a sensitive system.

Tensed to run, I pushed the door very cautiously, just enough to set off an alarm, but was met with silence. Another second saw me safely inside. Having spent so long gaining access to the flat, I had to work quickly. I closed the door behind me and began my search. The bedroom or the kitchen seemed the most likely places to find something that was hidden. Hurriedly, I found the bedroom. It wasn't easy, searching with only the dim light from outside, but I was afraid to switch on an overhead light. There was a double bed with a lumpy duvet thrown carelessly over it, bunched up on one side as though the sleeper had dragged it over to that half of the mattress. On the side of the bed with the lion's share of the duvet stood a small pine cabinet, on top of which was a lamp and a phone charger.

With trembling fingers, I opened the cupboard door. In the pale light from the window, my hands looked ghostly in their rubber gloves. Inside the cupboard, I found a packet of contraceptive pills, a bottle of aspirin, a Penguin book of short stories, a few combs, a pair of nail scissors, a pack of emery boards, dental floss, and a sheet of small photographs of Rosie herself, with two missing. Her severe expression suggested they had been taken for a passport. There was nothing else in there. Closing the bedside cupboard, I turned my attention to the floor to ceiling wardrobes fitted along one wall of the room. It would take a long time to search them all, top to bottom, but the phone might be concealed somewhere in there.

As I looked around, wondering where to search next, I heard the scraping of a key in a lock and the muffled sound of voices and faint laughter. A light was turned on in the hall. Rosie had returned, and she was not alone. I listened, but the pounding of my heart seemed to drown out every other sound.

I was trapped.

Chapter 32

Once again I had run out of options. My plight was desperate and entirely of my own making, but there was no time for self recrimination. With no possibility of escaping through a window on the third floor, my only hope was to conceal myself somewhere inside the flat until Rosie left for work the next morning. If she found me hiding, along with tools for breaking in, it would be obvious what had happened. What made it worse was that she worked for a magazine so she was bound to have contacts with the local papers. Before long everyone in the region, if not the whole country, would know I had forced an entry into her private residence. It was hard to see how Nick's position could remain tenable after that. The headmaster of Edleybury must be a role model for young people. He couldn't possibly survive the scandal of being married to a burglar.

Hurling myself through the bedroom door into the living room, I flung myself down behind the sofa. Had it not been placed just to one side of the door to the bedroom, it would have been impossible to hide behind it in time to avoid being seen, because a second later I heard the door open. The voices grew louder as they approached my hiding place but they were muffled through the sofa so that, although I could tell a man and a woman were talking, I was unable to distinguish a single word until the woman said, quite clearly, 'Let's go to bed.' It sounded as though they were just the other side of the sofa. Not daring to breathe, I froze, praying they would not see me. If they sat down and the sofa shifted backwards, it would crush me. Tensing myself, I waited. Whatever happened, I must not cry out.

Cursing my stupidity, I realised that I should have revealed my presence as soon as the front door opened, inventing some story about finding the door ajar when I had arrived to speak to Rosie. She would almost certainly have been annoyed at my intrusion, but that would have preferable to being discovered hiding there. It was too late to reveal myself, and too late for regrets. I dared not turn my head to look, but heard them going into the bedroom. Silently I begged them to close the door but it remained open. Any sound I made might alert them to my presence. What I had to concentrate on was extricating myself from this potentially ruinous situation. Rosie had only to return to her living room and as she came through her bedroom doorway she would see me cowering on the floor. There could be no talking my way out of that. Nothing short of an invisibility cloak could help me.

As my eyes grew acclimatised to the low lighting, I stared at the back of the sofa, praying for a miracle to rescue me. The sofa was thankfully a large three seater, upholstered in brown and cream fabric. Craning my neck past one end of it, I could see the door that would take me to the hall and out of the flat. But first I had to cross the living room, and once I had clambered out from my hiding place, I would be exposed. The light went out in the bedroom.

It was fortunate for me that Rosie and her companion were more interested in each other than in what else might be going on inside the flat. I heard a faint rustling and plopping as they dropped their clothes on the floor and fell into bed, their laughter and inconsequential chatter quickly replaced by grunts and gasps. Had I not known better, I might have interpreted the noises they were making as the dying breaths of some hunted animal. Fiercely restraining an impulse to giggle, I told myself that discovery would not only lead to intense embarrassment, the consequences would be catastrophic. The heavy breathing continued. If my situation had not been so precarious, it would have been farcical.

My problem demanded an immediate resolution. Either I could try to sneak away while they were busy under the duvet, or else I could wait it out until they fell asleep. But they might go back in the living room to drink and talk or watch television for hours, while I remained behind the sofa, not daring to stir, while my muscles grew stiff from keeping to one position and I struggled not to cough or sneeze or betray my presence by the slightest movement. Besides, as long as I remained skulking behind the sofa, sooner or later Rosie was going to look out through the bedroom door and discover me hiding there. Once again, I was left with no choice. One way or another, my only hope of escaping detection lay in getting out of there.

Cautiously I dragged myself forwards. Beneath me, the floorboards creaked. I held my breath. The noises in the bed stopped for a second, then resumed. It wasn't clear whether they had heard my stealthy movement, but the pipework in buildings often rumbles and squeaks and, besides, if they had heard anything, they would probably assume it was the noise of the bed shifting beneath them.

Pulling myself up onto my hands and knees, I stole around the sofa, doing my best to move silently. With the sofa between me and the bedroom door, I lowered myself to the floor once more and slithered forwards on my front, trying to keep my head below the top of the sofa while inching my way towards the front door. Rosie and her visitor had turned out the light in the bedroom, but light from the hall helped me to find the door. It also increased the risk of my being spotted crawling across the room.

They were still occupied between the sheets when I reached the hall. Scrambling silently to my feet, I ran lightly to the front door. Thankfully the man with Rosie didn't suffer from premature ejaculation or my escape plan might have been scuppered. Offering up a silent prayer of gratitude for his prowess, I reached for the handle. Only then did it occur to me that if the door was double locked it would be impossible to open without a key. I tried to remember whether the door had been locked after it was slammed shut, but at the time I had been too focused on avoiding capture to notice what was happening elsewhere.

My head swam as my hand slid up to the handle and turned it. The hinges groaned when the door swung open. Summoning all my remaining energy, I threw myself out of the flat and closed the door behind me as quietly as I could. I was alone. Leaning against the wall, I pulled myself up onto my feet but my legs were shaking so hard I could scarcely walk. It was foolish to linger right outside Rosie's flat, shaking and crying, but my legs refused to move.

Only a few minutes could have passed but it felt like hours before I managed to stagger to the lift and summon it. If I hadn't been trembling so violently I would have hurled myself down the stairs, but I couldn't trust my legs to carry me. Another age seemed to pass until, finally, the lift arrived to carry me down to the ground floor and freedom.

Safely in my car, I leant my head on the steering wheel and sat there for a while, trembling and sobbing with relief.

By the time I reached home, it was nearly ten o'clock. Luckily, Nick was not yet back. Hurrying indoors, I went straight to the bathroom and took a long shower. It was hard to believe I had succeeded in breaking into a virtual stranger's flat, escaping almost certain discovery. The fact that I was still no further ahead in my investigation seemed unimportant. All that mattered was to be home and safe. No one suspected where I had been, or what I had been doing, that evening. Once again I couldn't control my tears; they were carried away by the shower.

About an hour later, Nick came home. Flopping down on a chair, he launched into a diatribe about his day and the incompetence of the bursar. Finally he asked me how my day had gone.

'It was fine,' I replied.

'What have you been up to?'

'Oh, not a lot,' I lied. 'I did some clearing up around the house, odd chores here and there, nothing very interesting. And I did some shopping, again nothing much, a few bits and pieces for myself.'

'Good,' he replied. 'I'm glad you went out.' He hesitated. 'Did you go into school at all?'

'No, I had every intention of going in, but somehow I didn't have time.' I laughed. 'I'll go tomorrow, I promise. I've been meaning to get in touch with Angela. It's time I started to play tennis again. And, of course, Julie needs support. I want to go and see her and find out what I can do to help.'

And after a little more desultory conversation, we went to bed as though nothing much had really happened that day. And in a way, I suppose, it hadn't, if every action were judged only by its outcome.

Chapter 33

The next day there was a ring at the front door. I recognised Detective Sergeant Hilary Woods at once, although her appearance was altered. Her hair was arranged differently and she was wearing lipstick.

'What is it now?' I asked, struggling to quell my alarm. 'Haven't you seen enough of me?'

'Shall we go inside and talk?'

'This isn't a good time. My husband's at work and I'm busy.'

I saw her smile, her face transformed by that minuscule movement of her muscles. No longer hostile, she turned into a potential ally. We not only tell lies to others as well as to ourselves, we are all chameleons displaying changing faces to the world around us. But some of us are more skilful at camouflage than others.

'You're the one I want to speak to,' she said.

She smiled again, her dark eyes alight with curiosity. In spite of the fact that I warmed to her, I remained wary, telling myself the inspector must have sent her to play the good cop and lure me into letting my guard down. They hoped she would persuade me to confess, woman to woman, ostensibly in confidence.

'Why would you want to speak to me?' I asked, without budging from the doorway. 'The inspector sent you, didn't he?'

Her smile faltered as she shook her head. 'I can see why you might think that but, actually, this is my day off. I'm not on duty. I've come here of my own accord, and in my own time.'

'Why?'

'I'm curious.'

'I don't understand. What are you doing here?'

'Please, can we go inside and talk.' She took a step closer. 'There's a chance I may be able to help you.'

'What do you mean?'

'It's complicated.'

'Why should I trust you?'

'No reason. And if you don't like what I have to say, that's up to you. I can go away and you can forget all about my visit. But something about this doesn't make sense.'

Either the police had discovered my lies about my visit to Sue's house on the day she died, or Rosie had found out about my break-in and reported it to the police. I tensed, expecting the worst.

'I don't want to talk to you without a lawyer.'

The sergeant let out a sigh of exasperation and spoke rapidly, in a low voice. 'I was in the room when you raised the possibility that Rosie White might have stored the missing photos on another phone. I'm talking about the photos you allege she showed you before Sue's death.'

This was a surprise.

'Are you saying you believe me? Because the inspector obviously didn't.'

'Shall we go inside and talk?'

Without another word, I led the sergeant into the living room. Sitting on comfortable armchairs, we faced one another.

'So, do you believe me about the photos?' I asked.

'To be honest, I'm not sure what to believe. But the DI agreed to my following up your suggestion and I did discover a couple of interesting things. First off, Rosie bought a second-hand smartphone seven weeks ago, although she already had two, one for work and one for personal use. This third one was purchased under a different name, although it was paid for out of Rosie's own personal account, and she made no mention of it when we spoke to her. The name she used when she bought it was Philip White, which is her brother's name, but my tentative enquiries led to me to believe he knows nothing about it.'

'Tentative enquiries? What do you mean?'

She looked faintly annoyed at the interruption. The mobility of her face both surprised and heartened me, leading me to believe she was dealing honestly with me. But I remained wary.

'We didn't want Philip White to suspect there was anything going on, in case he alerted his sister to the fact that we were investigating her phone, so we just asked him whether he had recently purchased a Samsung phone.'

She hesitated, before adding that Philip White had been unaware that he was talking to the police. He had been led to believe he was speaking to a telephone salesman.

'And he told you that he hadn't recently bought a phone?' I finished the train of thought.

'Exactly!'

'Doesn't that confirm what I told you? And what was the other thing? You said there were a couple of things that you found interesting.'

'A week after it was purchased, the credit ran out on the phone Rosie purchased in her brother's name and nothing has been added to the account since then.'

'So the line has been discontinued?'

'Not exactly, but if the phone isn't used for six months, the line will automatically be cancelled. She could top up at any time before then, but she hasn't used it for two weeks, not since she called the phone company to report the phone stolen.'

'Stolen?'

'Yes. She reported it stolen and the phone company told her that since there's no credit on the line and the handset was second hand and there's no evidence she even made the purchase, there's no further action to be taken.'

I sat forward. 'What do *you* think happened to the phone?'

'She reported it to the phone company as lost or stolen,' the sergeant replied, her expression blank.

I nodded. 'Yes, so you said, but what if she didn't lose it? And why did she buy another one in the first place? That sounds suspicious, doesn't it?'

The sergeant shrugged. 'Not necessarily. People sometimes want another phone for its different features. The screen was larger, for example.'

'Easier for displaying images,' I muttered. 'It all makes sense.'

'She already had the use of a phone for her paper, plus her existing personal one, so she purchased a reconditioned handset, which she claims to have lost a month after she bought it. She discovered she couldn't make an insurance claim on the second-hand phone, so she gave it up as a bad job and stuck with the one she already had. It's all perfectly plausible, but—'

'But it does mean it's possible she used a third phone to take photos of Nick and Sue deliberately to mock up fakes, all of which she could have done without using her work or her personal one.'

'Yes, it's possible.'

'And in her work she would have had access to all the software needed to photoshop and alter and create images.'

'This doesn't prove she did anything of the kind,' the sergeant said.

'But it does mean it's possible.'

We stared at one another for a second.

'It's possible,' she repeated slowly. 'Tell me what you know about Rosie.'

I hesitated. 'Why should I speak to you and not the inspector?'

'Because I'm here,' she replied simply. 'We could do this at the police station if you prefer, but we thought it might be easier to talk to you here. So, tell me about Rosie,' she repeated. 'Tell me everything you know about her.'

In as much detail as possible, I told her all about my interview with Rosie and our encounter the following day where she had told me about the love letter she claimed to have seen in Nick's desk, and our subsequent meeting where she had shown me the photos.

When I finished, the sergeant grunted. 'Can you remember what make of phone she used?'

'No. I was so focused on the images, and so shocked, I didn't notice anything else.'

The sergeant had admitted my story was possible. Strange and unsettling though the truth might be, it was preferable to thinking I was crazy enough to have imagined everything Rosie had shown me.

Chapter 34

Nick had arranged for me to see a second psychiatrist, even though I assured him there was no need to consult anyone else. In my opinion, Dr Scott's report had been thorough enough. The truth was, I had gone down the route of doubting my own sanity once before, and wasn't prepared to revisit that dark place. Even so, I agreed to attend the appointment to humour Nick.

This time we travelled to a different area of London, somewhere near Soho. Neither of us knew exactly where we were going. Nick was following the directions on his phone and we got lost several times as we trudged along streets devoid of road signs, accosting tourists who were barely able to understand English, let alone to confirm our exact location.

'Where the hell are we?' Nick asked, red-faced and unusually irascible.

It was early afternoon on a hot day in mid-July and we were both sweaty and thirsty, having drained the small water bottles I had brought with us for the journey. I held back from complaining that this was an unnecessary waste of time and money, having already made the point at some length on our train journey, no doubt increasing Nick's exasperation.

'Perhaps we should take a taxi,' he suggested at last, scowling with frustration.

'And waste even more money on this pointless excursion,' I muttered.

Finally we arrived at our destination, a four-storey white block that must once have been elegant, but looked grubby and slightly neglected. Although the exterior of the building had seen better days, the interior was decidedly upmarket, the wallpaper smart and tasteful, the furniture solid wood, with a dusky blue carpet and matching drapes at the windows. No expense had been spared on the decor and furnishings.

Unlike Dr Scott, this psychiatrist matched my preconceptions, and the visit felt more like an interrogation than a consultation. White-haired, sharp-eyed, wearing a worn grey suit and a bright red cravat, the psychiatrist gestured at me to recline on a leather sofa. It was not very comfortable, but I obliged without demur. Seated just out of my line of vision, he set about questioning me.

Before Nick and I left the consulting rooms, the psychiatrist offered to share his findings verbally.

'I'll be sending you a full written report in due course,' he said, 'but you might like to hear a brief summary straight away.'

I nodded nervously, regretting having agreed to attend his clinic. My mouth felt dry and I could feel my head spinning with the stress of waiting to hear whether he judged me to be sane or not. My anxiety was misplaced because his conclusions were more or less the same as the earlier report from Dr Scott.

'So you don't think I'm suffering from delusions,' I said.

The doctor gave me a genial smile. 'Oh, we probably all suffer from delusions, to a greater or lesser extent, wouldn't you say? Who can look at himself in the mirror and accept the truth? But as for your question, Mr Kelly,' he went on, turning to my husband, 'on the basis of this one consultation, I can't say I've found any evidence that your wife may be suffering from any psychosis.'

'So I'm not crazy,' I said.

He chortled. 'No more than the rest of us, which admittedly may not be saying very much. Humankind cannot bear very much reality, as the poet said.'

'T.S. Eliot,' I murmured.

'Indeed.' The psychiatrist inclined his head.

'Yes, yes, we know,' Nick interrupted, a touch of irritation in his voice, 'no one likes to face reality.'

'Especially the reality pertaining to oneself,' the psychiatrist replied genially enough, but giving Nick a shrewd glance as he spoke.

I could have kissed the man.

Despite my elation, I was pleased to walk out of the building and, as the train carried us home, I asked Nick if we could agree to stop the psychiatric assessments which were proving a pointless waste of time. He nodded and smiled, taking my hand. And, just like that, we seemed to have come through the horrible aftermath of Sue's death. Somehow it no longer mattered whether Nick had been having an affair with her or not. I was tired, and just wanted us to get back to normal.

We went out for a quiet pizza, and I certainly drank more than was sensible. Nick was more restrained as he was going to drive us the few miles home, but he was clearly over the limit.

'If we're stopped, you could lose your licence.' I giggled.

'We'd better make sure we're not stopped then.'

He drove back along quiet country lanes, confident that his position would protect him. I wondered if he was right. These days, nothing seemed certain, and I was afraid his confidence would one day prove his undoing.

'We're living on shifting sands,' I said.

'Everything's going to be all right from now on,' he assured me, not really taking in what I was saying.

'Let's go away for a few weeks,' I suggested.

'You know I can't for a while.'

I had forgotten he was going off to attend a headmaster's training course at the weekend.

'Why don't you go and see Jen while I'm gone?' he added. 'She'll be back from Wales at the weekend.'

'Maybe. I'll think about it. I don't mind spending time at home and you'll only be gone for two nights. Angela's around, and

I want to pick up where I left off and get back to how things were before– before all this.'

'Yes, it's important to carry on as though nothing happened. Apart from Sue's death, of course.' He sighed.

Although we might forget briefly, we were nowhere near returning to the life we had known before Sue's death. We weren't even close to it. Nick was probably thinking the same as me, and we drove the rest of the way home in silence.

That night, when we went to bed, we had sex for the first time since recent events had shattered our equilibrium, forcing us apart. But as I closed my eyes, I saw the picture of Nick lying with Sue, and imagined their naked bodies moving in harmony, as ours were. Once I had thought of it, I couldn't banish the image from my mind. I wanted to yell in his ear, asking him if he had ever had sex on a flowery chintz bed cover, and whether he still thought about her. Perhaps she was in his mind while he was with me. 'Was she tender? or passionate?' I was tempted to ask. 'Did she make any sound while you were screwing her?'

But of course I didn't. Whatever had happened between Nick and Sue, we needed to focus on the future and find a way of moving forward until we found our way back to our shared past. So I said nothing. Some things are better left unsaid.

If only it had been as easy to silence the voice in my head.

Chapter 35

True to my word, the next morning I went to the school office to speak to Julie. If she was surprised to see me, she did not show it. Perhaps Nick had forewarned her to expect me. In any event, she paused in her typing to give me a taut smile, pushing her curly hair off her face with an impatient gesture.

'It's lovely to see you, Louise, really it is,' she said, her enthusiasm just a tad overdone. 'I'd love to stop and chat but I'm up to my ears at the moment and I need to crack on.'

I interrupted her. 'Nick told me you're a bit overrun at the moment.'

'You could say that.'

'So I wanted to see if there was anything I could do.'

Realising this was an offer of help rather than an unwelcome social call, Julie's expression lightened. 'That would be brilliant! We could certainly do with another pair of hands around here.'

All signs of irritation gone, she gazed up at me, her eyes narrowed in shrewd calculation. 'How much time can you spare?'

'I'm free all day.'

'I tell you what, you could start by entering these details – you do know how to use the database, don't you? Obviously you know your way around the system–' She broke off, flustered by her unintended gaffe.

This was exactly the kind of comment Nick had been worried about, but I was more mentally robust than he gave me credit for.

'That shouldn't be a problem,' I replied easily, ignoring her discomfort. 'Can you do the first one or two, just to make sure I understand exactly what needs to be done.'

I spent the rest of the morning working on data entry. The task was mind-numbingly boring, but it was essential to the smooth running of the school that we had a complete profile of all new pupils entered on the system, along with the appropriate security filters so that teaching staff could access the information at one level, the accounts department another, while the medical staff needed yet another area of access. Julie was grateful for my help, even more so when I offered to return the following day and put in another session. 'A few more days like today, and the job will be finished. I can't tell you how grateful I am,' she said. 'You've been a real help.'

I smiled. 'We're all on the same team.'

At one o'clock, Julie and I went across to the school dining room where a light buffet lunch was provided for staff who lived on site. In the evenings, an early supper was on offer for those who signed up for it before midday. Like Nick and I, most of the staff who were still around ate at home in the evenings if they weren't going out, but at lunchtime the dining room was quite busy, even in the holidays.

Nervous about going in there alone, I felt bolder accompanying Julie. I needn't have worried. No one gave me the cold shoulder, and Sue's name wasn't mentioned once. I was pleased to see Angela and we arranged to play tennis later on, assuming the weather stayed dry. A light steady rain had been falling all morning. It had stopped just before lunch, but the sky remained grey and overcast.

At half past one, Nick came into the dining room. He didn't betray by so much as a flicker of an eyebrow that he noticed me sitting there, but I knew he was pleased. Only as I stood up to leave did he look up and smile.

'See you later,' I said.

Both of us behaved as though no unpleasantness had rocked the smooth running of our marriage, or our lives at the school.

The rain stayed away, and I met Angela at three o'clock. We agreed to have a short knock up and not play a set for fear of slipping over, as the ground was still wet, not that she ever went full out against me anyway. She was a PE teacher and a tennis coach, while my skills stretched to a passable serve and the ability to hit a reasonably easy ball over the net. We played ostensibly to improve my game, but neither of us was really there to play tennis. Angela was no doubt pleased to be on good terms with the headmaster's wife, while I was keen to find out everything I could from her about the staff and, more importantly, the gossip at school. So we hit a few balls around and then went to the staff room to make coffee, as usual. We had hardly run around at all. It was an easy, pleasant way to spend a couple of hours in convivial company.

Angela must have been very pretty when she was younger. Even now she was attractive, in spite of pouches under her smiling blue eyes and a myriad of fine wrinkles in her skin. Being sporty, she had kept a youthful figure and moved gracefully, and she seemed to be permanently serene. Only on the tennis court did she display any sign of animation, shouting out encouragement and praise, and offering advice when my hits went wild.

'Focus on the ball,' she would call out, and 'Follow through, always follow through!'

When she wasn't commenting on my tennis strokes, she bore an air of patient forbearance, as though she had suffered and survived. I actually knew little about her personal life, beyond the fact that she was divorced and childless. She must surely have been upset when she and her husband split up, but it was hard to imagine anything disturbing her equilibrium. I tried to picture her in a temper, hurling plates across the room at a shadowy figure of a man, but somehow I couldn't envisage Angela as anything other than gently smiling, her mood shifting from serene to enthusiastic only when she was on the tennis court. Although I only ever saw her when she was in her comfort zone, it was difficult to believe she could be different in other circumstances. There was a consistency about her that was reassuring.

As we sat over coffee, I wondered whether she had tried to picture my expression when I had composed nasty emails in a fit of jealous pique, as I had wondered about the depths that must surely lie hidden below her composure. But we didn't speak of such matters. Delving beneath the surface of the human psyche is a dangerous game. We were better off playing tennis, and engaging in desultory chatter about school.

Just as with restricted levels of access to the school database, there was information we were not allowed to share and, as long as we kept to permitted levels of communication, we could maintain our superficial friendship. Perhaps I should have accepted the same limitations in my relationship with Nick and taken our love at face value, without fretting over whether he was seeing anyone else. If I had left undisturbed whatever lay hidden between us, we might have skated over the darkness and followed an easier path through life.

So Angela and I sat drinking coffee, and chatting companionably enough about the weather, minor improvements Nick was planning for the sports facilities, and gossiping about other staff, carefully avoiding the one topic that was probably uppermost in both our minds. We agreed to meet at the same time the following week, weather permitting, and parted with a friendly smile. Life definitely seemed to be returning to normal, at least for me.

On my way home, I passed David by the abandoned cricket pavilion. He was walking in the opposite direction to me, and we stopped.

'I heard you were back,' he said, as though I had been away on holiday.

'How are you?' I asked.

'Me?' He sounded surprised at the question. 'Me? I'm fine. Why wouldn't I be?'

His response seemed to imply that of the two of us, *he* was not the one who had been unwell. Dismissing my suspicions as foolish paranoia, I smiled at him. David had always treated me with an old-fashioned courtesy which I found quaint and, at the same time, reassuring. Like Angela, he was predictable, which made him safe to be around. It was easy to see why he was so well respected, and even liked, by both pupils and staff. Even the younger teachers treated him with a good-natured tolerance, although they were often at loggerheads with some of the other more established members of staff.

'Are you going away at all this summer?' I asked him.

He shook his head, his hazel eyes solemn. 'I was planning a trip to Italy but, with all the difficulties that cropped up towards the end of term, and the additional workload that's caused, it's unlikely I'll be able to get away. I can usually just about manage to keep on top of things at this time of year when Mandy's working for me full time, but she's been up against it, taking some of the load off Julie, and now she's away, and we're nowhere near finalising the timetable. It'll be a struggle to get it done in time for September. Of course I'm being hassled about it already. Some of the staff always want to know their commitments in advance, but they're going to have to wait. I can't work miracles. I hear you've been helping out with admin.'

'A little.' I smiled, pleased that my small contribution had been noticed.

'I'm sure it's not how you planned to spend your summer, stuck behind a desk, but it's all hands to the pumps. The temp is doing what she can, and Julie's doing a great job, but we're all going to be under pressure until we find a suitable replacement for Nick's secretary.'

Like everyone else on site, he seemed to want to avoid mentioning Sue by name, and I appreciated his restraint. None of us wanted to think about what had happened. We chatted for a few minutes and then continued on our separate ways across the deserted cricket pitch.

The clouds had drifted across the sky, allowing the sun to throw a shaft of golden light over the pitch. I breathed deeply, enjoying the transient perfume of summer: the smell of grass mingled with tantalisingly familiar scents that I couldn't identify. On a sudden impulse I called the only person who could clear up the confusion that was still festering in my mind. I called her extension at work and was surprised when she answered straight away.

'Rosie? This is Louise Kelly from Edleybury.'

'I'm sorry to tell you–' she began.

'No, don't refuse me again. You can't. I just want to talk to you,' I blurted out. 'I have to see you.'

Perhaps she responded to the urgent desperation in my voice but, whatever the reason, she didn't hang up straight away and I seized the instant to throw myself on her mercy.

'I really need your help. I want you to tell me the truth,' I said.

'The truth?' she repeated, as though I had made an outlandish request. 'I'm sorry, who did you say you were?'

'It's Louise Kelly, from Edleybury. Rosie, you know who I am.'

'Hold the line please.'

Her oddly impersonal tone convinced me that there was something wrong with her. Mental illness is said to be infectious, and I wondered whether I had traced the source of my recent disturbance. Perhaps Rosie was the one who was divorced from reality, not me. I couldn't believe it hadn't occurred to me before.

The voice on the line returned. 'I'm afraid Rosie isn't here,' she said, and I gathered I had been talking to a complete stranger, begging her to help me.

'Oh, never mind. I'm so sorry to have bothered you and thank you for your time.'

As I hung up, a wave of clarity swept through me as though I had been shown the answer to my problem. If strangers were not prepared to help me save my marriage, I was going to have to confront Nick himself, and this time there would be no more secrets. If it turned out that he had been having an affair, we would decide together how we wanted to proceed, but our decision would be based on the truth, not on some nebulous speculation.

I walked back to the house with the sun warming my back. Light fell across a vast swathe of grass, and foliage on surrounding trees shone vibrant in the golden glow of a late afternoon. Whatever transpired, I realised then what I had known all along; I was never going to abandon my marriage.

Chapter 36

Nick was busy finishing off a report he was writing for the governors when I arrived home. He read parts of it out to me.

'Do you think the tone is too bullish?' he asked.

I felt a bit sorry for Nick, the new boy on the block, who was trying to convince the governors to change the school, and its traditions.

'Change is always hard,' I said.

'This goes beyond the normal resistance to change. We're dealing with a load of dead wood here. Oh, they're solid to the core, the lot of them, and the school's in safe hands with them. A bit too safe, and that's the trouble. Individually they're decent enough, but as a body they're very resistant to change. And we have to move with the times. Burwood have gone co-ed and it's been a roaring success.' He grew animated as he spoke. 'If we phase the girls in, year by year, five years from now we could be fully co-ed and we'll have doubled our pool of pupils to select from. With overseas pupils increasingly looking elsewhere, and ever fiercer competition to attract home-grown talent, it's the only way the school can survive in the long term. But they're all too stuck in their ways to see it. If I'd suggested turning the school into a zoo, they couldn't have been more shocked when I first raised the idea with them.' He gave a mischievous grin. 'But I'm going to do it, and we'll turn this place around. It's the only way forward. If we want to compete, we have to move the school into the twenty-first century. They've been bleating about sports facilities, and changing rooms, and boarding houses, saying what I'm proposing is impossible, but it can be done. We've already got our sixth form girls, and plans are in place to convert one of the boarding houses. I'm not saying it's going to be easy. Girls won't tolerate the living conditions boys put up with, I know that much. Burwood had a bit of trouble on that front in the early days.' He chuckled. 'But seriously, we can learn from their mistakes and get this right. There's no point in reinventing the wheel. Listen.'

He read out a section from his report which focused on figures and forecasts. With the increased pupil population, he argued, a bank loan for extra building work could be paid off within a few years. It sounded a bit optimistic to me, and I told him so, but he assured me he had gone into the matter in detail.

'The chair of the governors is sympathetic to the proposal,' he added, 'so I'm sure we can swing it. David's against it, of course, along with all the rest of the dead wood.'

There was a contingent of about eight members of staff who had been at the school for several decades, whom Nick had dubbed "the dead wood", in his conversations with me.

'He may be the deputy head, and old friends with the governors—'

'But you're the headmaster,' I completed his sentence.

'Exactly.' Nick smiled. 'And the chair of governors supported my appointment for a reason.'

'Are you saying he knew about all this before we came here?'

'We discussed my vision for the school before my appointment, yes. He warned me some of the governors would be difficult to persuade, but only a fool will insist on fighting the tide of progress. And they're not fools.'

It sounded rather grandiloquent to describe going co-ed as "the tide of progress", but I didn't say so, asking instead, 'What about persuading the dead wood it's a good idea?'

Nick gave a dismissive shrug. 'Never mind about them. We're looking at the bigger picture. Most of them won't be around for much longer. They'll have retired, or kicked the bucket, before the new scheme is even half done.'

He would probably have continued talking about his vision for the future but Jen called me, as she had done most evenings since my brush with the police. We chatted for a while, and then I went to see to our supper. Unbelievably, and rather wonderfully, life was returning to normal. Once I had spoken to Nick, and persuaded him to tell me the truth, we would settle back into our former happy relationship. Of course we would have to sit down and have a serious conversation about what had happened, if it turned out that he had indeed been unfaithful, but I had already decided to forgive him, as long as it never happened again.

'It's been a challenging year for you,' I planned to say. 'Sue was a tremendous help to you in running the school, far more than I could possibly have been, and deep gratitude can easily be confused with love.'

At which point I would pause long enough to allow him to interrupt me to say that he had never loved her, had never loved anyone but me.

'It was just a fling,' I imagined him protesting, perhaps with tears in his eyes, although he never cried. 'She meant nothing to me.'

It felt wicked to imagine a conversation like that about Sue, as though my thoughts were somehow disrespectful to the dead, but Nick was my husband. No other woman had any claim on his affection and, in any case, nothing I said or did could make any difference to Sue now.

Onions were frying, garlic crushed, and I was chopping tomatoes, when the doorbell rang.

'Can you get it?' I asked. 'My hands are wet.'

'Okay.'

A moment later, Nick called out to me. 'Lou, it's the police. They want to talk to you again.'

He sounded agitated, but I was eager to see the sergeant. Hoping she had made progress with her investigation into the pictures on Rosie's missing phone, I switched off the gas, wiped my hands, and hurried to the hall where I balked, catching sight of the detective inspector standing on the doorstep. The sergeant stood impassively at his side.

'Hello, Inspector,' I said, stepping forward slowly. 'What do you want now?'

'May we come in?' he asked.

We seemed to be trapped in a time warp, repeating the same conversation over and over again.

I hesitated. At the risk of sounding uncooperative, I said, 'I was just making dinner.'

'Thank you,' the inspector replied. Deliberately mistaking my meaning he added drily, 'but I'm afraid we won't stay.'

We sat down in the living room and the inspector looked from me to Nick and back again. Nick was frowning, as though he was struggling to understand what was going on.

'What is this about, Inspector?' he asked.

'Something has happened to Rosie White.'

The two detectives sat watching me without saying a word.

Nick broke the uncomfortable silence that followed. 'What's this got to do with us?'

'Your wife alleged Rosie White showed her photographs that proved you were having an affair, Mr Kelly.'

'Rosie White?' I repeated slowly as though trying to remember who she was. 'Oh yes.' I turned to Nick. 'She's the journalist who interviewed us for the county magazine.'

I wondered if they knew I had tried to meet her, several times, or that I had broken into her flat.

'What about her?' Nick asked.

The detectives looked at one another, and the inspector gave a slight nod.

'I'm afraid she's dead,' the sergeant said. Her words fell softly through the air between us. 'She died three nights ago. Her editor reported her missing when she failed to turn up for work two days in a row and he was unable to reach her.'

For a moment I didn't know what to say.

'Oh Jesus, not another one,' Nick burst out. 'What the hell happened this time? I take it she was murdered too?'

The inspector gave him a curious look. 'What makes you say that?'

'You wouldn't be here otherwise, would you. But, Inspector, my wife and I didn't know this woman. We barely even met her. It's decent of you to come here and let us know, but all she did was interview us for an article–'

The inspector's expression remained fixed as he turned to Nick with a single word question. 'Article?'

'In a magazine. That's how we met her. She came here to interview us for the Hertfordshire Style magazine.'

'She's dead now,' the inspector replied curtly.

'I'm so sorry,' I said, struggling to find the right words for the occasion. 'How did she die?'

It was the most appropriate response I could think of. And all the time I was casting my mind back, desperately trying to recall whether I might have left any evidence of my presence in the flat. It wasn't the first time I had seemed to be caught in a horrible invisible trap in my dealings with the police. Once again, my head swam and my sight grew blurred, as though I was looking at the world through water.

'And what has this got to do with us?' Nick added, almost under his breath.

'She was smothered with a pillow,' the inspector replied in a chillingly matter-of-fact tone. 'In her own bed.'

'Oh my God,' I cried out, horrified.

'We wondered whether either of you had been in touch with her or might know anything about who she was seeing,' the inspector said.

I hesitated, not knowing how much the sergeant had passed onto her boss. Nick had no such reservations.

'No,' he replied promptly, 'we don't know the woman. I can only surmise that it's a sad coincidence, her being killed so close on the heels of Sue's murder. We'd like to know if you've made any progress with that. I've tried to contact her family to find out whether they've made any funeral arrangements, but as far as I can gather, the body still hasn't been released.'

Nick's attempt to deflect the discussion from Rosie had only limited success. The inspector assured us that Sue's body would be released "soon".

'Soon?' Nick repeated, sounding irritated, 'that's vague.'

The inspector greeted the implied criticism with a shrug before returning to his own enquiry.

'Have either of you seen Rosie since she interviewed you here?'

It was impossible to deny that I had spoken to her, so I answered as boldly as I could, hoping no one would pick up on my nerves.

'Actually,' I said, in an unnaturally high voice, 'yes, I saw her.' I cleared my throat and continued, forcing my voice to go lower. 'We had a drink in the pub near her office in Watford the other day. She said she had something to ask me.'

For a second, no one spoke and I realised they were all waiting for me to continue.

Nick was looking at me with an expression of faint surprise. 'You never mentioned it.'

'It wasn't that important. She has a cousin, or a friend.'

I amended my statement quickly in case the police checked with Rosie's cousins. Perhaps she had no cousins.

'And this other woman, I don't know who she is, anyway, she was asking about Edleybury because she was thinking of sending her son here and she wanted Rosie to ask me about the school, unofficially. Of course I gave her the usual response,' I added, with a quick smile at Nick before turning back to the inspector. 'Edleybury offers an all round education catering for pupils with a variety of talents. Naturally we strive for, and attain, excellent academic results, but we don't focus exclusively on academic studies. Our sports and arts facilities are–'

'Thank you, I've read the prospectus,' the inspector cut in abruptly.

I made no reference to my night-time visit to Rosie's flat, and breathed more freely when the discussion moved on. During the police visit, I made several unsuccessful attempts to catch the sergeant's eye, but she either didn't notice, or else deliberately declined to exchange any significant glance with me, and eventually the inspector left, with her trailing behind him. I hoped she would look over her shoulder in the doorway and give me a smile, or a nod, to reassure me of her discretion, but she didn't look round.

Chapter 37

That weekend Nick was away attending a conference of headmasters, which sounded like a pretty dull affair. None of the other spouses would be there, and he told me I would be kicking my heels in the hotel on my own all weekend if I went with him. It wasn't even a particularly nice hotel, with no spa facilities or cultivated gardens, so it made little sense for me to accompany him.

When Nick had originally planned his trip, it hadn't occurred to me that I would want to do anything in his absence other than sit in the garden, walk in the school grounds, and generally make the most of the lovely weather, or perhaps use my sewing machine if it rained while he was away. For months I had been intending to make some new curtains for the guest bedroom but had not yet got around to it, although we had purchased the fabric a few months after we moved in. Those plans had been made long before our interview with Rosie and everything that had followed. But there was another way to take advantage of Nick's absence to follow up my suspicions.

More than mere curiosity compelled me to set off on Saturday morning. There was still a real danger the police would discover I had been to Rosie's flat. I might have got away with it by claiming to have paid her a social call. After all, she was in no position to deny it. However, since I had said nothing about any such visit when the inspector had last questioned Nick and me, that was going to be tricky to carry off. The fact that the police had not yet come knocking at my door to quiz me about it led me to hope they might not discover any trace of my presence in her flat.

I had been careful to wear rubber gloves while I was there, and had kept my hood up in the street. Only when crawling across the carpet had I had much direct contact with any of the surfaces there, and that had been unavoidable. Looking back on that evening, it was hard to believe what had happened, with my breaking and entering, and then hiding in the living room while Rosie was having sex on the other side of an open door. Just thinking about it made me cringe.

It sounded as though she had been killed the night I broke into her flat, in which case the man who had visited her that night might have murdered her, given that she had been smothered with a pillow. With a cold shiver, I realised that I was possibly in possession of information that could help the police to find her killer, but I was powerless to share what I knew. In any case, I told myself that I had seen nothing of the man who had been in bed with her, so my account could add nothing to what the police already knew.

Without much idea of what I was doing, or why I was going there, I drove to the street where Rosie had worked and found myself pulling into a parking space, my hands and feet seeming to move without my control. Feeling as if this was all a dream, I walked back to the pub where I had met Rosie only five days earlier.

Although it was not yet midday, I sat down at a corner table with a glass of red wine, and tried to remember my last conversation with Rosie. We had been sitting, face to face, at that same table. As I recalled, she had not been very forthcoming, but had insisted she knew nothing about the photographs she had shown me. After that, she had said she never wanted to see me again. Her wish had been granted, although not in the way either of us had expected or wanted. I sipped my wine, which wasn't particularly nice, and thought about my marriage. As I sat quietly musing, a familiar figure entered the bar. Detective Sergeant Woods looked around and, as soon as her gaze lighted on me, she came straight over to the corner where I was sitting.

'I thought I spotted you coming in here,' she said, shuffling into a seat beside me. 'What on earth are you doing? You must know Rosie worked just up the road.'

I cursed myself for my stupidity. What was I doing there, running the risk of being seen by the police? There was no reason why I shouldn't be in the pub having a drink, but perhaps I had come there subconsciously hoping to come across the sergeant. Everything was so confusing.

'You should have come to the police station,' she said. 'I've been wanting to talk to you. Listen, my DI has asked me to warn you to stay away from the case, and to have nothing more to do with our investigations into the deaths of Sue or Rosie. Otherwise you're only going to attract attention and cause a distraction. If you interfere again and force us to look into your connection with Rosie before we're ready to do so, we'll be down on you again like a ton of bricks, and next time we're not going to let you walk away from us so quickly. You might get away from the DI once, but...' She shook her head. 'He doesn't forget anything. If you were in any way involved with what happened to either of these victims we're investigating, we'll find out. But in the meantime, you need to keep out of the way.'

For a moment we sat, each lost in our own thoughts. A couple of young men came in. Hunched in her chair, facing the wall, the sergeant took a hand mirror from her bag and glanced in it. Guessing she was checking whether any of her colleagues had entered the pub, I realised we did not have much time.

'You told me Rosie bought a phone in her brother's name,' I said, leaning forward and speaking in an urgent whisper.

'We don't know she bought it herself, only that she paid for it.'

'Which means she bought it.'

'In my job you learn never to believe anything that hasn't been proved beyond doubt.'

'If you ask me, only a fool would question whether she bought that phone herself.'

'Listen,' the sergeant glanced around, 'I'm not comfortable talking to you about this.'

'In case someone sees us?'

She shrugged. 'Feel free to tell whoever you like that I've been talking to you but, now Rosie's been murdered, my boss might start to wonder why you're asking so many questions about her. So unless you have an undeclared reason for this curiosity of yours, take my advice and drop your interest in her. If you had nothing to do with Rosie's death, then I don't understand your obsession with her,' she added, turning to stare at me and study my response.

'I want you to help me to prove my innocence, and I want to know whether those photos of my husband that Rosie showed me were genuine.'

'It's my job to find out who's guilty of murdering these women, both of them known to you. I'm not interested in whether or not your husband was unfaithful to you.'

With that, she stood up and hurried away.

Chapter 38

Even though she had warned me to stay away from the investigation, I called the sergeant the next morning. Nick wasn't due back until the evening and, after refusing to come to my home again, she finally agreed to meet at five o'clock in a small room upstairs in a country pub. It was not far from the school, and I thought it would be a suitable location for a discreet rendezvous.

Feeling like a spy, I made my way to our clandestine tryst. As I glanced furtively around the downstairs bar, I was dismayed to see the head of maths sitting at a table with another member of staff, deep in conversation. In their late fifties or early sixties, they were members of the group Nick referred to as the "dead wood". It was hardly surprising to see them there since we were only a few miles from Edleybury. Regretting having agreed to meet the sergeant in a pub so close to the school, I stole past them, hoping they wouldn't look up and notice me hurrying up the stairs. The sergeant was already there, waiting for me at a table in the corner.

'Have they– have you– has anyone found the phone yet?' I asked as I sat down. 'You have to tell me what's happened. You can't just leave me in the dark like this.'

She shook her head. 'I only came here to tell you that it's time you let this go, Louise. You need to leave us to get on with our job. There's nothing more to say. I'll contact you if we find anything. And now if you want to speak to us again, you need to call the police station and go through the usual channels.'

She stirred in her seat, and was about to rise to her feet; only the desperation in my voice detained her.

'No, wait, wait!' I cried out.

I glanced around the room. It was empty apart from us but, even so, I lowered my voice and pressed on. 'That phone must be somewhere. It can't have just disappeared. You said she bought a phone in another name. Why would she have done that if she wasn't planning to do something she wanted to keep hidden? It stands to reason, doesn't it. That's the evidence you needed to prove to you that I'm telling the truth about those photos, and Rosie was lying about it. And now we have to find that phone, or we'll never know if the photos were genuine or not.'

I paused for breath, aware that my voice had risen in agitation. The sergeant took the opportunity to try to scotch my interest in the missing phone, but I remained adamant that the police had to search Rosie's flat, her car, her office, anywhere she might have hidden the phone.

'Did she have a boyfriend?' I asked, 'or a sister, or parents? What about her brother? We know she had a brother. She might have hidden a phone in someone else's house. It has to be somewhere,' I insisted, although we both knew Rosie might have destroyed it any time after she had shown me the photos. 'The longer we leave it, the more chance there is that it'll be thrown away by someone who doesn't realise its significance. That's why you have to search for it now. Surely you understand, I need to know if I can trust Nick and this is the only way to find out. Rosie was the one person who could have told me the truth, and now she's dead. Please, you have to help me.'

'There was nothing in her flat, we've already looked,' the sergeant said coldly. 'The search teams are thorough. Believe me, if there was a phone hidden there, they would have found it.'

'It must be somewhere. They were searching the flat for evidence of her killer, weren't they. But they weren't looking for a missing phone. And it could be in her car, or in her office, or–'

'Or she could have disposed of it at any time during the period between her showing it to you and her death.'

That certainly seemed likely. After Rosie had shown me the photos of Nick and Sue, over a month had elapsed before she was killed. In the meantime, she had succeeded in convincing me Nick was unfaithful. What I still didn't understand was why she would want to do that, unless it were true.

'There must be another explanation,' I said. 'What was Rosie's relationship with my husband?'

'I've been looking into her background,' the sergeant replied. 'There's nothing to suggest she ever came across your husband before she visited the school to interview you both. But in any case,' she added impatiently, 'what difference does it make? We still don't know who killed Sue, or Rosie, and that's what matters. Finding Rosie's phone isn't going to help further our investigation.'

'Finding out whether those photos were fake might help you to solve the murder case,' I suggested hopefully.

'That's hardly likely. And anyway, I told you Rosie never met your husband before your interview, so there was no obvious reason for her to fabricate those images.'

'But you don't know she *didn't* fabricate them. Rosie could have had a grudge against Sue and wanted her to lose her job–'

'You really need to get over your obsession with Rosie White,' the sergeant said firmly.

'The truth is, I need to know whether my husband was having an affair.'

'Perhaps you should ask him.'

I did not tell her that I had already asked him, but was not sure whether to believe his reply.

The sergeant lowered her voice and leaned forward. 'Listen to me, Rosie's dead, and you're going to get yourself in trouble if you keep poking around in a murder investigation. All that will happen is that you'll attract attention, and unwanted police attention is never a good idea. It tends to lead to questions. My colleagues will want to know why you're so interested in this murder victim. They'll want to know why you won't leave it alone. And then they might start investigating you, and who knows what dirt they'll dig up from the past, things you probably don't even know about. And don't think for one moment that they'll be content with looking into your circumstances. They'll investigate your husband as well. Is that what you want?'

'No, of course not. That's why I'm asking you, in confidence. You have to tell me—'

'No, Louise, I don't have to tell you anything. I'm not working for you. And we're not talking again, we're not meeting again. I've told you we haven't found Rosie's phone, which is more than I should have said, and now this relationship is over. Nothing that passes between the two of us is in confidence. I work as part of a team. If you want to know whether your husband was having an affair, you'll have to ask him.'

'I'll tell the inspector you met with me in secret,' I said, aware it was a forlorn threat.

'Go ahead. Be my guest. Tell him whatever you like. Just don't contact me again.'

She left me sitting there alone. I had gone to meet her with high hopes that she would help me to get to the truth, but once again I was left in ignorance of Nick's relationship with Sue. The sergeant had not been exaggerating when she described my interest as an obsession. I couldn't stay there much longer if I was going to be home before Nick arrived back from his weekend away, so I finished my drink and stood up.

The head of maths and his companion had left by the time I went back downstairs. My relief at not being spotted only served to highlight my unease, and I realised the sergeant was right about something else as well: the need to change my approach. It was no good hounding her for confirmation that the photos were fake. I would have to confront Nick and discover the truth from him. Admittedly, if he had been unfaithful, I would have preferred to learn about it from someone else, so that I would have time to think about what to do. In addition to that, if the allegations weren't true, it would be far better if he never found out I still suspected him of having an affair. While I longed to believe his denials, I had to be sure. There was no way of learning the truth, other than from Nick himself. I steeled myself to tackle him as soon as he stepped through the door.

When Nick arrived home, tired and disgruntled after a difficult journey, I realised it was not the time to challenge him about his relationship with his secretary. He told me his first train had been delayed, meaning he had missed his connection, and then when he had finally reached his car, he had been stuck behind a slow-moving tractor for miles. So I decided to wait until the next day to ask him, straight out, whether he had been unfaithful to me. There would be no more procrastination. One way or another, I was going to put an end to the uncertainty that was plaguing my waking hours and stalking my dreams.

Chapter 39

Nick went out early the following morning before I had a chance to speak to him. It didn't matter. We could talk later, over supper. After breakfast, I worked on some more data entry for Julie until lunchtime. Once again she was pleased with my help. Nick had interviewed several shortlisted candidates with a view to replacing Sue as soon as possible, but had not yet offered the post to anyone. He needed to make an appointment soon, if his new secretary was to be settled in before the beginning of the next school year. Although Nick insisted that he would rather wait and appoint the right person, a suitable candidate was proving difficult to find.

Julie and I went into lunch with David's secretary, Mandy. Just as I was finishing my dessert, my phone rang. I answered, and recognised the sergeant's voice.

'We need to meet,' she said without any preamble.

'Why?'

'There's something we want to discuss. You could come into the police station, but I thought you might prefer somewhere more discreet. Do you want to meet for a drink?'

I hesitated. The last time we had seen each other, she hadn't been able to get away from me quickly enough, and she had left telling me not to contact her again. She must have suggested meeting in the pub thinking I was more likely to be on my guard if they questioned me at the police station. I was intrigued, but she was wrong if she thought I would be less wary in a relaxed environment.

'Okay. When? Where?'

'Are you free this afternoon?'

'Yes. All afternoon.'

We arranged to meet at the same place as before, and this time I arrived early. I carried a glass of red wine carefully up the stairs and sat down at a table in the corner, facing into the room so that I would see the sergeant arrive. A couple of girls were seated on the far side of the room, talking in short bursts interspersed with long periods of silence. Their voices were so loud, I couldn't help overhearing some of their brief exchanges.

'She never!' one of the girls said.

'I'm telling you, she did!' replied the other.

There was a pause.

'You're kidding, aren't you?' the first girl asked.

'She did.'

'No, she never. Not Karen. She never.'

'I'm telling you, she did,' her companion repeated, as though it was the refrain in a duet.

Before I could hear any more of their monotonous conversation, the sergeant arrived.

She spoke so softly I had to lean across the table to hear her. 'The search team found the missing phone you've been talking about.'

'So Rosie *did* have a third phone. I thought so. Where was it?'

'In her car. So you were right all along. The photos had been deleted, but we restored them.'

'Can I see them?' I asked, eager yet reluctant to look at them again.

She shook her head. 'I haven't got the phone on me. It's being held as evidence. But they were pretty much as you described them. The two of them standing together, side by side, then the two of them embracing – kissing – and finally the two of them in bed together.'

'Was it definitely them in the final picture?'

'The woman was definitely Sue. The man could have been him, but the images weren't that clear. There's no way of knowing for sure.'

'I might be able to tell, if you let me see them. He is my husband.'

She shook her head. 'No, it was too blurred.'

'Can't your technical team tell whether they're genuine or not?'

'They were taken on an old phone,' she said dismissively. My personal problems were not her problem. 'But that's not why I wanted to see you. I could have told you all this over the phone. The reason I wanted to see you was to tell you about something else the search team found at Rosie's flat.' With a horrible sensation in my stomach I waited, terrified that they had come across something I had left behind when I broke into Rosie's flat.

'Oh God, not another photo,' I muttered. 'What's it of this time?'

'No,' she replied, 'not another photo. But this may help to clear your name. The search team found a number of hairs in Rosie's bed. Some of them belonged to her, but there were others, male, Caucasian.' She nodded grimly. 'So we have the DNA of a man who was in bed with her, and there are traces of semen on the sheet as well as evidence of sexual activity before she was killed. We don't have a match. But we know a man was with her at her flat on the night she died.'

Actually more than one person was there, I thought, but I didn't tell the sergeant that. I could hardly say it had slipped my mind until now, and I certainly couldn't explain what I had been doing there, hiding behind the sofa in the living room. A horrible thought struck me. Nick had been out that evening, and he hadn't arrived home until eleven. What if the man I had heard in bed with Rosie had been my husband? I hadn't recognised him at the time, but their voices had been muffled by the sofa, and I had seen only a brief glimpse of the back of his head, in the dark. In my panic, I could have seen my own sister in the room without recognising her. Desperately I tried to remember whether the police had ever taken a DNA sample from Nick.

If Nick had been having an affair with Rosie, then everything else made sense. Rosie had discovered that he was also having an affair with Sue, and had contrived to take photos of them together to show to me, in revenge, or maybe hoping to force him to stop seeing Sue. Perhaps it was plausible that Rosie had killed Sue. Discovering what Rosie had done, Nick had killed her, either in anger or, what was more likely, to protect his position. He might even have killed both of his lovers, to keep his infidelity a secret. Even though I couldn't bear the thought that anyone else might believe that of my husband, it made sense. And if I had worked out that scenario, the police were bound to come to the same conclusion.

'You're telling me a man was there, in her flat, on the night she died,' I whispered, wondering fearfully who he might have been.

'Exactly. She arrived at the flat in the company of a man, and we're wondering whether this visitor could have killed her. We've been studying the security cameras in the block, and two people went there that night whom we've been unable to trace. We've checked with all the residents, but two other people entered the block on the evening Rosie was killed, two unknown people.'

Forcing myself to sit still, I could feel my chest shudder every time I took a breath, and I felt like throwing up.

'Are you all right?' my companion asked me, and I nodded.

'This is just all so awful.'

'Shall I go on?'

'Yes, please.'

'Rosie entered her block at eight thirty-six, accompanied by a man. We don't know who he was. He was carrying an umbrella which unfortunately shielded his upper half from the camera. It's not a very sophisticated system, just a camera outside the entrance recording everyone who enters the building, and if you ring and look directly at it, people in the flats can see who's calling. Otherwise, it just picks up that someone is there.'

'What about when he left?'

She shook her head. 'The umbrella again. He was probably carrying it deliberately to hide his face. But we know she went inside with an unknown man.'

'What about CCTV outside?'

'We're checking cars driving in the area at the time but it's like the proverbial needle in a haystack because he could have caught a bus, parked a mile away, picked up a taxi at the station, ridden a bike, or walked there across the fields. We're doing what we can, but all we know about him is his DNA and we can estimate his shoe size and a few other details from the CCTV image. He's got particularly large feet. We're also interested in a hooded figure who was in the building that we haven't yet accounted for. He entered the building an hour before Rosie, and emerged shortly before her visitor left.'

I listened with growing unease. I could have told her I already knew a man had gone there to have sex with her, and any attempt to trace the hooded figure was pointless. If I had known she was about to be killed, I might have been able to prevent it, but there was no way I could have predicted what was going to happen. Now I was facing another terrible prospect. The time of Rosie's death was probably an estimate, which meant the man who had been in bed with Rosie on the night she had died, the man who might have killed her, could have been my husband. He had told me he was at a meeting, but he could have taken a detour on his way home.

'What about the hooded man?' I asked, in an attempt to lead her away from the truth; I knew that the hooded figure wasn't a man.

I hoped my curiosity wouldn't arouse her interest. As the sergeant had already pointed out, it wasn't a good idea to attract attention, especially from the police.

She frowned. 'We haven't managed to identify him yet. The face was impossible to view, but we've excluded all the residents by taking DNA samples from them. None of the residents saw anything unusual but it's possible that this missing hooded man might have seen something. We need to find out not only who he was, but what he was doing there that night.' The sergeant paused and then looked straight at me. 'It looks as though Rosie knew the man who was in her flat on the night she died. Do you know where your husband was last Monday evening between eight and ten?'

I hesitated, because Nick had arrived home about eleven that night. His car might have been picked up on CCTV so there was no point in lying.

'Is that when Rosie was killed?'

'Please, just answer my question,' the sergeant snapped.

I wondered if the police had really found photographs of Nick and Sue on a hidden phone, or whether the sergeant had deliberately reminded me of Nick's suspected adultery, hoping to persuade me to incriminate him.

'My husband was at a meeting at school. He would have been with a number of his colleagues all evening,' I answered coldly. 'I'm sure he'll tell you the same, and any details he gives you about his movements will be corroborated by the senior management team at the school.'

'He is being questioned, and his alibi will be checked.' She glanced at her phone. 'They should be finished by now.'

The police had made sure Nick and I would have no way of communicating while he was being questioned, so they could see if our stories matched.

'You were keeping me out of the way just now,' I said.

'We don't trust anyone,' she replied, adding gravely. 'You would be wise to do the same.'

It wasn't clear if she was checking up on me or Nick. If he had been out of the house until eleven, I might also have no alibi for the time of Rosie's murder.

Chapter 40

The afternoon had become overcast by the time we left the pub. I was tempted not to go home at all, but drive straight to the station where I could catch a train across London and retreat to my sister's house and play truant from my life, like a child avoiding school. I imagined my sister welcoming me without question, telling me she was delighted by my unexpected arrival and inviting me to stay with her for as long as I liked. But that was never going to happen.

Besides, I wanted to see Nick and tell him that I still loved him, whatever he had done. Just as he had said to me, when we had both believed I was going mad, we would get through this together. In spite of my determination to stand by him, I was afraid to confess that I knew about his affairs. The man waiting for me at home was not the man I had married. My husband had changed into someone else, entirely other, a stranger to me. He was a cheat and a liar. It seemed I was clinging to a reality that had never existed outside of my own imagination, a fantasy of a man who had never been real. The sergeant had been right to warn me to trust no one.

There was a boom of distant thunder and it began to rain heavily. My windscreen wipers were poorly adjusted, making it difficult to see the unlit road. Angered by the thought of Nick in another woman's arms and in her bed, I put my foot down. Unable to see clearly ahead, I was too late to notice a shape dart across the road right in front of me. There was a sudden loud thud and the car juddered before skidding on the wet road as I slammed on the brakes. Shocked at the collision, I reversed and felt the car jolt as the tyres moved backwards over a bump in the road. Shaking, I stopped the car and climbed out to see what had happened. The light from my headlamps fell across a fox lying in the road. It wasn't moving. I froze, reluctant to move closer to see whether it was still alive and suffering.

All the shock and upset of recent events overwhelmed me and I stood in the road weeping, my tears washed away by the rain. The life of a fox was so random, yet so complex a creation. The matted fur on its body had grown with the sole purpose of protecting it, but despite centuries of evolution designed to ensure its survival, nothing could have saved it from the impact of a vehicle travelling at forty miles an hour along a wet and winding road. I had been driving irresponsibly.

'It's just a fox,' I told myself.

If a dead cyclist had been lying in the road, I would have been prosecuted for dangerous driving, but manslaughter was just what the name stated, the slaughter of man, a crime that didn't extend to other living creatures. The wanton killing of a feral animal didn't matter. All I had to do was get back in the car and go home, leaving one less fox prowling the fields for its prey.

I wanted to feel guilty but, as I sped away from the fox, my overriding feeling was relief that no one would ever find out what I had done. A few other motorists would notice the cadaver lying in the road as they drove past, before scavengers disposed of the rotting corpse and it disappeared, as though it had never existed. My remorse converted to anger; after my own death I would join the fox in eternal oblivion.

'Hello, love. How's your day been?' Nick asked me when I reached home. He looked up. 'You're drenched.'

'I got caught in the rain. I need to change out of these wet things.'

After a hot shower and a cup of cocoa, I felt a lot better, and was trying to decide whether to raise the subject that had been nagging at me, or tell Nick about the dead fox. While I was dithering, he told me the police had been to the house again.

'What did they want?'

'They had some questions about my meeting with the governors, and they wanted me to give them a DNA sample. They explained it was routine elimination.'

Fear gripped me suddenly, twisting my throat until it seemed to close up, yet my voice sounded surprisingly normal as I asked, 'Did you give it to them?'

'Of course,' he replied, looking surprised but not afraid. 'They explained it was just for the purpose of elimination. They're hoping to get samples from every man who has met Rosie White.' He laughed. 'I wished them luck with that. She must have spoken to hundreds of thousands of men in her job.'

I remembered him claiming that he was an expert liar, but if he *had* been in Rosie's bed that night, his present bravado was positively breathtaking, when he must realise the police would soon return to arrest him for murder. I was not sure what to make of his boldness. Assuming he was doing everything he could to conceal his guilt from me, not to mention his terror, I offered him an opening.

'I thought we were going away this summer, not for work but for a proper holiday,' I ventured, hoping he would understand my meaning.

'I want to, but you know I've been busy with interviews. As soon as I can get away, we'll go. Give it a few more days.'

'Don't you think now might be a good time to make our escape?' I pressed on, choosing my words with care yet trying not to place too obvious an emphasis on the last word in my question.

I steered as closely as possible to what was on my mind, without actually coming out and saying that we might need to get away, leaving the country if we possibly could before it was too late. But instead of seizing the opportunity to avoid arrest, Nick laughed. Hearing the familiar sound, I wondered whether he was the crazy one in our relationship.

'It's not that bad here, is it?' he said. 'Listen, Lou, as soon as I've sorted out the staffing situation, we'll take a few days off, I promise, a week if we can, and we'll go anywhere you like, just the two of us. But I'm afraid it'll have to wait. And we can't go for long. You know I need to be here when the results arrive.'

I nodded. Afraid that Nick was guilty, I couldn't believe he was thinking of nothing but his staff appointments and the examination results which were due in towards the end of the month.

'But we should be able to fit in at least one long weekend before term starts,' he went on. 'And next year, I promise we'll nip off the day after the summer term ends.'

Going away as soon as term ended had been our plan this year, only outside events had prevented us. Listening to him talking about staff and holidays and the future, a tiny flame of hope flickered in my darkness. A man worried about being arrested for murder was unlikely to be talking so cheerfully about plans for the following year's holiday. The police had taken a sample of his DNA and he was completely at ease.

Wondering whether I might have been mistaken about him, I was glad I hadn't accused him outright of murdering Rosie. Perhaps, after all, I had been wrong about him. The more time passed without the police knocking at our door, the more convinced I became that Nick might not be guilty after all. Now it was the thought that I might have unjustly accused him of murder which made me shudder.

That afternoon I met Angela for our weekly game of tennis. She was encouraging as usual, even telling me my game had improved which, given everything that was going on, would have been little short of a miracle. I didn't believe her but was too anxious to laugh at her unwarranted praise.

'I don't think so,' I replied. 'I'm playing like a wally today.'

As if to illustrate my point, I hit an easy ball straight into the net.

'Let's play that point again,' she said kindly.

Had she not approached our games with such generosity, she would have won every point, but playing tennis, she told me, was not solely about winning. It was as much about improving skills as about gaining points. It was, ostensibly, a really lovely way to spend an afternoon, playing tennis with a congenial partner in a beautiful setting on a lovely summer's day. But my mind wasn't on the game.

I was thinking that when I got home Nick might not be there. If he were, I still needed to tackle him about his alleged affair with Sue, and about Rosie as well. We had to be completely honest with each other. I didn't know what to think or who to believe but I knew I couldn't continue much longer in this blithering uncertainty. Even if he had committed no crime, he might still have been unfaithful, and if he *was* apprehended on a murder charge, we might not have much time left together before the police came looking for him. The fact that they hadn't arrested him yet might not mean anything. The sergeant had warned me to trust no one. I didn't even know whether to trust my own judgement about my own husband.

Chapter 41

Aware that I needed to proceed with caution, yet desperate to know the worst, I had a stab at tackling Nick about his extramarital relations that evening over supper.

'You must miss Sue dreadfully,' I said softly.

He grunted and swallowed a mouthful of pasta. 'No one's indispensable.' He reached for his wine glass. 'Oh,' he added, seeing my expression, 'apart from you, of course.'

'But you must miss her.'

'Yes, of course I miss her. We worked together every day. And in the sense that she was efficient, and pleasant to work with, she's going to be extremely difficult to replace. But I'm hopeful this new woman, Maggie, is going to shape up well. She's coming back for a second interview next week, to meet David, and Julie, but she seems just the ticket. I think it would be a good idea if you met her too,' he added with sudden hearty enthusiasm, pretending this was more than an afterthought. 'The good thing is, she's been a school secretary before. She worked for the head at Wolsey College for five years before she took a career break to have her family, so she knows the territory. We'll have to train her on the system, but that's going to be the case whoever we appoint. Someone who's worked in a school before could be ideal.'

'How old is she?'

'Mid-forties. She's been off work for a few years but she's had plenty of relevant experience, and being a mother won't do any harm when she's dealing with parents. Not that Sue wasn't excellent in that aspect of the job,' he added quickly.

He threw a glance at me that was almost furtive, as though checking he hadn't upset me by his tactless comment.

'Will she be focused on the job if she's got children?'

'That's a very misogynistic question,' he reprimanded me, with a grin. 'Your sister would be horrified if she heard you say that. Anyway, Sue didn't have children and I don't suppose she was entirely focused on the job all the time.'

'What do you mean?' I asked, suddenly very interested in the turn the conversation was taking.

'Don't you think Sue had other interests to occupy her mind?' he replied.

'Like a romantic entanglement with a man, you mean?'

'That wasn't what I meant, but yes, I suppose that would qualify as an outside interest.'

I decided to take a direct approach. 'Was she seeing anyone?'

He frowned lightly. 'Haven't I already told you I've no idea? We never discussed her personal life, difficult though it seems to be for you to believe that. At the risk of sounding misogynistic myself, I believe that's the kind of conversation she might have had with you, not me.'

'There must have been someone. She was an attractive woman.'

'Yes, I suppose she was, in a pretty-pretty kind of way.'

'What does "pretty-pretty" mean?'

'Pretty. Like chocolate-box pretty, conventionally pretty. You know what I mean. So yes, I dare say there was someone, a man, or maybe a woman?' He raised a quizzical eyebrow. 'So to come back to your question, yes, of course I miss her, and not only because it's so time consuming looking for her replacement. But I'm determined to get this right. A lot hangs on it. I don't want to have to go through this process again in a hurry. Yes, I think we may have struck lucky with Maggie.'

The police had not yet come to drag Nick away, and he seemed more interested in finding a new secretary than in mourning the one he had lost. I was beginning to think I had been wrong in suspecting him of being unfaithful, with not just one but two women.

I went to bed that night feeling confused, but far less disturbed.

The next morning I went back to the office to help Julie again.

'One more day and the database should be up to date,' I said.

'Apart from the new pupils who need to be entered.'

'Typical. Just when you think you're finished, along comes a load more work.'

'It's only until September,' she said quickly. 'Once Nick has a new secretary, she'll be responsible for maintaining the database.'

'Oh, I don't mind,' I replied, afraid that I had given the impression I was helping reluctantly. 'It's actually very satisfying getting through it.'

She smiled. 'But you wouldn't want to spend the rest of your life on it.'

'No, probably not. Although it's not a bad job.'

'We would have given the task to the temp, but some of the information is sensitive. We're not really supposed to share it with outsiders.'

I nodded, gratified to be regarded as one of the inner circle.

We worked quietly for the rest of the morning then went to have lunch in the staff dining room, as usual, where no one paid any particular attention to me. My fear that people were talking about me behind my back had gradually faded. I sat next to David's secretary, Mandy, who was looking after the temp. Over lunch I heard them talking about her boss, the deputy head.

'David's a really nice guy, but you have to be prepared for extra duties,' Mandy said.

'Extra duties?' the temp repeated archly.

She was a smiling girl of about twenty with curly fair hair, a few years younger than Mandy who was thirty, dark-haired and plump.

Mandy laughed. 'Not like that! Nothing like that. What I mean is, there's always more to do. Every time you think you've finished, he hits you with something else. He never stops.'

'He sounds like a workaholic.'

'That's putting it mildly.'

'But you seem to like working for him,' said the temp.

'Oh yes,' Mandy replied. 'He's nice, and the pupils adore him. I've got no complaints. And he's really generous as well. You'll never guess what he gave me last Christmas.'

They carried on chatting, but I didn't hear the rest of the conversation because they stood up to leave.

'So, what are you up to this afternoon?' Julie asked me.

I shook my head. 'I'm not sure.' I hesitated. 'I could do some more data entry for you, if you like.'

She smiled at me. 'As long as you don't mind.'

'Of course not. I'm only too pleased to help.'

Chapter 42

Maggie smiled politely at me. 'It's very nice to meet you too, Mrs Kelly. Thank you for the tea.'

'Please, call me Louise. Nick tells me you spent seven years at Wolsey College.'

'It was just under six years, actually.'

Dark-haired and slim, she was dressed in a neat navy suit, everything about her traditional and conventional apart from funky red-rimmed glasses which added an element of fun to a studied image of practical efficiency. I liked the look of her straight away.

'Nick told me you worked for the head there?'

'Yes, that's right. Do you know him?'

'No, but Nick's spoken to him. I think they've met several times. And you have a family?'

'Yes.' Maggie smiled. 'A daughter. She's nearly six, and she's settled in well at her school, so I thought it was high time I returned to work. If I leave it much longer I don't think I'll ever do it. But I didn't want to take on just anything and end up changing jobs, so when I saw this post advertised I jumped at it. This is the kind of place I could see myself staying. I loved it at Wolsey and I wouldn't have left if it weren't for my family commitments.'

Her words could have been deliberately chosen to support her job application but she seemed genuine, and I believed she was sincere as she chatted pleasantly about her previous school and her daughter.

'What did you think of Maggie?' Nick asked me after she had gone.

'I liked her. She seemed perfectly suited to the role.'

'Yes, I think she'll fit in really well.'

'When can she start?'

Maggie was joining us two weeks before term began, which would give her time to finalise her childcare arrangements.

'How are you going to manage in the meantime?' I asked him.

'It gives us a window.'

'A window?'

Grinning, he pulled an envelope out of his pocket and flourished it above his head.

'We're spending a few days in Venice.'

'But how come—'

'It's all booked. We've had such a rough time of it lately, I thought we deserved a little treat.'

Our time in Venice was brief, but from the water bus that bore us along the canals to our hotel until our flight home, everything was magical. Our hotel was located by a narrow waterway off the main Grand Canal. After checking in, we sat at one of the tables outside and had a leisurely lunch and by the time we finished, our stressful year at school seemed to have faded into the distant past.

We visited St Mark's Square, which was uncomfortably packed with tourists, and took a trip on a gondola. Gliding along narrow side stretches of canal in utter silence, we could have been transported back in time to an era before mechanisation, the peace disturbed only by our gondolier's tuneless singing.

Later on, before dinner, we stood on a bridge to watch the sun set gloriously over the lagoon in a blaze of spectacular pink and gold.

'I can't believe how lucky we are,' Nick said. Leaning down, he kissed the tip of my nose and pulled back to gaze at me. 'Or is it luck?'

A green barge with a large metal construction on board went by.

'What's that?' I asked.

'A dredging boat,' Nick said.

I wondered what they would be dredging the canal for.

'Probably collecting silt, or they could be shoring up the poles, or transporting rubble.'

Gazing out over the dark flowing water, I wondered how many people had slipped – or been shoved – into the freezing water, and whether the dredging equipment ever brought up long-dead bodies. It would be an easy place to commit suicide.

'Well?' Nick repeated. 'Is it really just down to luck?'

'I'd say we're lucky. It doesn't get any better than this.'

'I'm not for one moment suggesting this isn't all beautiful, or that we don't have a wonderful life. What I meant to say was, perhaps we make our own luck.'

'To some extent, maybe. But there must be plenty of people who would love to have your start in life, and your job, only they never get the chance. Seriously, how many people are given the opportunities and advantages we've had?'

'Granted we started out ahead of the game. You didn't choose to be born both beautiful and clever, but there are a lot of beautiful clever women who don't achieve half as much as you. That's what I meant about making your own luck.'

His flattery made me smile. 'All I've achieved in my life so far is to marry you.'

He grinned. 'And what an achievement that was! I rest my case.'

Chapter 43

The morning after our return from Venice, I followed the gravel path to school as it had rained overnight and the grass was wet. By the time I made my way home in the afternoon, the ground had dried out, so I took the short cut across the cricket pitch, making a detour to look inside the disused pavilion. It was a ramshackle building, little more than a brick hut with an inner door leading to changing rooms, and Nick was planning a major refurbishment. He had asked me to get some quotes for the work, and I had already approached some local traders for estimates.

Meanwhile the school surveyor had declared the building unsafe in its present state of disrepair, so the windows had been boarded up and a strong padlock fitted to the door, to keep inquisitive youngsters out. It looked stable enough from the outside at a first glance, but inadequate foundations and the proximity of several tall mature trees had apparently disturbed the structure and a closer scrutiny revealed cracks running all the way up the walls. Opinions varied over whether the damage was irreparable, but Nick had decided, quite rightly, to err on the side of caution. In any event, he told me, the roof needed replacing, which meant that in its current state the pavilion was unusable.

'If just one surveyor says the building can't be safely restored, we'll knock the whole thing down and start again.'

'That won't be popular. It's a historic building.'

'A historic building on school premises,' he had replied with a quick grin. 'Preservation of life trumps preservation of bricks and mortar, especially when the lives of minors for whom we're responsible are involved. Thanks to Health and Safety we'll end up with a smart new cricket pavilion.'

Nick's words rang in my ears as I undid the strong padlock. I had never been inside the pavilion before. The interior looked far worse than the exterior. The paintwork was peeling, the flooring had lifted along one edge, probably due to damp, and the lockers were rusty and scratched. Graffiti scrawled on the walls added to the general atmosphere of neglect. Mustard-yellow curtains hung at the grimy windows, and the varnish on wooden benches along the walls was worn away from years of careless use.

More serious than the general state of dilapidation was the crumbling plasterwork and fractured ceiling. Only a couple of floor-to-ceiling iron struts prevented the whole edifice from tumbling down, and they hardly looked secure. A cracked cricket bat leaned against the wall by the door, that and a stray shin pad left abandoned beneath the bench the only indications that this had once been in use as a cricket pavilion. A few tufts of dry grass flitted across the floor, caught in a gust of air that came in through the open door.

Unaware that anyone had followed me in, I started on hearing footsteps behind me. A figure was standing in the doorway. With the sun at his back, his face was masked in shadow.

'Hello?' I called out. 'Who's there? You know it's not safe to be in here.'

He took a step forward and a shaft of light from the window fell across his square face, illuminating his hazel eyes.

'Louise,' he said, taking a step towards me. 'I wondered why the door was open. What are you doing in here?'

'Oh, hello, David. I was just taking a look around. Nick's planning to do it up in here. Long overdue, don't you think? It can't create a very good impression on visiting teams having to use the sports hall changing rooms, while the pavilion is out of bounds.'

He looked around. 'It could certainly do with a coat of paint.'

'Never mind the decor, it smells of damp and mould, and the whole place is falling down.'

'I hope not. This pavilion has been here for years.'

'It looks like it.'

He looked around. 'Let's hope we can find a builder who can do a sensitive job of renovating it.'

'It's going to take more than renovation to make it safe. It's going to need a complete rebuild.'

'Rebuild? What do you mean?'

'We probably need to knock it down and start again. The whole place is falling apart.'

'What? You are joking.'

'Oh, come on. Just look around. The ceiling's about to cave in for a start, and the walls are disintegrating. There's more dust than brick. Shoddy foundations, that's the problem, and all the trees.'

'I rather think you're missing the point,' David said coldly. 'There's a history to this pavilion. It has an atmosphere that's evolved over many decades.'

'An atmosphere of damp and mildew. Yes, I think it's time for a complete overhaul.'

He took a step towards me. 'And I think you should leave it exactly as it is. We don't need any more changes.'

I was beginning to find his tone offensive, even menacing. He might not think much of me personally, but I was the headmaster's wife and my position, at least, deserved respect. While I hesitated, wondering whether to tell him what I was thinking, or whether I should wait and speak to Nick about this altercation, David took another step towards me and paused, looking at me speculatively.

'You care about Nick, don't you?' he asked.

'Of course I do. I love him. He's my husband.'

There was a long pause before he said, 'You know this isn't the right place for him. For either of you.'

'What are you talking about?'

David gazed up at the unstable brickwork overhead, muttering about neglect, while I waited to hear what he would say.

He swung his head round to face me and began to speak very fast. 'I'm telling you what's best for you and your husband. If you want your marriage to survive, you need to leave here. You're the person best placed to convince him it's time to move on. Tell him he has to resign, go away and never come back. You can't want to stay here, knowing it's not the right place for your husband. He doesn't fit in here.'

'And I suppose you do? Do you really expect Nick to leave so you can step into the vacuum as acting head, and worm your way to being appointed headmaster?' I snapped. 'That's what this insane suggestion is all about, isn't it? Your selfish ambition.'

'No,' he cried out as though the words were torn from him. 'You couldn't be further from the truth. It's not about me. This is about what's best for Edleybury.'

'Oh please!'

'You have to listen to me. This place isn't right for you. Nick has to leave here, and you can help make it happen. You can persuade him. This has got nothing to do with me. I'm not an ambitious man. But I'd do anything to save Edleybury from the influence of a man like your husband, with his crude ideas and his lack of morals.'

Listening to David's wild words, I remembered Nick telling me that David had arranged our interview with Rosie. He took a step closer, moving across the shaft of light from the window and for the first time I noticed how large his feet were. The detective sergeant had told me that the man who had visited Rosie on the night she died had particularly large feet. David had known Rosie all along. And of course he had known Sue as well.

Chapter 44

I took a step away from David.

'I'm prepared to do whatever it takes to protect Edleybury,' he was saying, his voice cracking with suppressed emotion.

'You knew Rosie, didn't you?'

He scowled at me.

'You were the one having an affair with her. It was you, wasn't it? Admit it!'

'So? I'm not married. Not like your husband. I can have a consensual relationship with a woman if I want to. We're not living in Victorian times. What I choose to do in my own time, away from the school, is entirely my own business. It's not as if I paraded my promiscuity in school.'

'You gave those photos to Rosie,' I pressed on, ignoring his provocative comments.

'What photos?'

'It *was* you, wasn't it,' I cried out. 'You were with Rosie on the night she was killed.'

The expression that flickered across his face was familiar, a slightly indignant scowl coupled with a voice that rose, just a fraction, in tone and volume. I had seen that same expression of exaggerated innocence many times on the faces of guilty pupils denying their transgression while insisting, 'It wasn't me, Miss.' His expression darkened.

'I don't know what you're talking about,' he muttered.

But despite his protestations, I could see in his eyes that he knew I had grasped the truth. I should have kept quiet, but the realisation that David, and not Nick, had been with Rosie that night, gave me courage.

'You orchestrated this whole thing, didn't you? You gave Rosie those photos and told her to show them to me. You set the whole thing up. Why did you do it?'

'Nick was never the right man,' David replied, his eyes blazing. 'He had to be stopped.'

'What do you mean? Stopped from what?'

'He had to be stopped before he destroyed Edleybury. He was never right for us.'

'What are you talking about? He's the headmaster.'

'He has no understanding of decent values. He lacks any moral compass. How can we entrust the life of the school to a man like that?'

'What do you mean, "a man like that"? Like what? He's the headmaster– '

David interrupted me. 'He's lax, morally lax. And all the changes he's pushing forward, they're wrong. Edleybury isn't a school for girls. It's unthinkable. No one who had any understanding of the school and its long traditions would dream of proposing such an idea. It can't happen, not in my school.'

'But it's not your school.'

'You don't understand. How could you? As soon as he stepped foot in the place, he was talking about turning it into a completely different kind of school. What can he possibly know about the spirit and ethos of Edleybury? A man who flits around from school to school, pursuing his own small-minded ambition. What does he know about loyalty and honour and centuries of tradition, traditions that have made Edleybury what it is? I've been here for nearly a quarter of a century, and yet my objections to his plans are being swept aside without any consideration.'

'That's not true. You must know how much Nick respects you. He thinks really highly of you. We all do. And he knows you play an indispensable role in the life of the school.'

'You think he respects my opinions?' David repeated, with a harsh laugh. 'What does he understand about what matters here?'

'I'm sure we all agree that what matters is instilling decency and integrity into the pupils.'

'Decency and integrity? You and your husband have no idea about decency and integrity. You have no morals.'

'Don't lecture me about what's right and wrong. Don't you dare.' I glared at him. 'I know, you know. I know what you did.'

He shook his head. 'What are you talking about? You know, you know? What do you know?'

'You killed Rosie.'

'What– what are you talking about?'

'You know what I'm talking about,' I replied, as calmly as I could.

While we were speaking, I had been edging towards the wall, inching my way past one of the iron struts, ready to make a dash for the door. The fabric of the building was falling apart, a large section of the ceiling at that end only held in place by one metal pole with a small platform at the top. No attempt had been made to attach it to the rafters, presumably because any drilling or hammering of nails would have caused the rotten wood to crumble. It wouldn't take much force to dislodge the metal strut, and the whole edifice would come crashing down. Placing the palm of my hand against it and curling my fingers around it, I felt the pole wobble in my grasp. Suspecting my intention, David lunged at me, but he was too late.

'Decency and integrity,' he repeated, spitting the words at me as I wrenched the pole from its position and made a dash for the door.

David's eyes glared at me in mute terror and his mouth gaped in a silent cry as, with a tearing roar, a section of the roof fell in behind me. A chunk of masonry landed on my shoulder with a sickening thud, missing my skull by inches, knocking me to the floor. I heard screaming and realised it was my own voice, sounding shrilly above the din of falling bricks and plaster. Numb with shock, I forced myself to crawl in the direction of the door while shards of brickwork clattered and ricocheted around me in a maelstrom of falling debris. Blinded by dust and screaming in pain, somehow I managed to drag myself over the threshold, not daring to rest until I felt grass between my fingers. Fragments of brickwork showered around me as the old pavilion collapsed with a thundering roar.

Daylight faded into ringing silence until a tumult of voices filled my head. They seemed to come from a long way off, muffled by a booming in my ears.

'What's happened?'

'The pavilion's gone!'

'It's collapsed!'

Near me, someone coughed.

'Oh my God, there's someone there!'

'Call an ambulance and get the school nurse here now!'

A burning sensation throbbed in my shoulder. Drifting in and out of consciousness, I heard the wail of a siren which was followed, a long time later, by Nick's voice calling to me.

Through a fog I saw him, tiny wet runnels glistening in the dust on his face. I tried to tell him that everything was all right and we were safe now, but I couldn't speak. Pain was raging through me like a fever, reaching me in waves that blotted out everything else.

Chapter 45

I must have regained consciousness in the ambulance because I have a vague recollection of vomiting on a red blanket, and Nick's voice telling me where we were as I strained to raise my head, while an engine droned faintly in the background and some kind of medical equipment beeped and flashed above me. Other than that, I have only confused fragmented memories of what happened after the pavilion collapsed until I woke up properly to find myself in a hospital bed with my shoulder bound in a thick bandage.

'Are you all right?' Nick asked me. Turning, he called out, 'My wife's awake! She's awake!'

I tried to tell him that I felt sick, but a sharp pain in my neck prevented me from moving my jaw. Tears slid from my eyes but I couldn't move my face to cry. The doctors pumped me full of painkillers. Even though I was groggy with drugs, it was excruciating being manoeuvred into a wheelchair to be taken for x-rays and scans and blood tests. I endured the pain as quietly as I could, only yelling out when an unexpected twist or jolt stabbed me, like daggers slicing through my bones.

At last I was returned to bed and given another shot.

'Does she really need morphine?' Nick asked.

'Yes,' I replied through gritted teeth, 'she really does.'

It was true. The pain was unendurable.

The following day, a doctor came to report the results of the tests I had undergone. I was feeling considerably more comfortable although my shoulder still ached terribly.

'Good news,' the doctor said. 'Your injuries are not as severe as we feared.'

Beside him, I saw Nick had tears in his eyes.

'It's all right,' I whispered. 'We're safe now.'

My shoulder tormented me for weeks, agonising whenever I moved it, and painful when I didn't, but the doctors assured me I was recovering and the discomfort would pass. They gave me an exercise routine which was excruciating, and advised me to move as much as possible to prevent my shoulder from seizing up.

'Shoulders are not designed to stay still,' one of the doctors told me. 'You need to move it gently as much as you can, in spite of any discomfort the movement causes.'

If I could have laughed without causing myself intense pain, I would have been amused by the language the medical staff used.

'They talk about "discomfort" as though it hardly hurts at all,' I complained to Nick. 'I'd like to see them go through what I'm suffering here. Bloody liars. They're worse than politicians.'

Nick gazed wretchedly at me, hating to see me suffer, and powerless to help, but I was too overwhelmed by physical pain to offer him any respite from his misery. Pain was my constant companion. It possessed me like an evil spirit. Crouching on my chest, it drained my life force, an invisible vampire that usurped my mind and ousted my humanity, making me cruel to the man who loved me.

Slowly the doctors reduced my drugs, and I regained control of my thoughts and stopped insulting the medical staff at every opportunity. It wasn't their fault I was in pain. Even with Nick's insistence on paying for additional sessions, and the ferocity of my physiotherapist, my progress was slow. Lying in bed at night was the worst. It was almost impossible to get comfortable. Whatever position I lay in the pain kept me awake, along with a blistering regret for everything that had happened.

Still, apart from my battered shoulder I was, miraculously, physically unharmed, although it took me weeks to recover from the psychological trauma of my experience. For months my sleep was disturbed by recurring nightmares of collapsing buildings.

Sometimes in my dreams I watched a fox vanish beneath an avalanche of bricks, while I wept bitterly for its pointless death.

One morning Nick asked me about my nightmare. 'You were mumbling something about a fox.'

I nodded, too tired and dispirited to explain.

Everyone told me I was lucky to have escaped with my life, and it was true. David had not been so fortunate.

Nick was even more horrified than I was. He blamed himself for failing to ensure the pavilion was safe. 'I should have knocked it down straight away. What was I thinking of, letting such an important decision be influenced a load of old men?'

I knew he was referring to the members of staff who fought against any change to the customs or fabric of the school. David had been their ringleader, but neither of us remarked on the irony of his fate, after David himself had argued so strongly against the pavilion being pulled down.

'What were you doing there?' Nick asked. 'You knew it was unsafe.'

I told him I had been taking a close look at the interior, preparatory to showing some builders around.

'And what about David? What was he doing in there?'

'He told me he saw someone go inside. That was me. But he couldn't see who it was, and wanted to check everything was okay.'

'He wanted to check everything was okay,' Nick repeated flatly.

'Yes, well, anyway, he came in, and we started arguing about whether the place ought to be knocked down. You know how he felt about it, resisting any changes, when suddenly– you know what happened.'

Nick sat by the bed in silence for a moment.

'What a horrible way to go,' he said at last. 'I wonder if he knew what was about to hit him.'

'I don't think so,' I lied.

When I closed my eyes, I could picture David, his face plastered in brick dust, staring at me in mute horror, before the roof caved in and he disappeared beneath a torrent of falling masonry. I couldn't have saved him, even if I had wanted to. His crushed body was recovered from the ruins of the pavilion, his face shattered almost beyond recognition. If I had lingered, even for a second, I would have suffered the same fate.

'So just when I sorted out a replacement secretary, now I've got to appoint a new deputy,' Nick grumbled. 'And that's not going to be any easier than replacing Sue.'

Forcing my way out of dark memories, I smiled at him. 'You'll manage. You always do.'

Chapter 46

Unlike his face, David's DNA remained intact, and on the afternoon of my return home from hospital, Nick and I received a visit from the police.

'I wanted to tell you in person,' Inspector Jarvis said, after making polite enquiries about my injuries. 'You have recently been affected by a most unfortunate series of events, but we have at last established the facts. We have a match for the DNA found on Rosie White's body, which has given us the identity of her killer.' He paused for a second. 'I'm sorry to tell you that the man who killed Rosie White was your deputy head, David Lancaster.'

'David?' Nick blurted out in disbelief. 'That can't be true. No, it can't have been David. I'm sorry, Inspector, but that's a preposterous suggestion. The man's dead and can't defend himself, but I can vouch for his character one hundred per cent. I assure you, Inspector, David was a good, decent man.'

The inspector shook his head, looking almost apologetic. 'That doesn't alter the facts, sir.'

I put my hand over my mouth to hide my smile. The niggling doubt that Nick might have been with Rosie on the night she died had now been eliminated. With proof that David had been in Rosie's bed that night, the police were satisfied he was responsible for her death. Having uncovered evidence that pointed to him having an affair with Sue as well, they concluded that he had also killed her. According to the detective inspector, David had been a sexual predator subject to fits of jealous rage who had pursued both women with vicious determination, reacting violently when provoked. Nick listened to the detective with a stunned expression.

'I don't know what to say to you,' he stammered at last, 'except that I don't believe it. I can't.'

'Your loyalty does you credit, sir, but I'm afraid it's true.'

The police seemed pleased to close the case, but none of this was good news for Edleybury, and Nick was not alone in wanting to suppress the story of David's killing spree. Having a deputy head who was a serial killer was hardly the kind of publicity the school was seeking. The governors must have had a connection with someone higher up in the police force than Detective Inspector Jarvis, because the story never appeared in the media. In addition to that, something Nick said left me with the impression that the school had passed money to the families of the murdered women to compensate them for their loss, and also, no doubt, to persuade them not to talk to anyone about what had happened.

Gradually the pain in my shoulder faded, as did the memory of David, glaring at me in terror, realising he was about to be buried alive. But my shoulder still ached when I moved it too strenuously, and my sleep continued to be plagued by nightmares. Any sport was out of the question for me for a while, so Angela and I met in the staff dining room instead of on the tennis courts.

'We must start playing again as soon as I can move this dratted arm properly,' I told her.

She nodded. 'Of course. That would be great. I've missed our games. How long do you think it'll be until you're fit again?'

'Oh, not until Christmas, at least.'

'That's a shame. But still, you're lucky to be alive. It must have been terrifying.'

'I know, it's just awful.'

'What actually happened?'

I hesitated.

'If you'd rather not talk about it, I quite understand.' She gave me a sympathetic smile. 'It must have been terrible. I'm sorry. I shouldn't have asked. It was insensitive of me.'

'No, no, it's not that I don't want to talk about it,' I hastened to reassure her. 'It's just that I don't really remember very much about what happened. They think one of us must have knocked into a metal support which slipped from its place and caused the ceiling to cave in, but I have no recollection of that happening. I was in the pavilion with David, discussing what we ought to do about the place, and whether it would be better to restore the building or knock it down and start again, and the next thing I knew, I was in an ambulance feeling as though I had been battered all over my body. I was in so much pain, I didn't even wonder what had happened to David. I suppose I assumed he had got out. I couldn't believe it when Nick told me later that David had been killed.'

I shook my head and winced as the movement prompted a twinge of pain in my shoulder.

'You were lucky to get out of there alive,' Angela said once again.

I nodded. It was a refrain I was to hear many times over the next few months.

The older members of staff were devastated at the loss of the deputy head, who had been their champion for so long. A bevy of them decided to retire that year, claiming the school was never the same after David's death. Nick expressed public regret at losing them but privately he was delighted.

'Another one going. It means we can recruit a newly qualified teacher,' he told me. 'They're younger, half the price, have double the energy, and are less set in their ways. It's a win in every respect!'

As deputy head in his previous school, he had frequently expressed irritation about the number of newly qualified teachers joining the staff, complaining that they lacked the experience to control and teach classes. As a headmaster with budgets to juggle, and no longer involved with minor disciplinary matters in the school, his priorities had changed.

Officially, it was said that Sue had died of some rare congenital condition which wasn't contagious. David was reported to have been killed in a tragic accident while he had been checking the safety of the pavilion. Legends soon spread around the school that the secretary had killed herself in the wake of a disastrous love affair, while the deputy head had sacrificed his own life rescuing me from the collapsing pavilion. Such a heroic fiction seemed fitting for a deputy head of Edleybury. It was certainly better than the picture painted by the police, of a psychopathic sexual predator.

New members of staff knew little about the victim of the collapsed pavilion apart from what they heard in Nick's eulogy, that David had been an exceptional deputy head, and a true servant of the school. As for the pupils, they moved on up through the school ignorant of the true facts of David's life and death. Spinning sensational fantasies about the staff, they never suspected their stories were nowhere near as lurid as the truth.

Epilogue

Faint cries reached us from a group of boys playing cricket on the far pitch. Behind them the paintwork of a new pavilion gleamed white against a bank of rhododendrons, its leafy profusion dotted with splashes of scarlet. Everything looked vibrant in the afternoon sun.

A cluster of Japanese boys strolled across the near pitch in the direction of the boarding houses.

'I had a letter from the agency in Tokyo recently,' Nick said, as the boys disappeared among the silver trunks of a copse of birch trees. 'They want to send someone over to look around the school.'

'Is everything all right?'

He nodded. 'They say they want to do more to promote us in Japan, so they're coming here on an information-gathering visit. I don't think they're checking up on us.' He gave a low laugh.

'Who are they sending?'

'I don't know. But whoever it is, we'll make them feel welcome.'

'Of course.'

In silence we watched white-clad figures waving bats and running around in the distance.

When Nick spoke again, his voice was so low I had to strain to hear what he was saying. 'I didn't really love her, you know.'

Several years had passed since tragedy had struck in our inaugural year at Edleybury, but I knew straight away who he meant.

He continued hesitantly, as though choosing his words with care. 'It was never going to last... I thought you would have understood, would have been more patient. Everything that happened... there was no need.'

'I wanted it to end, but not like that,' I replied. 'Not like that.'

He sighed, and above us a breeze whispered in the leaves of the birch trees.

'It was you, all along,' he said.

He could have been declaring his enduring love, or telling me that he had always known I had murdered two women to protect our marriage and preserve our way of life.

The breeze in the birch trees died away; only occasional cries from the young cricketers disturbed the peace. Staring straight ahead, Nick no longer seemed aware of my presence beside him, or of the shouts from the cricket pitch. Perhaps he was remembering a different game, played out in front of a rickety old pavilion, in a lost world of innocence and tranquillity.